THE WATCHING BIRD

Thomas Spademan

stella isle press

The Watching Bird

ISBN: 978-1-967376-04-9

CONTENTS

For Ruby, who always sees.

"Nothing is but what is not."

—*Macbeth*, Act 1, scene 3

"Accustom your tongue to say: I do not know, lest you become entangled in a web of deceit."
—Berakhot 4a

PROLOGUE: THE VESSEL

The night Selene was born, the village's scholar-priest came to her family's cottage on the rocky coast of the Brine to bestow the traditional blessing upon the baby and bring gifts new parents often find useful: a small basin in which to bathe the child, two warm, rough spun woolen garments, a plain bunting bag suitable for the sea climate, and a small leather pouch of cloth diapers and safety pins. The scholar-priest also brought a gift of preserved apple-like thryssal fruit. Thryssal was thought to bring good luck, and thryssal preserves were always welcome at firstmeal, especially in a Briner village far from the orchards near Academy City. After chanting an invocation that had been greeting infants to Erden long before the reach of living memory, the scholar-priest declared Selene to be "a wondrously beautiful child" and "a true blessing to her parents and our village," before accepting and gulping down an ungainly, hand-thrown ceramic mug of hot brew and passing back into the night.

In short, Selene came into the world in a way not noticeably different from any other of the thousands born every year in the Principality of the Academy—the Prinship, as it was called by its citizens.

Soon, Selene was walking and talking, ocean-hued eyes brilliant behind dark hair. Her quiet, loving nature gladdened her parents' hearts. As a young student, she was invariably cheerful; her teachers praised her patience and judged her to be above average, though not gifted. In due time, she came of age and, at sixteen, was found of sufficient intellectual capability and possessing the virtues in proper measure and balance, and was admitted to the Academy, where she would enter as a registrant, opening many doors for a future career as a carer, healer, creator, server, or even scholar-priest, although all who knew her judged that last career unlikely; she was thought not to have the *gravitas* of soul exemplified by those destined to become leaders of the Academy and the Principality.

In the waning days of summer, Selene's parents watched as their only child left in the charelwayn that would carry her to her new residence in the first-year students' dormitory in Academy City, far from the Reach.

"The years have passed so quickly," her mother observed as the cart passed out of sight. It was partly a lament and partly an expression of deep appreciation for the quiet joy their family life had brought.

"Yes," was Selene's father's taciturn response.

As they turned back to their cabin, they failed to notice the mist that had collected around them in the otherwise clear, warm night air. Nor did they notice when fibrous halos appeared around their heads, nor when the halos softly prismed through the spectrum, turned deep red, and then faded. As the charelwayn rumbled out of sight, Selene's parents returned to their fire, their minds at peace, memories of their daughter dwindling with the strange mist.

CHAPTER ONE

THE REGISTRANT

The Academy—or, to give it its full name, the *Academia Veritatis et Cognitionis* (the *Academy of Truth and Knowledge*)—was a cloistered collection of buildings of similar architecture and indefinite antiquity that together presented an unnavigable maze for new students. Whatever architect had decided, centuries ago, that the buildings should present a unified appearance but be laid out in a chaotic pattern so inscrutable as to not actually *count* as a pattern, clearly had not been thinking of the inconvenience they would be causing generations of fresh registrants desperately trying to find their dormitories, homerooms, classrooms, and departmental offices. At least the dining rooms were easily found, simply by following the smell of succulent vegetable-meat pies and savory root soup that filled the air at lastmeal. Without that unintended guide, one might expect the inexperienced students to starve to death during their first weeks at the school, so illogical was the plan of the campus.

Even so, the chaos of move-in day always came to an end, and, for the most part, the registrants arrived where they were supposed to be.

This included Selene, who was neither the first nor the last to find Celestine Hall, her assigned dormitory.

From the moment she first passed through the three double doors of the main entrance, Selene felt she was home. She was entranced by the beautiful, ornate arched doors covered with carved scenes from Erden's history, and the stained glass windows above the entrance depicting *Lux's* consort, the sky goddess *Caelestis*, wearing a crown, riding a lion, and clutching the moon, with *Lux* in an expanse of light contemplating from high above. Just inside the doors, up three broad marble steps and to the left, was the building's main desk. Climbing the stairs, Selene noticed a distinctive and beautiful owl icon, a relic carved from lustrous reddish-brown wood; the owl, depicted perched on a pile of books, seemingly watched over the students as they came and went.

"I heard a story about that owl," came a voice from behind her. Selene turned to see a student of about her age grinning lopsidedly.

"Hi," he said brightly.

"Uh...hi?" Selene responded.

"So, do you want to hear the story?" the man-boy asked.

Selene was always kind and certainly didn't mind making a friend on her very first day at school, even if that friend was less than prepossessing, which fully described the person facing her. He had a lanky, coltish quality about him. *As if he has not yet fully grown into himself,* she thought. His face, however, was open and expressive, his eyes a mixture of curiosity and enthusiasm, and his smile crooked and slightly too broad. Selene found it charming. He needed to button his shirt properly, however, a fact made more evident when he gesticulated a bit too much when talking, which action also encouraged his apparently uncombable sandy hair to greater chaos. Selene immediately decided that, all in all, she was going to like this curious individual.

"Sure. What's the story?"

"Well, I was told this by an adept—but I am sure you know all the class levels here, right?"

"Sure. We're registrants, just starting out. In our second year, we will be initiates. The third-year students are adepts, which is when we will finish our foundational studies. After that, we can apply to train for one of the specializations: carer, healer, creator, server, or scholar-priest. That training takes another two years. I actually saw some apprentices and fellows in the various colored tunics of their specializations as I came to the school today. They seemed so busy, carrying piles of books with them as they were walking to...well, wherever they were going."

"Hey, you know your stuff," the lad nodded appreciatively. "My name's Ichabod. What's yours?"

Ichabod! What a strangely old-fashioned name, thought Selene. *He must be from one of the villages far from the Academy. Like me. But*, she concluded, *the name fits him well*.

"Selene."

"So, Selene, this adept told me we have to be careful not to stand directly under the Watching Bird—that's what she called it—before our first exams, or we will fail the exams and get expelled."

"What? It's just an old hunk of carved wood. That seems silly."

"Well, *you* go ahead and stand under it. I sure won't," Ichabod smiled.

Selene laughed. "OK, Ichabod, I promise. I won't stand under the Bird if you won't. Might as well take every precaution. I feel like I am going to get kicked out of here, anyway. I wasn't the brightest in my primary school, you know. I wasn't even sure I would make it here in the first place." *I am blithering*, thought Selene.

Ichabod, whose smile and raised eyebrows made him look a bit puppyish, either didn't notice or didn't mind. "Who did? I guess we should check in at the front desk."

In a matter of minutes, they had received their keys. They were both assigned rooms looking onto the campus from the third of four floors, just around the corner from each other, although in different houses—Selene in Adamus Women's House and Ichabod in Elisius Men's House. Selene was pleased with what she saw when she found her room: spare but inviting after the stresses of a long day in a new place.

Celestine Hall—a large, old brick dormitory—housed more than a thousand students. From above, it looked like a giant block figure eight with two inner courtyards. It was said to be the second oldest building on campus, and Selene and Ichabod soon discovered some of the quirks you always find with old buildings. While their rooms, for example, were literally around the corner from each other, because they were in different houses, they'd normally have to descend and then ascend three flights of stairs to visit each other; but on their very first day, Selene discovered a narrow ledge with a decorative parapet that ran just outside her window, encircling the building and providing a direct route between their apartments. They weren't supposed to be on the ledge, she knew, but they certainly weren't the first students to discover it. The ledge immediately became their usual mode of travel between each other's rooms when Ichabod was startled by Selene's face poking in through his window.

"Whoa," he exclaimed. "What's that? Are you sure it's safe? Are you sure that's *legal*?"

"Yes, and maybe," Selene responded as she hopped into Ichabod's room. "Probably not, though. Unpacked yet?"

"Yeah. Didn't have much to unpack, really." It was true. Selene peered into Ichabod's open wardrobe, which contained exactly two pairs of pants, three plain shirts made of heavy cloth, a weatherworn sweater, a much-mended coat, and socks and such in the open lower drawer, all in varied, muted colors that suggested a village in the Greenward. A worn canvas and leather knapsack of the sort farmers use hung on a hook on the inner door of the wardrobe. Scanning the room, Selene saw a bed against the wall to the left of the wardrobe, covered by a thick, plain woolen blanket. Across the small room, against the opposite wall, was a notebook and hand-carved stylus on a low wooden study table, which also supported a battered oil lamp and a chipped ceramic mug of uncertain color. Adjacent to the table was a washbasin. And that was it. It was clear that Ichabod, like Selene, had earned his place at the school through hard work alone—unlike many other students, who were "legacy" admissions or whose parents had made large donations to the scholar-priests in the name of *Lux*.

Should I ask Ichabod about his home and family? Why not? she thought. "Ichabod," she started to say, when from the hall came a stentorian voice.

"All registrants to the Universe. All registrants to the Universe. Hey, you!" called the voice, knocking on Ichabod's door. "Finish unpacking and get to the Universe Room."

Ichabod smiled wryly at Selene. "See, it's good to travel light. Mist!" he exclaimed, using a phrase Selene's parents had severely discouraged as vulgar. "Where is the Universe Room, do you suppose?"

"No idea. Guess we can just follow everyone else and find out."

"This is the Universe Room for Adamus and Elisius Houses. Usually referred to as 'the Universe.' Be sure you know how to find it." The scholar-priest who was speaking had ponderously introduced himself as Professor Thallos. He was, he said, the head of both Adamus House and Elisius House, and was "here to see to it that you succeed in—or at least survive—your registrant year."

The professor's appearance unnerved Selene. His was a substantial, almost looming presence. His broad features reminded Selene of a large farm animal, although she felt a twinge of guilt at the idea. *Even so, it's true*, she thought. *He looks like a kind of scholarly ox.* From between crease-lines earned from years of long, hard study, his un-blinking eyes slowly scanned the group of ill-at-ease registrants while the rest of his body barely moved. *He is like a statue with a mechani-cally animated ox head*, thought Selene. She found it unsettling and, glancing around, realized she was not alone in this.

The professor wore the dun-green and reddish-orange teaching tunic of a scholar-priest. It was exceedingly simple in cut and design, however, unlike the attire of most other scholar-priests, who tended to adopt elegantly tailored clothes decorated with colorful patterns representing various aspects of *Lux* or the history of the Academy. A closer examination of Professor Thallos's tunic revealed that there were, in fact, subtle patterns symbolic of the omnipresence of *Lux* embroidered into the fabric. So, he had not completely foregone the traditions of his profession. A heavy leather belt held his book pouch, with a stylus inserted through a loop. Around the professor's neck were the chain and pendant that marked him as a Head of House. The pendant was in a style Selene had never before seen; it was certainly an antique and, Selene thought, must be centuries old.

A small young woman with long hair so deeply black it was almost dark violet raised her hand and, without waiting to be recognized, asked, "Professor, why is this called the Universe Room?"

Professor Thallos's head swiveled to face the young woman. He contemplated her steadily, almost sadly. When she started to blink her eyes in obvious discomfort, without breaking his gaze, he opened his book pouch and removed a well-creased volume and a small pair of wire-rimmed spectacles.

"Registrant, I am sure I need not tell you that 'patience is the scholar's quill.' Or, perhaps I do need to tell you. I would ask that all of you withhold your questions until I am done speaking, but, as you are all *incunabula* here, as it were, I will humor you this time."

"Doesn't seem very humorous to me," Ichabod whispered.

"How can she not know what a universe room is?" Selene whispered back, but Icabod merely shrugged.

Professor Thallos held up the worn volume. "As you leave here today, you will all receive a copy of this book, commonly called the *Go-With*. It is properly titled the *Vade Mecum Veritatis et Cognitionis*." The professor looked at the young woman again. "Can you translate that for me, Registrant...?"

"Elara, sir," said the dark-haired student. "It means 'go with me to truth and knowledge.'"

"Yes, Registrant Elara. Carry it with you at all times. It is a complete manual of all things Academia. Let us consult it to answer your question."

He donned his glasses and began reading in a monotone voice. "'Each dormitory hall shall be composed of two or more houses. Houses shall be associated as pairs, one for men, one for women, governed by a Head of House.' Such as myself, of course. 'For each pair of houses, there shall be a Universe Room to be used as a general-purpose space; it shall serve any function deemed necessary by a Head of House or, upon application, by any pair of residents, one from each house.'" Professor Thallos looked up. "There's more here, but I hope that answers your question, Registrant Elara, and that in the future, you will refrain from wasting our time with questions the answers to which you will find in the *Go-With*." Elara nodded weakly and attempted to make herself even smaller as Professor Thallos returned to his previous stance.

"Once again, this is the Universe Room. When it is necessary for us to meet to discuss issues affecting your life here in Celestine Hall or the Academy more generally, we will meet here. You may also apply to me with specific requests for its use, but I should tell you: I will regard most such requests as frivolous." The professor sounded serious, but

Selene wondered if he just might have been joking, just a little. His voice was grim, but his eyes were not.

"I suspect that some of you come to the Academy already conversant with our ways and rituals. I also suspect that most of you who think you understand the Academy are misinformed. And I believe I can infer that many of you are *wholly* ignorant of our ways; so profoundly ignorant that you are not even aware of your ignorance." Here, Professor Thallos leaned forward and regarded the young woman Elara once again, who had failed to make herself small enough to avoid his scrutiny.

"Ignorance of one's own ignorance is the natural state of humanity," Professor Thallos continued with a small smile. "This is the first and most important lesson you shall learn as registrants. You may think you already understand what I am saying, but you do *not*." He folded his glasses with a snap and stowed them in his pouch, a wry grin on his face. "I have seen *whole cohorts* of registrants fail to achieve the proper mental state of educated puzzlement called *aporia* until mere days before the end of the term. I expect such mediocrity to continue with this cohort."

"Well, as long as he doesn't expect much from us, I can live up to that," whispered Ichabod. Selene had to repress a snort.

Professor Thallos became grave and allowed his eyes to sweep slowly across the entire group. "I have also seen many registrants simply fail. I can tell you why they failed. I will say it again: 'patience is the scholar's quill.' This year, you will learn many things, and they will not all initially sit easily together. You must remember this: you are in no position to judge the truths you will learn until you have encompassed the whole. This you will not achieve until at least three years of study have passed, if you achieve it at all. You will, I should add, lest you become too discouraged so early on, glimpse aspects and even elements of the outline of the whole by the end of this year. But it will be only hints and contours of the Great Source and truth that binds us all and is the bedrock of our society and our being: the benevolence of *Lux*."

"You may think you come to the Academy knowing and understanding *Lux*. I will repeat myself. You do not understand *Lux*. Embrace this truth, and you will profit from your year as registrants. Otherwise..." He shrugged.

"Your task now and for the next three years is to imbibe. Not to question. This has ever been the way of our society, and you now have the deep responsibility and privilege of contributing your small part to the reproduction of that society. The order and well-being you have enjoyed in your lives up to this point and which have made your presence here possible, all of that now begins to depend on you. You are no longer passive beneficiaries of our society's peace and abundance. You now join those who actively create and recreate it. You are thus now responsible for it. And this, I should point out, is the meaning of the relic you have all certainly seen when entering this building; I would ask you to think of your responsibilities whenever you pass by the Watching Bird."

CHAPTER TWO

MIASMA

B efore they knew it, Selene and Ichabod were deep into their studies. Courses at the Academy were unlike anything they had ever encountered. Each course combined a theoretical component with a practical component; Professor Thallos called it "why and how" education. The "why" part was invariably elucidated through *socraticum elenchi*, texts which presented truth through a dialectical method of claim and counterclaim that, according to the *Go-With*, guaranteed truth. As Professor Thallos was wont to ponderously propound:

"The *socraticum elenchi* is the beginning of all discovery and the end of all knowledge."

The students were not to even think of criticizing the *elenchi*, of course. This was especially true for lowly registrants. Their task was merely to memorize specific *elenchi* that, they were told, were incontrovertibly true and, for all they knew, had been handed down since the founding of the school in deep antiquity. Ichabod wasn't about to respect this prohibition, of course, not when the *elenchi* offered so many possibilities for humor, and he would frequently engage

Selene in mock debates about everything from the quality of Professor Thallos's lectures ("Monotonous but useful," he declared them) to the evening meal options ("Invariably an adventure").

"I'm going to have the root soup, and I recommend it for you as well, Registrant Selene," Ichabod would say in a mock-professorial tone.

"And why is that, Registrant Ichabod?"

"The wholesome nature of the broth distinguishes the root soup as a superior source of nutrition, which is the primary function of food, as any adept will, at excruciating length, tell you. Much more important than any subjective aesthetic pleasure that might accrue from its consumption."

"Registrant Ichabod, please acquaint me with the meaning of the term you have so obtusely used: what, please, is 'food'? For I suspect that root soup does not fall within the category of 'food,' or only falls within it by overly generous analogy, as one of your jests may be only generously thought a profound insight."

In truth, their banter provided much-needed relief from the stress of their daily work, which spared few moments for personal time or relaxation.

Institutional routines in the academy, as in the Prinship as a whole, followed the course of the weekdays. The week began with *Fiat Lux*, named in honor of *Lux*. As young children, both Selene and Ichabod had been taught that all things, including the week, begin with *Lux*, the embodiment of truth and knowledge. Both high and home rituals honored the Great Source on *Fiat Lux*.

Fiat Lux was followed by *Fiat Stella*, on which day the citizens of the Prinship were taught to consider themselves as points of light reflecting *Lux*, as stars and Erden's twin moons were thought to reflect their sun. As a child, Selene loved thinking of herself as a star, high in the nighttime sky, reflecting the light of Lux.

Then came *Fiat Veritas* (truth), *Fiat Kalamos* and *Fiat Liber* (named for the stylus and book of learning, respectively, symbolizing the power and primacy of the scholar-priests), and, finally, *Fiat Caelestis Dies* and *Fiat Caelestis Nocta* (both consecrated to the sky goddess consort of *Lux,* who causes the moon to pour rain and crops to grow). Each day had its special meanings and rituals. And so the week cycled around, again and again, each cycle another manifestation of *Lux's* benevolence.

Selene's and Ichabod's classes also followed thematically the round of days of the week:

- On *Fiat Lux,* the registrants learned about the omni-properties of *Lux* (always through rote memorization of relevant *elenchi,* of course).

- *Fiat Stella* was spent on moral philology, again through the memorization of relevant *elenchi.*

- *Fiat Veritas, Fiat Kalamos,* and *Fiat Liber* were spent on such things as geometry, observational learning of the *essentia* of all things, and dialectical philology.

- The first hours of *Fiat Caelestis Dies* were to be spent synthesizing the previous week's lessons into a coherent whole, while students spent the later hours in service to their houses and the campus.

- Finally, Selene and Ichabod were allowed all of *Fiat Caelestis Nocta* for their own purposes, although those activities were usually monitored by Professor Thallos or other scholar-priests at the Academy. Some students would take this time to participate in the various religious ceremonies and functions of the Order, although Selene had never found any interest in it; *Lux* knew that her parents had dragged her to high rituals of the Order enough as a child.

The new students found the workload unexpectedly brutal. "Ugh," Selen exclaimed over lastmeal at the end of a particularly long week. "I am so tired!"

That night, the miasma came.

For the previous two weeks, Selene and Ichabod had been studying the history and properties of the miasma in Professor Thallos's observational learning class.

"Like there's any use in studying this," Selene commented.

"Oh, I don't know about that. The mist is not something I'd ever wish on anyone," Ichabod observed darkly. But he and Selene and the other students dutifully poured over their texts, committing complex conceptual schemas and long lists of dates and events to memory. Primary among their texts was the *Amaraeus*.

Amaraeus, a Dialogue on the Nature of Miasma and the Plague

Persons of the dialogue: **Amaraeus**, *Lucerna Scientia, and* **Timalus, called "The Moth,"** *his student.*

Amaraeus: Timalus, the miasma has returned this year, as we predicted, and once again taken the life of a student. It has taken the lives of many here at the Academy over the centuries—yet always only those in their first three years of study. You observed the Death drifting through our streets and across our courtyards, did you not? Although its origin remains hidden to us, we can at least now confirm its four-year cycle: three years it will skip, but the fourth year inevitably brings the Death. Do you agree?

Timalus: Yes, great teacher. We have confirmed the four-year cycle. I have observed the Death in the past, as a young child, but never before with the discipline of a scholar. This time, as I watched it form, move, and disappear, it struck me as if it were almost a living being, and I wondered. What could be its purpose? Surely it cannot come from *Lux*. I fear I err in so speaking, for do not all things come from *Lux*? And yet, how could something so malevolent be of *Lux*? Surely, then, it is a force apart. And thus, pendulum-like, my mind swings between two untenable beliefs, and I feel only the pain and uncertainty of ignorance.

Amaraeus: Your questions show you to be a wise student, Timalus, for knowledge of one's ignorance is a precious and rare thing. Long has the Death puzzled even our greatest scholars. Not one has yet been able to place it within the order of things, although many have been the attempts. There is one understanding that I favor, however: it has been posited that it is not of *Lux,* but is simply a force inherent to Erden itself—a vapor, perhaps, produced in the depths, rising to trouble the surface.

(Interlinear gloss by Scholar-Priest Alorex, known for her knowledge of Caelestis: Many, in their haste, claim that *Lux* must be the origin of all things, for *Lux* is the source of all light. Yet we must remember that even the light of *Lux* casts shadows, and there are places beyond the reach of *Lux.* The Death is such a shadow.)

Timalus: If the miasma is not of *Lux,* then what is its nature? Our studies of Erden have revealed mysteries enough, yet not a scintilla of evidence for the natural origin of the Death. Are these two the only possibilities—it is of *Lux* or it is of nature?

Amaraeus: Indeed, Timalus. There are many possibilities to consider; Erden is older than our understanding. You have heard that Being was at first a great chaos? I say that the miasma is a primal aspect of that initial chaos. Thus, in harmony with the fourfold being of nature, it, too, appears every four years as nothing more than a natural phenomenon.

Timalus: Then, teacher, does it not follow that the miasma is something wild which exists outside of *Lux*? We should fear it and attempt to tame it, for *Lux*, and for ourselves.

(Interlinear gloss by Scholar-Priest Eliana, known for her wisdom of Divine Reason: *Lux's* will extends as a potential in all things but need not be actualized in all things if, for example, the remnants of the initial chaos serve a purpose. Student Timalus speaks incorrectly, though not unwisely.)

Amaraeus: No, Timialus, fear is unjustified and unworthy of followers of *Lux*. Fear is a poor companion to wisdom. We must approach the Death with caution, and yet with commitment. Though the Death be but a remnant of chaos, and though we may conclude that it serves a purpose, yet it is still something to be studied and eventually controlled.

(Interlinear gloss by Scholar-Priest Seraphis, founder of the Great Archive of the Academy: Herein lies the tension between reverence and inquiry. The miasma humbles us, for it reminds us that there are forces and knowledge beyond our grasp. But to disregard study would be to yield to ignorance. *Lux* demands that we gain knowledge, but only that which is knowledge of *Lux*, through which all truth is revealed.)

Timalus: Ah. So, we must accept the Death as part of the natural order, although it stands apart from *Lux*, and we must at the same time seek to understand and overcome it. And what of those who have suffered and will suffer the Death? Each cycle reveals our continued failure. Are those deaths just? How can they be? Why does it only affect registrants? Why is only one generation in four born at risk? And the one generation out of every four that it affects; is it not impudence to act to protect those young people, freshly come into their time of reason?

Amaraeus: Protection is prudence. *Lux* would ask for no less. If burning sweet herbs, ingesting healthful tonics, and demarking thresholds have brought only partial mitigation, it is clear by the result that in applying these, we are giving effect to the will of *Lux*. It differs not from wearing a cloak to protect against the winter wind; would *Lux* have us suffer from the frost? We shall, in due time, understand and thus master the Death fully; in this I trust in *Lux*.

(Interlinear gloss by Scholar-Priest Delos, greatest of the leaders of the Order: Here, Amaraeus speaks wisely. To protect against the unknown is the first duty of those who serve *Lux*. The miasma is no ordinary ailment; it respects no boundary and obeys no command. Protection is the path of wisdom, not presumption.)

Timalus: Then, even if we cannot know its origin, we may still defend against its effects. But I wonder, master; will there ever be a time when we might fully uncover the miasma's secrets? Might there come a scholar who can pierce the veil and find its source?

Amaraeus: Ah, the question of hope. *Lux* has given us minds to question, but has also given us limits. We must strive, yes, and in striving, come closer to the truth. Yet some truths, Timalus, lie hidden because they must be so, at least for now. The miasma's nature may be one of these—a mystery that humbles us, keeps us vigilant, and reminds us of the frailty of life.

(Interlinear gloss by Scholar-Priest Marconis, author of *Commentaries On the Death*: There are mysteries that will never yield to human knowledge. The miasma, as a force left over from the time of chaos, is a reminder of boundaries we are not meant to cross until the proper season comes. Let us seek understanding, but with caution and humility.)

Timalus: I understand, teacher. The miasma is a challenge not only to our faith but also to our wisdom. *Lux's* light only illuminates that which needs illumination to maintain the world of great beneficence in which we live. A thing may not be *of Lux,* but it will be *for Lux.*

Amaraeus: Precisely, Timalus. The Death is a boundary marker, a lesson in the limits of human inquiry, expansive though they be. We shall study it and defend against it, but we must not presume that we shall ever fully know it. And therein lies our place: as seekers within boundaries, students of that which can be known, and respectful of both that which is known and that which cannot be known.

(Interlinear gloss by Scholar-Priest Tiberon the Silent: To think one can master the Death is folly. The Death is no mere force but an agent of the unknowable, the chaos that borders the order of *Lux.* To try to know the unknown is to attempt to square a circle. What fool tries to step into the same river twice?)

(**Response by Scholar-Priest Alorex:** Again, Tiberon the not-so Silent reveals his apostasy!)

———————◆———————

"Registrant Selene, what are the three protective measures?" Professor Thallos was grilling the students. The unfortunate student who had asked about the Universe Room on their first day—Elara—had again wilted under the professor's fierce questioning, and it was now Selene's turn. At least the question was an easy one to answer.

"Burning herbs, ingesting healthful tonics, and demarking thresholds, Professor," she was able to blurt out from her seat high in the back of the lecture hall.

"That is *mostly* correct, Selene. But what kinds of herbs? Surely burning bitter yarrow or black cabbageleaf would not produce a salutary effect."

"I'm sorry, professor," Selene had turned beet-red. "I should have said 'sweet herbs.' My mother used to burn basil, coriander, and mint," she finished with a rush.

"Yes, well," Professor Thallos cleared his throat, "I'm sure your mother is a very wise woman." He turned to Ichabod. "Registrant Ichobold," he began.

"Ichabod, Professor," Ichabod corrected him for what seemed like the twelfth time.

"Yes. Ichabord. Would *Lux* have us suffer from the cold? Think before you answer, young man."

That's straight from the text. Professor Thallos seems to have developed a very low opinion of Ichabod, thought Selene. *I wonder why.*

Ichabod was not at all troubled by the conversation or the question, however, and immediately answered, "No, professor. The cold is not of *Lux,* although it is *for Lux,* and hence, we not only may protect ourselves from it, it is our duty to do so. Which makes me wonder, professor, if I may revive the fire in the stove?"

The class laughed as Professor Thallos looked less than pleased, but he nodded sharply at Ichabod, who proceeded to stoke the fire while clearly enjoying the warmth proximity to the rotund stove granted.

And so the questioning continued, each student demonstrating their understanding of the dialogue (or lack of it). In the end, all were excused with the imperative that they work on their memorization of the text.

The miasma came in the late evening two weeks later, just before veil, the middle hour of the night (short for "scholar's veil," the *Go-With* said). Long past lastlight, when all students were supposed to be in bed, Selene, unable to sleep, had skirted the third-floor ledge around the building to Ichabod's room to share the miseries of a young scholar. He didn't mind in the least.

"How am I supposed to keep up with all this work?" Selene complained. "We are expected to know everything already."

"You are nearly the best student in the class, Selene," Ichabod attempted to reassure her.

"Oh, easy for you to say, mister smarty pants. You *are* the best student in the class. And still, Professor Thallos seems to hate you. 'Ichabord.' What's up with that?'

"I dunno. I've been wondering..." But Ichabod was never to finish the sentence, interrupted by a bone-chilling scream that came from the direction of Selene's room, through the window and around the corner. In an instant, both students were out the window and hurrying around the ledge, and tumbling through Selene's window into her room, where all was empty and still. They quickly traversed the room, opened her door, and entered the hallway.

"It's Elara. It's the Death!" a student shouted. Rushing down the hall, Selene and Ichabod pushed Elara's door fully open to see a fine mist that, to Selene's eyes, glowed bright red and then dimmed until it reached a deep pulsating red. And then Elara was gone.

At that moment, Selene saw the world wobble—that was the best she could describe it later—and felt herself passing out. As she was losing consciousness, she peered into the dark mist that was now so deep into the spectrum that it was like black rust. She saw...she was not sure what she saw. She, like every citizen of the Prinship, had heard descriptions of the miasma before, but this was different; it didn't at all match how she had heard it described. First was the color. It was supposed to be gray, not red like this. And it seemed like a living thing, but without the shape of any living thing she knew. *It has the shape of a mind*, she thought. *That makes no sense at all. But that's what it is...an agent without a proper body. A duality in reality.* It was too much, and she fell into blackness and nonexistence.

CHAPTER THREE

PURIFICATION

The next morning, the students worked at the direction of the faculty to purify the entire school. A great quantity of the sweet herbs the students had been discussing just days before—basil, coriander, and mint—was provided to cleanse rooms and hallways. For firstmeal, the students were served a tonic made from those same herbs. Selene was surprised that the taste was so repulsive but dared not say anything; a pall hung about everyone, and even though the students were traumatized and burning with questions, hardly anyone spoke. When they did, it was not more than a subdued word. Nor did the faculty encourage discussion.

Selene felt overwhelmed. She found herself hiding in the Universe, cleansing the same table repeatedly, her mind replaying Elara's first interaction with Professor Thallos and wondering if it had anything to do with why the Death had taken her. Why Elara? She had proven herself to be a hard-working student, and had at least survived Professor Thallos's relentless questioning, even though she had been quiet and barely interacted with the other students. She just seemed so harmless.

It makes no sense at all, Selene thought as she sat with her head in her hands. Absorbed in thought, she did not notice when students from both Adamus House and Elisius House quietly filed in, followed by Professor Thallos. The professor put a hand on Selene's shoulder and, when she looked up, waved her to a seat with the other students. When they were settled, he addressed them.

"You all knew this was the last year of the cycle. That this was a Death Year," he began. "Knowledge does not always deliver under-standing, however."

"You also know from your recent studies that the Death and the miasma that brings it are not fully understood. Perhaps one day, one of you will contribute to a greater understanding of these things, and you will look back to today. Perhaps it will then make sense—make full sense to you. I have held that hope in my soul since I was a registrant like you. Oh, yes, Registrant Maris. I, too, was once a registrant. I was, in fact, a resident of Elisius House."

"Fifteen times I have lived through the cycle of the miasma and the takings. Not all cycles have seen a taking from among my students, but enough have to fill me with inextinguishable sadness. For this reason, I have devoted the entirety of my scholarship for many years to unraveling the puzzle that is the Death."

The students looked at the professor with surprise. None had ever considered Professor Thallos's life outside of teaching, much less what he was like when he was their age. They all knew in some abstract way that scholar-priests have duties other than seeing that the students suffer as they memorize their elenchi, but that he would spend his time on something so concrete, so real, and so very unpleasant, never occurred to them.

"Please, professor," came a voice from the back of the room, "We all have memorized the *Amaraeus*, and we all know the true doctrine. But is there anything more?" At that moment, it was the most important question of all. The students regarded Professor Thallos intently.

"The true doctrine teaches enough for life," he said in a measured voice. "There is a balance between knowledge and error, as the *Amaraeus* teaches. You must learn to live within that balance. Trust *Lux*. Trust your teachers. Trust the Academy and the Principality. If, during a life of service in your chosen field, you are given a deeper understanding or new answers beyond the old, then know that it is as *Lux* intended. Know that it is thus right and good. Know as well that just as your sorrow now is right and good, all that has happened and all that will happen are also right and good."

"There will be no classes this afterzenith. I suggest you stay with your friends and take time to heal. Remember Elara. Be kind to one another. As *Lux* is kind to us."

As the class was leaving, Ichabod walked up to Selene. "Come with me?" he asked. She nodded, forced a deep breath slowly in and out, and followed him out of the Universe.

"We need to get out, I think," Ichabod observed. "Have you been to the Arboretum yet?"

"No. What's the Arboretum? And when did you get a chance to go there?"

"It's a place full of trees. Where did you think I was always going after lastmeal?"

"Uh...you sure you want me to answer that?" she responded.

"Come on, we can be there in just a few minutes," Ichabod strode briskly ahead.

"Hey. Wait!" Selene yelled, trotting to catch up.

Selene thought the Arboretum lovely. The branches above were filled with activity, and the trees...the trees! They must have been ancient. Some reached hundreds of feet into the air. Nor were they all of one kind. Selene saw every species of tree she knew and even more that she didn't. Some spread slender branches of velvet purple covered in lavender needles. Others had stout trunks covered with thick bark of mottled browns and greens, and waxy leaves as big as serving trays. The ground cover was a riot of colors, formed, as Selene saw when she inspected it closely, by innumerable tiny wildflowers spread across the forest floor like a patchwork blanket.

The flittering in the trees turned out to be tiny birds with iridescent heliotrope bodies, heads a deep red hue, and vibrant yellow legs and feet. They twittered above the two registrants like squeaky wheels as Selene and Ichabod made their way deeper into the woodland along a well-kept path. The Arboretum wasn't quite a forest, but it wasn't quite a park, either. Selene had never seen anything like it.

"Those are aedon birds. They love the needletrees," Ichabod offered.

"Are we allowed to be here?" Selene asked as her head swiveled around, trying to follow the birds as they tag-teamed through the canopy.

"Oh, sure. Yes. I am sure we are. I mean, no one has stopped me yet. Of course. I didn't actually *ask* anyone. But it's a park, right? So, it's here for people to enjoy it, right?" Ichabod hadn't entirely convinced even himself.

Selene laughed. "Oh, of *course* it's OK. Why did I even bother to ask the question? Say, what's that?" She was pointing at a rocky formation set back about 50 feet from the path.

"That, Selene, is our destination."

It was a bit of a scramble to reach the rocks, but once there, Selene found herself in a natural alcove hidden behind a particularly large boulder. The two registrants, winded from their hike, sat down on low rocks that formed almost perfect benches deep in the alcove. There was no evidence that the formation was anything but natural, although the beautiful marbling and veins of copper-colored metal lent an almost regal splendor to the stone. *It really seems almost too perfect*, thought Selene. After getting comfortable, she looked up at Ichabod.

"Ichabod, something weird happened to me in Elara's room last night. I think I am going crazy."

"Why? What happened? You mean when you fainted?"

"Yes. I mean, it's probably nothing. But when we opened her door and saw the mist all deep red and pulsing, I..."

"You saw what?" Ichabod interrupted. "Selene, the miasma looked the way it always looks—like a dark gray mist. It wasn't red, and it certainly wasn't pulsing."

"Not red? Ichabod, it was deep red, at least at the end. So deep that it was almost black. And it *was* pulsing. At least, that's what I saw. You didn't see it?"

"Okay," he replied, holding up his hands in surrender. "If you say that it was red and pulsing, then it was red and pulsing. But, no, it was gray and just kind of fuzzy, the way it always is. At least, to me. Did anything happen after that?"

"Well...I was probably hallucinating, but I could have sworn that the mist wasn't just a thing. It...*felt*...like a mind. Like a mind without a body. Like...I don't know. A nightmare in which the mist was threatening us." She was looking at her feet by this point.

Ichabod thought for a long moment. "Well, I still say it was just your mind playing tricks. But you *did* faint. That was weird. I just assumed it was the stress, but you were the only one who fainted. And no one really understands the Death. I wonder if there was something unusual about where you were standing, something about the air, maybe, that allowed you to see the mist in a way that no one else ever has. Maybe it was the lighting? Maybe that distorted your view?"

Selene was grateful that Ichabod hadn't simply dismissed her. "Yeah. Maybe. I don't know. But it sure felt real. I've seen the mist before, although I was little and don't remember it much. But this was different. You didn't feel or see anything weird about it?"

Ichabod shook his head slowly. "Nope. The thing is, I have seen the Death before, and it was pretty much exactly the same as this time. Not red. Just gray. And not pulsing."

Selene sensed that Ichabod was about to tell her something important to him and gently prodded him. "Was it someone in your family?"

"Yeah," he said sadly. "My cousin." Selene waited for him to continue.

"It wasn't all that long ago. I was 12 years old, and it was my older cousin Vespera. Named after the river, of course, and it fit her. She always just seemed to flow through life so easily. She was my absolute favorite. Actually took time to talk with me and never talked down to me, even though she was four years older. She had just started her registrant year and was visiting our house with her parents over the weekend. They had her sleeping in my room while I slept on the couch in the living room. Everyone had gone to bed just a few minutes before, and I needed another blanket. So, I went to my room, and when I went in, I saw the mist, and then Vespera was gone. But the mist was gray, Selene." Tears dimmed Ichabod's eyes. "It devastated my aunt and uncle. I guess you never think it's going to be someone you know—or, at least, you think it won't be someone in your family."

Selene felt sorry for him, but she was also quite interested in his description of the miasma. She knew she shouldn't press him on the issue. She did anyway.

"Ichabod, I saw what I saw. The miasma was a deep, pulsing red. I really don't think it was in my mind or a trick of the lighting or anything like that. It felt *real*, as did my sense that there was something there. I think this is important, Ichabod. In fact, I *know* that it's important," she asserted emphatically.

Ichabod shook off the sad memory. "How do you know it's important?"

Selene grunted in frustration. "I don't know how I know it. I just know it! You know the feeling you get when you just know you've done a good job on a test? You just *feel* it? I feel this, Ichabod. That's all."

"Hm. Well, let's assume that what you perceived is really what was there. It's possible, I guess. After all, according to the *Amaraeus elenchi*, no one has discovered anything new about the Death in...what, a dozen centuries?"

"More than that."

"Well, then, it's about time that someone unearthed something new about it. And if that someone is you, just think: you will be the star student of the school. And just a registrant, too!"

Selene grimaced. "Uh. I don't really care about that. I'd rather not have the attention." She became thoughtful. "Anyway, the Death has come and gone for this cycle. The next three years are skip years. It's not like we can do anything about it for now. Not for another four years—by which time we'll probably have graduated. So, I guess it really doesn't matter. We might as well just..."

Ichabod interrupted her before she finished her thought. "I think what we need is to find out if anyone has ever had an experience like yours. I bet no one has, but if they have, where would we look that up? Who could we ask?"

Selene looked at Ichabod, puzzled, until he answered his own question. "Professor Thallos, of course."

Professor Thallos listened to Selene's account of the miasma but brushed away their questions. "I believe we have established in our class discussions, Registrant Selene," he began heavily, "that truth is a matter of patience. You are a new student, so this may be hard for you to understand, but wisdom is not the work of a day. Remember, the parts of a picture never tell the whole story, and unless you can see the whole picture, you are not in a position to judge, merely to receive passively. This is an important principle, Registrant Selene..."

As Professor Thallos settled into what Selene was sure would be a long, discursive treatment of the virtues of patience and passivity, her mind wandered. She looked around his office. The professor had occupied the space for many, many years. Selene idly wondered how many. The furniture was old-fashioned, and clouds of dust had billowed when she and Ichabod first plumped down in the antique high-backed chairs. The professor sat at an ancient desk, the heavy wooden top of which was gouged and stained in places, evidence of many accidents with ink and ceramic mugs and plates. Behind Professor Thallos and to his left were two walls of shelves, books haphazardly placed on them with no discernable organization. The shelves, like the desk, gave a general impression of disorder. Except for the bottom shelf behind the desk: it contained a neat row of file folders, some new and some old enough that the covers had yellowed significantly.

To the right of the professor was a large window which reached the ceiling of the office about twenty feet above them. The only view through this window was of vines that had taken over and through which daylight filtered, casting a purplish hue on everything. In front of the window was a small cabinet on wheels, on top of which were a few mugs and a pot. Beneath the students' feet lay a worn carpet that originally had some design on it; the only part Selene could now pick out was the profile of a building with a dozen once-bright windows and a chimney. All in all, the office felt like a battered survivor from centuries past.

"...And so I would ask you to think about this, reflect on it, and make it the creed by which you conduct your life as a student at the Academy, Registrant Selene. You, too, Registrant Ichibard. Now, I must ask you to return to your studies. Please do not hesitate to come to me should you have any more questions. As you leave, you can tell whoever has been waiting in the hallway to enter." And with that, Selene and Ichabod thanked the professor and headed for the door, letting the student, a fifth-year fellow who had been waiting impatiently, know that the professor would see him. As the student entered, Selene could see he was carrying a very old edition of a dialogue she'd never heard of before; it had the odd title *Meditations on First Philology, in which the lucent path and the eternal Lux are demonstrated against the Malicious Deceiver.* She couldn't quite read the author's name.

"Hey, Ichabod, did you notice the old book the fellow was carrying? Something about *Lux* and a Malicious Deceiver?"

"No. Sounds like a weird topic, though. I wonder what it's about," he replied.

"So do I," responded Selene, as she and Ichabod made their way back to Celestine Hall.

·· ———————◆——————— ··

Later, after he had satisfied the impatient fellow's curiosity, Professor Thallos closed and latched the door to his office, cleared off a miscellany of student work that had collected on his desk, turned to the shelf behind him, and pulled out one of the more yellowed folders. He scanned the label carefully, although he already knew what it said: "Miasma Incident, y2298 AL." For sixty years, Professor Thallos had focused his scholarship on the Death. It was more than a focus, however. It was his life's work. Having neither a spouse nor a family nor even any close relatives, his work on the Death filled all of these absences. The study of the Death was his best and worst friend, and his best and worst enemy. Teaching had become almost meaninglessly repetitive over the years; it was as rote for him as was the memorization of the *elenchi* for the first-year students. Not that he was a poor teacher. His students invariably left his care as well-trained as they could possibly be, and he hoped they found him a reasonably compassionate mentor. But the moments of instruction years earlier had become, for him, interruptions in the more important task of understanding the Death. Questions about the miasma, about its four-year cycle, about its appearance—these were omnipresent in his thoughts. Even when he was teaching, these questions lurked somewhere in his mind, always ready for an unexpected connection to be made.

Disappointingly few had been those connections over the years. He had personally collected excellent records of each appearance of the miasma on campus, and many occurring elsewhere, spanning his sixty years of tenure, and had added many records—some excellent, some only fragmentary, some lifted surreptitiously from the Great Archive—going back further centuries. But, on the whole, these records told him little. *If the head of the Archive discovered me in possession of some of these older documents,* he chuckled to himself, *there would be some uncomfortable questions asked.* Still, Professor Thallos felt that he had at all times remained within the ambit of *Lux* and had always acted with the utmost reverence while simultaneously seeking a proper understanding of the great scourge of their otherwise idyllic society. *Well, they can have the records back when I am dead,* he thought, privately amused by what he imagined would be a fair amount of consternation among those administrators when they realized how much had been purloined. *Anyway, I am the only scholar-priest who has thought to investigate the Death so systematically, and did so even though the chancellor frowned upon it.*

The Miasma Incident of y2298 AL...now forty years ago, he thought idly. Professor Thallos had interviewed everyone he could at the time—not just those few people directly involved, but everyone and anyone he could corner. *It's wrongly named, though,* he thought. *The important events occurred four years earlier, in y2294. But no one want-*

ed to admit it, then or now. The misnaming was just part of a desire that it all be kept as quiet as possible. Professor Thallos had not been fooled then, and he wasn't fooled now.

The first item in the folder was a list he himself had created in y2298, after the student—Ravian was his name—had been taken by the miasma. Two things about this case were very curious and had caused Professor Thallos to come back to this file many times over the years, until the folder itself was half-disintegrating.

First, Ravian had been a fellow—a fifth-year student and twenty years old. Never before, at least according to any official record anywhere in the Principality, had a twenty-year-old been taken by the Death. Always, the miasma would descend on a young man or woman of sixteen or seventeen years of age. Several theories for the age anomaly had been advanced at the time. Ravian had been a small, philosophically inclined young man who was often absorbed in his own thoughts to the exclusion of the world around him. Those who didn't know him were often surprised he *was* a fellow; they usually took him for a second-year initiate or, sometimes, a first year registrant. So, suggested some, perhaps he just *seemed* younger than he was, and this caused the miasma to collect around him. Maybe the records of his birth year were wrong.

Another theory held that the taking was caused by something Ravian himself had done. Perhaps it was his too-great interest in matters of dialectical philology. Perhaps something about his mind attracted the miasma.

A third theory said that it was just a random mistake and that there was no explanation for it beyond that, and "Thank *Lux* it has never happened again."

However, during the many interviews Professor Thallos had conducted, he had discovered something no one else knew, something which eliminated the various theories that had been floated at the time. Four years before the Death had come for him, Ravian, much like

Selene, had witnessed a taking, and in a moment of incaution, had asked a classmate, "Is the mist always red like that? Does it always vibrate? I heard it was colorless and indistinct." Ravian's classmate, an apprentice named Perian who later became an important carer in Academy City, had looked at Ravian with horror on her face; he put her off with a joke and never mentioned it again.

Now, forty years later, Professor Thallos was the only person on all of Erden who had full knowledge of the Miasma Incident of y2298 AL and who also knew that something similar was happening again. He pondered its significance. *Does this mean that Selene is in danger? But not immediate danger,* he thought. *If the same pattern holds, then Selene won't be taken by the Death for another four years—but she might well be in danger then, even though she should be too old to be taken. Perhaps there is no pattern here at all, anyway. Can there be a pattern when there is only one datum? But there is a pattern: three skip years and a taking. That's held for centuries. Ravian's is the only case I know of, in which this pattern was broken.*

As Professor Thallos mulled over Ravian's case, he shuffled through the rest of the file, finding nothing of interest until he reached the last page in the stack. He unfolded a poem that Ravian had written shortly after his first encounter with the miasma in y2294. Scrawled next to the poem, in a hurried, scratchy, and uncertain hand that may or may not have been Ravian's, were the words "First Philology - Malicious Deceiver!"

Of red, no one but I know;
Why should this secret be only mine?
To share it would be to breathe as a fool,
To withhold, to all would be unkind.
My mind is tormented, e'en as I sleep,
In waking, the image is fire,
Oh! *Lux*, please release me, release me, release me!
To whom the whole of Erden is a briar.

What's always before my eyes and my mind,
Must soon become silt in the ocean.
To *Lux*, I commit my whole heart and soul;
To *Lux*, my complete devotion.

Perhaps, thought Professor Thallos, *the young man's emotional pain did indeed attract Lux. Perhaps the exception for a fifth-year student was a kind of divine kindness.* The professor was not satisfied with this explanation either. *How many people have suffered through the ages, even in a world as gentle and kind as Erden? Why would Lux grant mercy to only one person, whose suffering, based on his poem, may have been greater than most knew but certainly was not extraordinary?* The professor shrugged mentally. *This time, it will be different. This time, I am forewarned and can do what should have been done in y2294. Information. Information is key. I need to collect as much information as I can...*

He pulled a stack of clean folders from a drawer in his desk and labeled them: "Selene," "Ichabod," "Elara," and so on, a folder for every student currently under his care, every student who resided in either Adamus House or Elisius House. He then created a form on a blank piece of paper, at the top of which he placed columns for the names, ages, and remarkable characteristics of each person. Repeating this on page after page and placing one in each of the folders soon produced a substantial stack. The clocks had tolled several hours by the time Professor Thallos set aside the folders and returned home, where he ate a cold lastmeal of treeleaf pie leftover from the day before, and fell into a troubled sleep.

CHAPTER FOUR

LASTLIGHT DREAMS

T hat night, the nightmares started.

Selene dreamed she was watching the miasma take another student, but not in the Academy of the present; this was many centuries in the past. She wasn't sure why she thought the nightmare was set so many years before; her surroundings in the dream looked much the same as the Academy in her time—the same brick and marble buildings, the same pathways, the same gardens. Even so, she knew it wasn't the present. The victim was another student. His dormitory room had the same simple furnishings Selene's did: a wardrobe, a writing table, a bed, a washbasin, and a few other odds and ends, althogh an ancient edition of an *elenchus* rested open on the writing table. The mist had collected and hovered above the student's bed, progressing through the colors of the prism until it reached a deep, deep red, where it remained and pulsed until the student was gone, just as Selene had seen when Elara was taken. Selene had the same sense of a being emanating from the mist. She was unnerved, but she attributed the nightmare to recent events and said nothing about it to Ichabod.

The next night was much the same, although this time Selene dreamed of a taking from only a few years earlier. She was not at all surprised when, on the third night, the nightmare returned, but this night she dreamed of two takings, one from perhaps a century earlier and one from deep antiquity—so far back she really had no framework for it and could only say that it "felt" like it occurred near the time of the founding of the Principality.

Selene woke at call on the third morning, exhausted. Her pillow was wet with sweat, and when she ran her hands through her hair, she found it damp as well. *That was bad*, she thought. *The dreams seem like they only last for a few minutes, but these took up the whole night again.* She went to her washbasin to splash water on her face and, while she was dressing, thought about the last dream in particular. *That one definitely seemed like it was from long ago. The buildings—they were all so different. Not at all like today. Plain, and kind of blocky and gray. I've never seen such buildings. Everything was so featureless. And I remember a name; someone was saying it as the Death came. It was an odd name. Something like "Jonathan." Who has ever had a name like that? Whoever he was, he seemed too old for a taking. Maybe it was just my imagination. Or stress. But it all felt so real.* She shook her head as if to shake away the nightmares, finished dressing, and headed to firstmeal.

"You look like you've been walking the Wastes," Ichabod remarked as Selene approached his table.

"The Wastes! I bet I do. I didn't expect to hear that expression from you, though. You don't believe in that stuff, do you?"

Ichabod's face reddened. "No. Not really. My parents are lay members of the Order, though, so I sort of grew up with those stories. You know, how *Lux* split chaos in two to create the sky above Erden and the land below, and then scattered gems across the sky that became stars.

Or, the story of the thousand lost scholar-priests who simply stopped traveling out of frustration and ended up founding the Prinship."

"Yeah, but at least that story could be actual history. You don't believe those taken by the Death end up in the Wastes, though, do you?" Selene was genuinely curious. "My parents do. But I think people just disappear and cease to exist. You know how Professor Thallos would make us ask the question?" Selene mimicked the professor's sonorous lecturing style. "Why would their *essentia* be to wander an endless waste, completely isolated from *Lux*, truth, and knowledge? Why wouldn't that be ours as well? Why wouldn't that be the *essentia* of all life? Observational learning says that all life is of a piece on Erden. The inconsistency argues against the conjecture." She grinned and concluded, "Believing in the Wastes is such old-fashioned thinking. It's like we are trying to blame the victims of the Death while thinking of ourselves as superior."

Ichabod tipped his head slightly. "Well, anyway, you look awful, Selene. Are you okay?"

"Yes. No. I am not sure." *I still haven't processed this yet*, Selene thought to herself. "I have been having nightmares. But not normal nightmares. I swear, they have been lasting all night long, although when I am asleep, they seem to take only a few minutes. It's like my sleep-brain is moving slowly while the real world moves at the speed of a runaway cart." Selene laughed ruefully and told Ichabod about her dreams.

"Those don't exactly sound like dreams, Selene. Sounds more like you are actually experiencing takings."

"That's not possible," Selene pointed out, even though she agreed with him.

"No. But maybe you are experiencing, like, an *echo* of past takings."

"I guess. Have you ever heard of anyone..."

Selene's question was cut off by the arrival of another resident of Adamus House, a registrant with generous blonde curls named

Altheia. Neither Selene nor Ichabod had actually met her, but they knew she was a "talker" and braced themselves for a rush of words.

"Can I sit here? There aren't any other places to sit. But I don't want to interrupt you two! You always seem so deep in conversation. Is that why you are both so smart? Although Professor Thallos isn't very nice to you, Ichabod, which is weird because you always seem to have the right answer. I'm Altheia. I don't know if you know that, but you are Selene and—Ichabod. What a lovely old name. I just love it!" She glanced coyly at Ichabod, who was, to her great annoyance, oblivious.

Having seated herself next to Ichabod, Altheia's chatter continued. "Don't you just love the firstmeals here? I could load up every day on sticky buns and hot brew. But that wouldn't be good for the digestion, would it? At *my* house, we are very careful about what we eat, although we always have loads on the table. My pets get most of it after meals, anyway. They love me for it! Do you have pets? I bet you didn't know that my parents were students at the Academy, too. Ages ago. They met in moral philology, and my dad couldn't get my mom's attention, so he intentionally said that the purpose of life is to have fun, just to upset her, and when she was well-steamed at him, he asked her out to midmeal to talk about it. Then, they fell in love and got married. Isn't that romantic? Oh, mist! I've spilled some hot brew on my clothes! Do you have an extra napkin, Icky?" Ichabod visibly flinched at the nickname. "Here, I'll just borrow yours. You are such a dear."

Selene wondered how Altheia had enough breath for this cascade of sentences and really had no desire to make more friends at school—one was enough, and she and Ichabod had things to do. But she would never be unkind, so she simply observed, "It looks like you got the stain out, Altheia. I can hardly see it now."

"Well, thank *Lux* for that. I wouldn't want to go to moral philology with a big target on me. I am doing poorly enough. If I can't start doing better, my parents are going to be very unhappy. They even might not let me visit the serveries in the market district over the weekend. Say, would you two like to start a study group? I'm not very good at moral philology, but I am a whiz with observational learning, especially when it comes to commerce. My parents own the big servery in the middle of the market district of Academy City, you know. You've probably been there. Everyone goes there."

"I've never been in the City proper," said Ichabod. "What's it like?"

"Oh, it's wonderful. You can get sweetnuts at my parents' store, of course. Everyone loves those, although the store mostly has regular things; furniture and clothing and toys, things like that. They just keep the sweetnuts to bring people in. There are all kinds of shops in the City. If we had a study group, I could tell you all about it. Maybe we could go there some weekend. My parents would like it if I had really smart friends."

By this time, Ichabod and Selene had finished their meals and needed to get to their morning classes. They agreed with Altheia that a study group might be a good idea without really meaning it, and then hurried off.

"I'll see you at lastmeal," Altheia waved to them as they left.

"Please, please, *please*, don't start calling me 'Icky,' okay, Selene?"

"Wouldn't think of it," she grinned. "Also, I had an idea in the middle of that inundation. I think I need to talk to Professor Thallos again."

"Why? Last time, all we got was a lecture about patience. A lecture we've heard seventeen times in his classes," Ichabod grimaced. "It was interesting seeing his office, I guess, but why would you want to go through that again?"

"Professor Thallos has spent—how many years did he say? A bunch, anyway, on the Death. My dreams, they match what I saw when Elara was taken. That should interest him. And my dreams have an added component, too: all the colors, the full spectrum. Not just red or gray."

Ichabod nodded. "I would expect him to be *very* interested in that. In fact..." Here, his eyes widened with a realization. "Why, he should have been way more interested in what happened to you the other day. If the Death has been the focus of his scholarship for however long, then isn't it weird that he wasn't more interested last time? But he just droned on about our duties as registrants and didn't ask you any questions at all. I mean, we've heard that speech at least a billion times from him already."

"I thought it was only seventeen," Selene laughed. "Here's another thought: what exactly got him interested in the Death all those years ago? Do you suppose something happened to him? Like, maybe he saw the mist up close himself, and saw something unusual about it. I'd like to know. Wouldn't you?"

Ichabod nodded. "Okay. We should talk to him again. I agree. But we can't just waltz in there and ask him, can we?"

"Why not?" Selene was energized. "Maybe that's the only way to get him to take us seriously. Maybe no one has ever asked him why he is so interested in the Death. I bet most people just take him for a peculiar, harmless old professor who wants to do something good for the world in the sort of abstract way that professors do. But doesn't it feel like there is more to him than that? We need to find out. Let's go see him this afternoon, after class."

Selene and Ichabod were anxious to finish their work and talk to Professor Thallos again, but the day seemed to drag on and on. Finally, after they had twice enumerated the antinomies of moral philology ("Moral law is composed of simples, yet all moral actions are compounds" and "*Lux* is the necessary ground of moral law, yet moral law is an eternal absolute"), they were out the door and trotting briskly to the professor's office.

Professor Thallos was not in, but, oddly, his door was ajar. When no one responded to their knocking, they pushed their way past the door and sat in the dusty seats with the tall backs, awaiting the professor's return.

"How long should we wait?" Selene asked after the first few minutes had passed. Ichabod shrugged, and the two spent a few more minutes listening to the sound of the blustery wind tapping a loose vine against the window. Soon, curiosity overcame them and they again looked around the office, more freely than they had during their first visit.

The bookshelves were filled with well-worn copies of all the standard texts that comprised an Academy education. There were *The Imperturbable Elenchi of Dialectical Philology* and *The Complete Observational Learning*, among other volumes. And then there were the neatly arranged folders. "What are all those folders? Look at them, Ichabod. They all have dates, and they are arranged chronologically."

"Hey, look here," he responded. "Here's one on the corner of his desk, labeled 'Miasma Incident y2298 AL.' Are they all about the mist?"

Selene got up and thumbed through the folders on the shelf. "Yes. Looks like it."

"Your story really must have had an effect on him, for him to have pulled this out; it can't be a coincidence. What are you doing?" Ichabod asked as Selene opened the folder on Professor Thallos's desk.

"I'm having firstmeal. What's it look like I am doing? Oh, this is interesting. Listen to this poem by some student named Ravian from forty years ago. 'Of red, no one but I know/Why should this secret be only mine?' Ichabod! Ravian had the same experience I had. It says here that he saw a taking *four years before he was taken.* And he described the miasma as red..." She flipped through more of the file.

"Oh. Ichabod, look, this is crazy. The Death took him four years later *when Ravian was a fellow.*"

"What? He was a fellow? A fifth-year? That's not supposed to happen."

"Nope. I've never heard of it ever happening. But that's what it says." Selene's face turned pale. "Does that mean...do you think...?"

"Nah," he replied, when he understood what she was implying. "There's probably more to the story. Or maybe Professor Thallos got the facts wrong. No way that's going to happen to you."

"Yeah. Maybe. I guess," Selene replied without conviction. No matter what Icabod said, the poem suggested she was still in danger. "'*Lux*, please release me, release me, release me...To *Lux*, I commit my whole heart and soul, to *Lux*, my complete devotion.' And look at what someone scrawled next to it: 'First Philology - Malicious Deceiver!' What does *that* mean?" It put her in mind of something, but what, she couldn't quite remember.

"I don't know, Selene, but I think the professor is not coming back to his office today, and I think it's time we got out of here."

The afternoon turned into evening as they made their way back for lastmeal, shooting down one theory after another about the "Malicious Deceiver" as they walked.

"I'm telling you, it was probably Professor Thallos who wrote that. He was accusing Ravian of being deceptive," argued Ichabod.

Selene shook her head. "No. The professor didn't write it. His handwriting is bad, but it looks nothing like that. The scrawl looked more like someone had written it years ago. It might even have been Ravian himself. Maybe he wrote the poem, decided that it was wrong in some way, and then wrote the comment in the margin."

"It's possible," agreed Ichabod. "Uh oh. Look out. Here comes Altheia."

"Hey, you two, I almost thought you weren't having lastmeal. Why are you coming from that direction? Oh. You got in trouble with

Professor Thallos again, didn't you, Ichabod? I really don't think he likes you very much."

"We were looking for Professor Thallos, but we couldn't find him," Selene tried to explain as they entered the food servery in Celestine Hall.

"Well, you sure do work hard on your school stuff. Wow, am I hungry. Look! They have eel and treeleaf pie!"

It took a few minutes for the three registrants to collect their food and make their way to a table in the crowded dining hall. Neither Selene nor Ichabod understood how it had happened, but Altheia had attached herself to them like a barnacle to a ship. They didn't mind all that much, except for the fact that Altheia really could talk nonstop. She was telling them again about her parents' servery, which seemed to be a general emporium for the well-to-do.

"Of course, last year we were almost able to buy out the old book-servery next door, and then we could have expanded *our* servery. But my parents decided against it. The bookserver is such a grump. And his store is just a chaotic mess. You can barely walk between the shelves. Who cares about all of those old books, anyway?"

This prickled something in Selene's memory. "You say it's all old books? What kinds of old books?"

"Oh, all kinds. Old school books, and a lot of books of the sort professors like to buy and put on their shelves, but never read. Nothing *good*. Probably some books people aren't supposed to have. No romantic stories or tales. I looked, and they don't even have my favorite, *Letters to the Thryssal Tree*." She looked meaningfully at Ichabod. "I can't imagine how they stay in business, really. My parents always say that you have to give the people what they want, and it's easier to do that if you just tell them what they want in the first place." Altheia seemed to think that this was a rather clever idea. "*Lux* eternal! That old bookstore mostly has things that no one could ever want, if you ask me."

Altheia's "*Lux* eternal" connected the dots in Selene's mind. The book the impatient fifth-year fellow had been lugging around when he visited Professor Thallos's office—what was it called? *Meditations on First Philology, in which the lucent path and the eternal Lux are demonstrated against the Malicious Deceiver. Somehow*, Selene thought, *that book, Ravian, my weird experience of the mist, and my dreams are all connected.*

"Say, Altheia," Selene said brightly. "Would you show us the market district in the City, and the bookservery, and your parents' emporium sometime? Neither Ichabod nor I have ever been to Academy City proper before. Our villages have hardly any serveries at all, and nothing like your parents' place, I bet. Would that be okay? It all sounds so splendid."

Altheia was quite pleased her new friends wanted to see her city and her parents' servery. "It *is* splendid! You have no idea! You will *love* it!"

Later, as they were walking back to their rooms just before lastlight, Selene whispered to Ichabod, "We need to go to that bookservery and see if they have a copy of the *Meditations* book. I don't want to wait until I am a fellow. Because...you know..."

Ichabod nodded. He knew exactly what Selene meant.

CHAPTER FIVE

ACADEMY CITY

S elene's nightmares continued, and the next few nights were nothing short of torment. Out of sheer desperation, she learned to force herself awake when the nightmares started and found she could then fall and remain asleep for the rest of the night. It didn't solve her problem, and it certainly didn't move her closer to an explanation for the dreams—which continued to feel entirely real to her—but at least she was able to function during the day.

Two weeks later found Selene, Ichabod, and Altheia in Academy City on a gorgeous *Fiat Caelestis Nocta*. The sun was shining high above, with only a few puffs of clouds scattered in the sky. The *Go-With's* description of Academy City was full of facts and figures and included a useful map, none of which prepared either Selene or Ichabod for how big everything was, especially the crowds. Neither of them had ever seen so many people or so many serveries, buildings, or carts in one place.

It was the day of the annual Vespera Regatta. In the distance, the three registrants could see Vesperan keelboats skimming the river—lean, easily driven, and carrying tall sails and spinnakers. They moved with grace and speed in the chop of the river as they passed out of sight behind the large warehouses of the market district. Looking to the center of the city, the giant Spire of Caelestis pointed to the sky, dominating everything, a moveable gnomon on top casting a shadow on the ground far below and acting as a giant analemmatic sundial. From the base of the Spire radiated the major boulevards of the City, each leading to different districts: market, city administration, the Academy itself, and several residential areas. Next to the Spire was the ornate, squat building of the Great Archive, containing the history of the Principality on thousands of hand-copied scrolls and books, some, according to the *Go-With*, more than two thousand years old.

Several small brooks wound through the city, arched stone bridges leaping across them here and there. By each of these bridges were statues representing various professions within the Prinship. The students noticed that the statues and bridges were all gaily draped with colorful flags and banners for the Regatta.

Selene and Ichabod were entranced. Her friends' naïveté amused Altheia, but, after long minutes spent following Ichabod and Selene as they gawked their way through the city, she guided them toward her home.

"What was it like where you grew up?" Altheia asked as they entered the Market District.

"It was just a Briner's village on the Reach for me," shrugged Selene, as if that explained everything.

"My parents are farmers," Ichabod said with pride. "We have three hundred and eight acres. It's the biggest farm in our division, coming right down to the edge of the Vespera River. We grow *everything* there. Mostly vegetables, but we have a section for roots, a copse that supplies wood, some fruit trees, and a bunch of chickens. I tell you, I miss the food. Nothing is as good as farm-fresh!"

"But..." Altheia hesitated, not wanting to insult the other two, but unable to squelch her curiosity. "What do you do for fun? If you don't have a market district like ours? And playhouses, and foodserveries, and..."

Selene glanced at Ichabod, who smiled gently in return. "Altheia," he gently explained. "Most people in the Prinship don't have much. Not like people in the City. But they are still happy. When I was young, I had endless paths through the fields to explore, and corvus birds to keep as pets, and while all we have in our village is a small servery, the primary school, the healer's house, the market, and our Universe Hall, we still have lots to do. We often have gatherings; people come from all around. They bring their music, and we share food and sing and dance. It feels like one huge, extended family." He sounded nostalgic, although he had only been away from home for a few months.

"When the Briners' boats come in after being on the water for a few days, nearly everyone in the village is there to greet and help them," Selene interjected, caught up in Ichabod's mood. "We build smokey bonfires to help them find the landing, and when the catch is unshipped and ready to send to market, people fill large containers over the fire with the best of the haul, all different kinds of fish and shellfish, all mixed together with roots and herbs. We throw sticks into the fire to send up sparks like stars into the night sky, and we listen to stories until the broth is done. Ichabod is right. The food at the Academy just isn't as good. Stuff tastes best when you can eat it right at the source."

Ichabod nodded in agreement. "Say, Altheia, maybe you'll visit our homes sometime."

"Oh. Yes. That would be very nice, I am sure." Altheia did not sound at all convinced and changed the subject. "Here's my parents' servery. Isn't it grand?" She smiled up at the large front of a three-story-tall building with a sign that declared EMPORIUM LUCANIS AURALIS in green and gold letters.

Selene and Ichabod were, in fact, quite impressed. The building wasn't nearly as large as most of the Academy's buildings, but Selene and Ichabod were used to the kind of serveries found in the villages of the Principality: small, disorganized, and chock-a-block with all sorts of unrelated things, both useful and useless. The front of the Emporium Lucanis Auralis must have spanned 80 feet, all of it display windows. In this window were beautiful (and expensive) clothes suitable for a fancy dress gathering; in that window was an entire sleepingroom's worth of furniture, elegantly carved from a deeply grained dark wood that much resembled that of the Watching Bird. The window right next to the double doors with shining bronze handles was filled with clever and unusual toys. Selene wondered what it would have been like to grow up with so much stuff around. *No,* she thought, *I wouldn't have liked it. You think you want a lot of stuff when you are young, but that's not what matters. Not really. Although Ichabod might disagree, the way he's looking at those toys.*

Selene was correct; Ichabod was entranced by what he saw, especially one toy in particular: a clever mechanical device that resembled a tiny charelwayn with miniature carved horses. It moved autonomously, but Ichabod at first couldn't determine how. It threw off sparks as it rolled, guided along a circular track with raised sides. Peering intently, he saw the cart contained a spring arrangement which turned the wheels. "Why don't they make one of those big enough for people?" he wondered out loud.

Passing through the doors, they entered a spacious sales area that took up the entire first level of the building. Toward the back and to the left was a wide staircase with a reddish carpet and a brass and wood railing going up to the second floor. The rest of the left side of the store was clothing—all sorts of clothing on circular racks, with a few shoppers moving around them. Selene and Ichabod saw work clothes, play clothes for lucky children whose parents could afford such things, more fancy dresses for important occasions, and a small collection of even more gorgeous wedding suits and dresses.

To their immediate right was a counter made of glass display cases in which were laid out all sorts of beautiful things for the home: elegant utensils with elaborate designs on their handles, gleaming polished brew pots (*but I bet the brew wouldn't taste any better from them than from my battered old pot*, Selene thought), and clever little boxes inlaid with iridescent shells that had no purpose as far as Selene could tell; she guessed that one would place them on a table simply for effect. Further back was another counter where customers could purchase sweetnuts of various kinds, and in the very back, Selene and Ichabod saw more of the dark, polished furniture.

The whole servery smelled of sweet spices, making their mouths water. Altheia stepped to the back counter from which the delicious aroma was drifting, Selene and Ichabod in tow.

A pleasant-looking, slim, middle-aged woman was behind the counter, stocking the sweetnuts for the day, two dappled hounds lying at her feet. The woman wore a stylish yellow work dress; she didn't notice the three registrants approaching until they were right at the counter.

"Altheia!" she said with loving surprise. As she came around the counter to give her daughter a hug, she was followed by the two hounds, whose tails were fanning the air like whirlijigs. "You didn't tell me you were coming home today. And with friends!" Altheia's mother turned to embrace Selene and Ichabod. "And who might you two be?"

"Selene and Ichabod," Selene responded, a bit flustered by Altheia's mother's energetic hug.

"Selene. And Ichabod. What lovely names. I am Auralis, but everyone just calls me Aury. You must be registrants at the Academy with my Altheia. Here, sit down, sit down. You should have a treat." Before they knew it, Atheia's mother had placed a large plate with an assortment of sweetnuts in front of the three students. The hounds sat nearby, looking at the newcomers plaintively. "What am I thinking? Here, you'll want something to drink with that. We have a new shipment of brew in. Fresh from the Greenward. It's Altheia's favorite." She placed three ceramic mugs in front of them and kept talking while she returned to her work.

"So, what are your plans today?" Aury asked. "You probably have favorite places you'll want to visit in the City."

"Well, no," replied Ichabod. "We've never actually been in the City proper. Just the Academy," Selene added.

"Never been in the City? Well, you are in for a treat. Altheia can show you everything. But don't go see the show at the playhouse. I hear that it's very 'contemporary,' as they say, and not at all something for serious students from the Academy."

"No, we won't," Selene and Ichabod mumbled.

"So, tell me. What are you two studying? What do you plan to do after the Academy? Altheia is going to be a server and help us here until one day, the Emporium will be hers. Aren't you, dear?" Altheia nodded happily in agreement.

"And then I can have sweetnuts anytime I wish," she joked.

Aury shook her head and chuckled. "Not unless you want to ruin profits." Altheia blushed, while Auralis turned to Ichabod. "And what do you plan to do, Ichabod?"

"Well, I am not sure. I never expected to be able to attend the Academy. My parents are farmers—my whole family has been farmers for as long as anyone can remember. I'm the first to go to the Academy in, I don't know. Forever. I expect I will try to become a carer and go back to my home to help folks out. Or a creator. Guess I'm just not sure. I'd really like to be a healer, but..." Ichabod's voice trailed off, and he shrugged.

"Very noble, Ichabod. I am sure that your parents are very proud of you. And you, Selene?'

"I don't know. I haven't thought about it much, honestly. I just like school. I'm from a Briner village on the Reach. Maybe I could become a creator, although I would miss home if I had to live here in the City. Really, all I want to do is get through the year."

"Nothing wrong with that, dear. Sometimes we don't know what *Lux* has in mind for us—not right away, anyway. I'm sure with hard work it will all turn out as it is supposed to. Mercy of *Lux*, speaking of which, I need to inventory the clothes. It has been so nice to meet you two. I am glad that Altheia found such delightful friends at school. Oh," she paused, "Here's Altheia's father and sister. Lucanis! Erynn! Altheia is here. Come meet her friends before they have to go."

Lucanis greeted them warmly while Altheia hugged her little sister and handed her a sweetnut. Erynn, who looked to be about six years old, was delighted by the treat and the attention as she perched on a stool at the counter, slipping bits of her sweet to the dogs. Lucanis and Auralis said their goodbyes and turned back to their work. As they were leaving, Selene overheard Altheia's mother whisper to her father, "Yes, a farmer and a Briner. But they seem nice anyway."

Back out in the fresh air, Selene and Ichabod headed for the book servery next to the Emporium when Altheia stopped them. "Hey, there's nothing down that way other than that old book place. Haven't you had enough of books already? Come on, I'll show you the fun stuff." So, the trio spent several hours looking at various clothing serveries, important Academy City Administration buildings, Altheia's favorite brew servery, and then, at Ichabod's request, the part of the market district where livestock and other farm goods were brought to the city along with fish all the way from the Reach. "I don't know why you'd want to see this," Altheia protested. "It's so stinky!" Finally, they stopped to look at a fountain near the Spire of Caelestis that was supposed to be an abstract representation of *Lux*—although neither Selene nor Ichabod could make sense of it, and Altheia just said that "It's fractal, whatever that is, but it's tons of fun to run through on a hot day."

The afternoon sun was lowering to the horizon when Selene finally convinced Altheia that they truly wanted to visit the bookservery. "Oh, all right. But let's not take too long, OK?" Selene agreed, and, tired and footsore, they went in.

What a huge fire hazard, was Selene's first thought as they stepped inside. *There are piles of books in front of piles of books in front of all the shelves.* "Um. Can either of you see how the books are organized?" Selene asked. "*Are* they organized? Where are the academic books?"

Ichabod pointed to some shelves. "Look, there are categories written on little pieces of tape on each of these. Here's a whole shelf called 'How to raise corvus birds.' I wonder if they know what they are talking about." He pulled a book more-or-less randomly from the shelf and started to open it. Selene gave him a small push.

"Remember why we are here, Icky. We don't have a lot of time."

Selene saw Ichabod roll his eyes. "Yep. Sorry! I do want to come back here and see what these books have to say, though. Anyway, what category should we look for?" He and Selene started picking their way through the crowded aisles, trying not to trip or knock over anything, which proved very hard to do.

"I am not sure. Probably just a section for *elenchi*. There. See those shelves? They are labeled *Elenchi By Level*. Looks like we'd want the top shelf, but I can't reach that high. Can you?"

Ichabod pulled over a small stool. "I got it. Remind me of the title again?"

"It's called *Meditations on First Philology, in which the lucent path and the eternal Lux are demonstrated against the Malicious Deceiver.*"

"Uh, nope," he said, scanning the highest shelf. "Nothing even close to that. Maybe it's kept somewhere else."

"Why would you want that book?" asked Altheia. "That's not on the approved reading list. And it certainly isn't a romance."

As she was saying this, the bookserver, a somewhat dusty-looking fellow with saggy eyes and a beard tucked into his belt, came over to them. "Time to finish. If you are going to buy something, now's the time. If not, then I'd appreciate it if you'd go, so I can go, too," he groused.

"We were looking for a particular book. It's for our studies," Selene lied.

"Oh? Is that so? You are students at the Academy, yes? Since when have students needed my books? Aren't yours supplied for you?"

"Well, we are not sure that we have the best edition, to be honest," Selene improvised. "The book is called *Meditations on First Philology, in which the lucent path and the eternal Lux are demonstrated against the Malicious Deceiver*. Do you have it?" She tried to make her question sound as innocent as possible.

The bookserver was having none of it. "No. I don't have that book. I have never had that book, and if I had, I still wouldn't have it, not for you. I'm locking the door now, and if you are not through it by the time the bolt is thrown, you'll be spending the night here." He started toward the door, his purpose obvious.

"Sorry! Sorry! We are going!" The three students were hastening to the door when Ichabod clumsily knocked over a pile of books. The bookserver growled at them as they passed and glared at Ichabod in particular, who was limping from the collision.

Selene was thus a bit surprised when Ichabod plonked a book on the counter and asked, "May I purchase this?" The bookserver examined the title and then took Ichabod's coin, but didn't even offer a bag in which to put the book.

"We'd better get back to the campus," Altheia suggested once they were out of the store, with just a hint of worry in her voice. "I really don't like that man very much. He's the one who refused to sell his servery to my parents."

"He sure is a grump, but look at what I found when I crashed into that pile!"

Ichabod was holding up a rather plain and uninteresting-looking volume with the unpromising title *The Death: A History*. Then Selene noticed the author.

"Professor Thallos wrote a book about the Death? Why didn't he tell us that? Why didn't we see a copy in his office? That's really odd."

"You can't take that back to Celestine Hall, Icky," Altheia was quick to point out. "What if Professor Thallos knew you had it? I don't think he'd like it at all. That's not a book for registrants. You're just going to have to throw it away now. Unless you *want* to get in trouble. There's nowhere to keep it." She looked peevishly at her friends. "I told you we shouldn't have gone there."

"Altheia's right, Icky," said Selene.

"Ah, you two," Ichabod was smiling. "I've got that covered. Come on, if we walk quickly, we can stash it and get back to the dorm in time."

After about 15 minutes of walking, Selene realized where Ichabod was headed. She wasn't sure about showing Altheia their private hiding place, but they needed to do something with the book. So, she kept quiet until they arrived at the Arboretum.

"What's here?" asked Altheia. "This is just the Arboretum."

Ichabod smiled at her and winked—at which Altheia instantly and visibly brightened—and said, "We have a secret place, Altheia. Promise not to tell?"

"You mean, like a secret place for just the two of you?" Altheia seemed just a tad put out.

"Nope. For the three of us," Ichabod replied just as they rounded the boulder into the hidden alcove.

Altheia meandered around the nook as Ichabod sought a good niche in which to hide the book. "This is a wonderful hiding place," she enthused, and then, more doubtfully, "I guess it's okay you bought the book, if you can hide it here."

Ichabod was tucking the book behind a rock and under a ledge, where it would be protected from the weather, just as Altheia finished speaking. "We'll come back as soon as we can and see what Professor Thallos has to say about the Death," he remarked, and, after looking around to be sure they were not seen, they slipped out and returned to Celestine Hall.

As they entered through the dorm's front door, the three students passed the ever-attentive eyes of the Watching Bird but, feeling a little guilty and a little excited about feeling guilty, were careful, even though it had been months since they had taken their first tests, not to walk directly under it.

Selene's nightmares had returned and were getting worse. Each night seemed an endless, chaotic parade of takings, and each morning she'd awaken utterly exhausted. The trick of forcing herself awake and going back to sleep was no longer working. She didn't tell Ichabod. *No use making him worry more*, she thought. Meanwhile, there had been a bad patch of weather for two weeks, and the three friends had not been able to return to the Arboretum.

Finally, the weather cleared up. Over lastmeal at the end of one particularly fine day, Altheia had been telling the other two a story about her sister "borrowing" one of the wedding dresses from a rack in the Emporium and surprising her parents at lastmeal by wearing it. Altheia and the others laughed as she described Erynn tripping over the long dress while pretending to be a bride. When Selene stepped away from the table to refill her cup, Altheia seemed to consider for a moment and then asked Ichabod, "Would you like to go to the Arboretum this *Fiat Caelestis Nocta*? The weather is supposed to be good."

"That's a great idea, Altheia. We really need to do that," he replied. Altheia wasn't sure exactly what he meant by his reply, but she was elated that he had said "yes" in any form and, having finished her meal, returned to her room with a bounce in her step to begin planning what to wear. Selene, having returned to the table with a second mug of hot brew, sat talking with Ichabod.

"We need to get to the alcove and see what's in Professor Thallos's book," Ichabod asserted. "And I have another idea..."

"What?"

"Well, we need to see what's in the *Meditations*, right? And we can't buy a copy. There are only two other places where we might find one, as far as I can tell."

Selene thought for a moment and said, "You mean the Great Archive, right? But students aren't allowed there. That's only for scholar-priests."

"True," nodded Ichabod. "Which leaves the copies that have been distributed to the fellows."

"What, are we just going to go up to someone and ask if we can borrow it?" Selene seemed unconvinced.

"We don't really have to *ask* to borrow it. We could just borrow a copy. Like Erynn borrowed the dress."

Selene was dubious. "Is 'borrow' really the right verb here, Ichabod?"

"Sure! We won't keep it. We will sneak it back as soon as we are done with it. If we do it carefully, no one will even notice."

Selene shook her head. "I don't think I really want to know, but—how exactly do you propose to do this?"

"You leave that to me. Just meet me in the alcove at zenith this coming *Fiat Caelestis Nocta*."

Having made sure she hadn't been seen, Selene waited in the rocky alcove. She had the copy of Professor Thallos's *The Death: A History* open on her lap when Ichabod and Altheia arrived.

"Oh, good. You're here," Ichabod exclaimed. Altheia was over-dressed for a walk in the Arboretum; neither Selene nor Ichabod recalled seeing her lavender cloak and patterned sash.

"What are you doing here, Selene?" Altheia was visibly put out.

Selene, engrossed in her book, didn't answer. "Hey, you two, listen to this. It's from Professor Thallos's book."

Records from the early years of the Principality of the Academy are sketchy and inconsistent, but they suggest that the people of the Principality came to the area from an unknown location about 2,500 years ago, around the year 150 before *Lux*. Those records also indicate that the original population was much smaller than today's, being between five hundred and one thousand people. No record mentions the Principality or the Academy until y1 *Anno Lux*; for convenience, we can designate the time prior to y1 AL as 'ante Luxian antiquity.' There is a single early reference from ante Luxian antiquity to a 'settlement,' which presumably became the Academy City, and something identified as a 'breakaway settlement,' which may be part of the same settlement or may be another, separate settlement, perhaps one of the first villages. Most notable for purposes of the present study, there is only one record in the ante Luxian period of a taking; this involved an individual named Jonathan Carthen. The record is anomalous and like-

ly corrupt given the unusual name and since it says he
was taken as an adult of 45 years of age.

Records abruptly become much more complete just
after y1 AL, essentially comparable to current records
in comprehensiveness and, thus, reliability. At that
time, the population of the Principality had reached
its present level (approximately 240,000), where it has
remained until now, 2,350 years later...

The book bored Altheia, but Ichabod was excited by what he had
heard. "Selene, does that mean that your dream..." he started to say,
but Selene cut him off, not wanting to talk about her nightmares in
front of Altheia. She changed the subject.

"What do you have in your pack, Ichabod?" She asked.

"I certainly hope it's our midmeal, Icky," Altheia remarked sourly.

Ichabod smiled and, to Altheia's chagrin, pulled out another book.
Selene glanced at its title.

"You didn't..." she started to say, but he interrupted her.

"Don't worry about it even a bit. I just 'borrowed' it. Shall we see
what it says?"

Altheia sighed ostentatiously without Ichabod noticing.

The author's name, Selene saw, was Renatus Lucerion, and the
copy of *Meditations on First Philology, in which the lucent path and
the eternal Lux are demonstrated against the Malicious Deceiver* was
well-worn, perhaps ancient. It easily fell open to a page at the beginning of the First Meditation, as if this were the most-consulted
passage; Ichabod gently and reverently smoothed the fragile paper,
while Altheia, still radiating disapproval, leaned closer despite herself.

Selene shifted her weight on the rock, torn between curiosity and unease.

Ichabod began to read aloud:

The First Meditation: On the Possible Existence of An Evil Deceiver

In every age, the scholar-priest must ask: Can we trust what is before us? For the eyes may err, the ears may deceive, and even the mind, in its reasoning, may twist truth into untruth. So, having secured for myself sufficient leisure and being free of all distractions, I have resolved to strip away all that might be false and to bracket each belief, until I find that alone which is certain and cannot be doubted.

Let us consider: if *Lux* the all-powerful exists, then is it not possible that He, in His infinite wisdom, permits illusions in guiding us toward ultimate understanding? No, it is not possible, for such would be contrary to *Lux's* nature. But might there exist a force—a Malicious Deceiver as powerful as *Lux* but as all-evil as *Lux* is all-good—that weaves falsehoods into the very fabric of our reality? Such a deceiver would be cunning beyond measure, presenting as truth what is false, shaping our perceptions, our memories, and even our reasoning to lead us astray.

I know not whether such a being exists. Yet the mere possibility compels me to doubt all that I perceive. For if it is even barely possible that a Malicious Deceiver manipulates even the lucent path, then what I take for light might, in truth, be darkness. I shall therefore resolve to accept as true, nothing which could be the effect of such an all-evil, maliciously deceiving being.

Ichabod paused, glancing at the others. "It goes on to talk about how only through the application of the principles of dialectical philology can one find the lucent path, and argues that those principles still need a foundation on which to rest."

Altheia frowned. "What *is* all of this stuff about doubt? No wonder the bookserver didn't want us to have this book. That's exactly the opposite of what we are taught. We registrants are supposed to be patient and question nothing. You know, like Professor Thalos says, *imbibe*. I really don't like that book."

"I know. It's weird," Ichabod agreed. "And anyway, in our classes, the *elenchi* never leave room for real doubt. They always resolve in absolute certainty. But this...it admits that everything we think we know could be a lie told by an all-powerful evil deceiver."

Altheia shivered, pulling her sash tighter. "Why would anyone write something like that? It's unnerving. If *Lux* is truth, then there can't be lies at the heart of truth, right? Can we stop reading this and just talk now?" Ichabod, caught up in the book, missed the earnest pleading in her eyes.

"Unless..." Selene hesitated, then continued. "Unless the deceiver isn't just hypothetical. What if it's real? What if there is something—or someone—that wants to keep us from seeing the truth? That would explain why it's such an important book. And other things, as well."

"What other things? That's ridiculous," Altheia interrupted. "*Lux* wouldn't allow it. Nor would the scholar-priests. There's no evidence of any deception, anyway. Things have been the same for thousands of years. We're safe. We're cared for."

"Are we?" Ichabod asked softly. "What if it is the Malicious Deceiver causing your dreams, Selene?"

"What are you two talking about?" Altheia asked, feeling at sea in the conversation.

Selene didn't answer immediately, and looked up into the branches that formed a canopy over their hiding place. Apart from the sound of the wind rustling through the trees, at that moment, everything was stillness.

Selene finally broke the spell, leaving Altheia's question unanswered. "We need to keep reading. There's more to this. I can feel it."

Altheia was about to voice a protest, but Ichabod nodded and turned a few pages until he reached the Third Meditation, the title of which seemed to promise an answer. He read:

The Third Meditation: Proof of the Eternal *Lux*, and Resolution of all Prior Doubts

Having established the method of doubt and bracketed all things about which I may possibly be deceived, I am left with one indubitable truth: *the self exists as a thinking substance*. From this foundation, we must now ask: what is the source of this thinking substance? Can the self exist without a cause greater than itself?

When I reflect upon my nature, I find myself finite, fallible, and incomplete. I recognize my own limits. My understanding is often clouded, my will is prone to error, and my perceptions are often fragmented. Yet, within me exists the *concept* of perfection: of infinite knowledge, boundless truth, and eternal light. How can a finite being such as myself conceive of infinity and perfection, save that such things exist and have been imprinted in me?

This conception of perfection cannot arise from me alone, for I am finite and flawed. A lesser cannot birth a greater; a being of limited understanding cannot originate the ideas of infinite knowledge and perfection. Therefore, this idea of perfection, of a light that shines without shadow, must have its origin in something outside of me. That something must itself be infinite and perfect.

I call this source *Lux*, the eternal light. *Lux*, the origin and embodiment of perfect truth and knowledge, therefore must exist, for only *Lux* can be the origin of my concept of perfection. The effect must have a cause of sufficient magnitude, and the only cause of sufficient magnitude for my idea of infinite perfection is the infinite perfection of *Lux*.

Moreover, *Lux* cannot deceive, for deception arises
from a lack or defect—a need to conceal, or a desire
to manipulate. But *Lux*, being perfect, has no need
or capacity for such defects. The light of *Lux* is pure,
unsullied by malice or falsehood.

From this consideration, I can conclude that I am not
deceived and that the world is as I perceive it; for the
contrary would be to deny every step in the chain of
reasoning so far established.

Some might question: Is it not possible that my conception of *Lux* arises merely from my imagination, or
from the teachings of others? Yet this cannot be. The
imagination can only rearrange what it has already
encountered. It cannot invent something utterly beyond its experience. Similarly, the teachings of others merely pass along what they have received. Again,
the original source of the idea of perfection must be
sufficient to produce the effect, and the only possible
source in this case is *Lux* Himself.

Furthermore, as an adjunct to this argument, I can
observe that the very act of reasoning presupposes the
existence of *Lux*. For reason depends upon the principles of truth, order, and coherence. If *Lux* were not
the ultimate foundation of these principles, reason

itself would collapse into incoherence, and we would be left with only chaos and shadow.

To this, I can add: the light of *Lux* is not only the source of our understanding but also the wellspring of benevolence. For, in favoring and embracing beings capable of reason and reflection, *Lux* has shared a portion of its light with us, enabling us to participate in the eternal order. *Lux*'s mercy is evident in the harmony of our society, the balance of our lives, and the constancy of the cycles that sustain us.

Let us, then, with absolute certainty, affirm the existence of *Lux*: infinite, perfect, and benevolent. In contemplating *Lux*, we align ourselves with the lucent path, dispelling the shadows of doubt and error. To live in *Lux* is to live in truth, and to live in truth is the highest good.

"Well, that's a relief," exclaimed Altheia. "I can see why they don't want us to read this until we are fellows. Although, honestly," here she straightened her dress, "Since everyone knows that *Lux* is...well, *Lux*, then I don't know what the point of questioning it is, especially with such a wild idea as a Malicious Deceiver. The book ends up where it started anyway: with *Lux*. What's the point of going around in circles?"

Selene, however, realized that the book raised more questions than it answered. Why was Ravian so interested in it? Had he found a flaw in the reasoning? It *had* to be his scrawl next to his poem. "First Philosophy—Malicious Deceiver" was a clear reference to the *Meditations*. Had Ravian had some sort of crisis of knowledge? Maybe that's why he was taken, even though he was past the age at which the Death normally visited.

The trio was quiet as they headed back to campus, Selene and Ichabod lost in their thoughts, and Altheia vexed that the outing had not been what she expected and that they were keeping something from her. When they neared Celestine Hall, Ichabod said he would catch up with them later and took off at a brisk walk, presumably to return the book that he had "borrowed."

CHAPTER SIX

ZENITH DREAMS

T he following week's *Fiat Stella* found Selene and Ichabod in Professor Rhadomis's morning Moral Philology class. The students liked Professor Rhadomis a great deal, although his deep voice and almost hymn-like oratory tended to act as a soporific, and students would more than occasionally nod off during his lectures, especially if the room were stuffy. His graying auburn hair gave him an aura of gravitas that suited the subject matter, and he had a dry sense of humor that especially appealed to Selene. Ichabod, too, enjoyed Professor Rhadomis's lectures since the professor, like Ichabod, had been born and raised a farmer, and he frequently illustrated difficult concepts with stories from his rural youth. The students could tell that Professor Rhadomis missed form life; he was often seen outside his campus home tending his extensive garden.

The core of Professor Rhadomis's worldview was based on what he called the "tripartite concordance": the unity of thought, word, and deed in a dialectical process that, he claimed, allows a practitioner to approach perfect moral truth, "the Being of which is *Lux*," as he would often say. Both Selene and Ichabod struggled with the course material, most of which was excerpts from Professor Rhadomis's book *The Lamp of Lux: Illuminating the Why and Way of Virtue*, which the professor said was written for apprentices studying to be carers, and so was "Perhaps a bit advanced for registrants, but there is nothing wrong with a bit of a challenge now and then, is there?" He'd sonorously intone this observation whenever the registrants seemed more at sea than usual. *Anyway*, Selene would think when his lectures seemed particularly obscure, *he's the easiest grader at the Academy.*

The professor was, once again, in the middle of a long, tangential explication of the tripartite concordance, and lethargy began to steal over Selene. She resisted impending unconsciousness and forced herself to focus on the lecture.

"We may thus identify three moments in the movement of the tripartite concordance. Consider, for example, your first encounter with something new. I remember the first time I took part in a harvest as a boy." The professor smiled broadly. "Although I had grown up with fields all around, the attention needed to harvest row after row of roots opened up a new understanding of the richness of farming. Perhaps you, too, have felt this way about something. This is the first moment of the Concordance: *aptertis*, the 'openness,' which names the initial encounter with an idea, experience, or mode of being."

Mode of being? What the mist is a mode of being? Selene was bewildered. *Ichabod seems to be getting it. I'll ask him later what it means.*

"And, after the harvest is done, you might then thoughtlessly pull yourself up to the table and—again, thoughtlessly—consume that which only a short time before had been growing and taking form in the ground. Such is a contrary mode of being; the connection with the field has been broken by your thoughtlessness. This is the second moment of the concordance, which we call *confractis,* or 'the breaking.' It exists in opposition to *aptertis*, or the openness."

Selene noticed Ichabod was doodling, drawing a row of root vegetables, ripe and ready for harvest, with an oversized goat eating them.

Ha, she thought. *He's having trouble following Professor Rhadomis, too.*

"So, does the *confractis* mode of being present a unity of thought, word, and deed?" The professor looked around the classroom and saw Ichabod hesitantly raise his hand. "Yes, Registrant Ichabod?"

"Well, professor, I think it does. And it doesn't." He paused, and Professor Rhadomis nodded and motioned for him to continue.

"It presents a unity of thought, word, and deed to the extent one thinks of the meal in front of them as food and acts upon that thought, but this unity is particular to that moment of the concordance and doesn't include what came before, the ground of the food's being, so to speak."

"And what came before, Registrant Ichabod?" asked the professor, clearly pleased with the answer so far.

"Well...the farming. I don't think most people in the City understand how much goes into growing and harvesting things. Sometimes I wonder if they just think roots and vegetables and leaves and meat magically appear in the market by the fiat of *Lux.*"

The class laughed at this, and the professor joined in. "No, I daresay many are quite ignorant of the processes of cultivation and harvesting. So, what could bring the *aptertis* and *confractis* to concordance? Not sure? No matter, you have answered well today!" Professor Rhadomis waved his arms in two wide circles, brought them together, and continued. "The *aptertis* and *confractis* are always, inevitably resolved in the *integris,* also sometimes called 'the wholeness.' Does anyone know why this resolution must always necessarily occur?"

At that very moment, as she was idly imagining all of reality as arms swinging around in big circles made up of innumerable smaller circles, Selene's vision fractured. A tiny, ragged, blinding spot formed before her, quickly expanding. She could no longer see the classroom; her eyes filled with a bright blob that covered most of her field of vision, her surroundings remaining visible only at the extreme periphery. She let out a sharp gasp.

"Registrant Selene, are you feeling well?" the professor asked, concerned. Selene shook her head, and the bright blobs exploded. Now she couldn't even see through the edges of her field of vision. "Registrant Ichabod, would you please see to it that Registrant Selene finds her way to the carer?"

"Yes, Professor," Ichabod replied, but Selene held her hand up to stop him. "What is it, Selene?" Ichabod asked.

Selene couldn't answer. The bright, ragged light disappeared for the smallest possible slice of time, and during that instant, she saw...what? It was like one of her nightmares. A taking! Even worse, the taking was of a fifth-year student—a fellow—and was happening in their very dorm, Celestine Hall! Selene sensed, or rather *knew*, that it was decades earlier, and she was absolutely certain of the location.

As quickly as it came, it was gone. *What was that? What the mist was that? A dream of a taking? But I was not asleep.* With her vision returned almost to normal, she allowed Ichabod to guide her out of the classroom.

"Ichabod." He didn't miss the urgency in her voice as they made their way to the healer's room. "I just had a...dream, I guess...of a taking. I think it was Ravian..."

"Here? I mean, back in the classroom?" Ichabod was nonplussed. "How is that possible?"

"How are the dreams possible at all? Why do they feel like actual history? I don't know what's going on, but there's something I haven't told you. I am still having them at night, and they keep getting worse. More detailed. More *real*."

"You mean they are changing?"

"Yes, I think so. What does that mean?" Selene was worried and not thinking clearly, and very much needed his help.

"They are changing?" He tried to make sense of it, using the framework for knowledge they had been studying. "I'd say that it means that what's happening to you is a process and not something static. And *that* probably means that it will keep changing until it gets to some end, some *telos*. It could get worse."

"Ichabod, what if the endpoint is that I am always in the dreams? What if I get lost in them permanently? Or—what if I am losing my mind?"

"Or they could kill you. They are dreams of takings, after all. Maybe this sort of thing happens to people before they are taken." Ichabod was not trying to scare Selene; he was just thinking through things, but he noticed Selene pale as he finished his thought.

"But I don't think they are going to hurt you; they haven't yet, anyway," he hurried to reassure her. "Here's the healer's room; let's see what she says."

The examination was brief. The healer used a small mirror to shine a light into Selene's eyes, had her read a jumbled bunch of letters on a poster from a few feet away, and found nothing of significance. "It's just a common visual aura. Nothing to worry about," pronounced the healer. "Probably from too much studying. You're perfectly fine, my dear," she repeated and sent the two of them out.

"Common visual aura? Since when is this common?" Selene muttered to Ichabod. Ichabod was remarking on how little help the healer had been when they walked squarely into Professor Thallos.

"Professor Rhadomis tells me you are unwell, Selene. I see the healer has attended to you. What was the problem? I trust you are better now." He was trying to be nonchalant but was failing; it was obvious to both Selene and Ichabod that Professor Thallos was keenly interested in Selene's illness, and very worried.

"Thank you, Professor. I think I just fell asleep or something, and my eyes went all whacky. The healer said I'm fine. It was just a visual thing. I should go get some rest."

Professor Thallos looked at her skeptically but, after a moment, he nodded and mumbled, "Fine. That's fine." The two students continued on their way. When the Professor was out of earshot, Ichabod stopped Selene near a side exit from the building.

"Say, Selene, *were* you actually nodding off?"

"Sort of. I was feeling sleepy, but I fought it off and tried to focus on the lecture. I was pretty much awake. Why?"

Ichabod nodded. "The thing is, I was wondering if there is a trigger, something that causes you to have the dreams. Because—think about it—up to now, the dreams have only happened at night. But you just had one while you were awake. Or mostly awake, anyway. See?"

"You think the dreams come when I am tired?" she responded.

"No, not exactly. I'm wondering if they come when you are relaxed. When your mind is quiet, if you know what I mean."

Selene shrugged. "What if that's true? I don't want them to come."

"You remember what Professor Thallos was talking about last week in observational learning?" Selene shook her head. "The poem. Remember the poem?" Ichabod started to recite:

The Path of Truth
(A Scholar's Aid to the *Method of Discernment*)

Observatio Primordialis, observe the world to make it clear,

Quaestio Essentiae, question purposes, *telos* here.

Concordia Primarum, what in books and minds abides,

Experimentum Veritatis, through essential tests, let truth be tried.

Dialectica Integris, tripartite concordance you must construe,

Illuminatio Luxae, from Lux all being shines true.

"Ugh. How do you remember that stuff, Ichabod?"

"Oh, I don't know. But, it's really useful. Think about it. We have *observed*—that's the first step. We have wondered what the *purpose* of the dreams is. That's *telos*, the second step. We have consulted books..."

"That's the third step of the method," Selene interrupted. "So, now we need some kind of experiment. What—you want me to go back to class and take a nap?"

"Ha! No, not that, not exactly. What if," Here, Ichabod lowered his voice. "What if you could *make* it happen?"

"Make it happen? How am I going to do that? *Why* would I want to do that? These dreams are terrifying, Ichabod."

"I know. But we need to learn as much as possible about them. Experimenting with them seems like the next step. It's the next step in the method of discernment, anyway. Otherwise, you just have to sort of wait and see what happens, and I really think that's a bad idea. Don't you?"

"I've just been waiting for them to stop."

"But they aren't stopping."

"True. OK. Alright. What experiment do you suggest?"

"Well, it seems like the dreams come when you are in a certain state of mind. Asleep, or nearly so, I guess, but I really think it's about being relaxed. I know it sounds kind of dumb, but try just spacing out."

"Sure. But let's go outside. We can sit on one of the benches on this side of the building. Just in case something weird happens."

"Agreed."

They sat down on a bench under a large tree with slightly translucent leaves through which the sunlight filtered down. *That feels wonderful; my skin feel so warm*, Selene was thinking to herself when Ichabod poked her.

"You still there? OK, try just clearing your mind. See what happens."

"Yes, but stop poking me!"

Selene had a feeling that Ichabod was right about this, so she pushed aside her nervousness, sat with her eyes closed, and tried to clear her mind. *No. Stop thinking about school*, she thought to herself. *Stop thinking of anything. Just feel the light coming through the leaves. Listen to the breeze fluttering through them. Quiet. Quiet. Still...still...still...*

Selene was in a sleepingroom in a villager's house. She knew—again, how, she was unsure—but she knew it was about 500 years earlier. The mist was brilliant red as it formed around a young woman. In a moment, it settled into a throbbing, deep red, and the woman was gone.

"Ichabod." Selene found that she could talk, although sluggishly. "I'm watching a taking."

"Observe everything you can. Anything could be important." His voice sounded thin and distant.

That's good advice, thought Selene. She looked around the villager's room and saw that it must be a farming village; she saw muddy farmer's boots and a rough coat by a wardrobe. She could hear the sounds of cooking from the other side of the sleepingroom door, and could smell breakfast. Meanwhile, the mist had disappeared. She looked out the window of the room. The sky was oddly tinged with red. *That's new*, she thought. Even more peculiarly, there were a few faint, fine reddish lines curling like jagged scrollwork through the atmosphere. Some stretched across the sky, but some seemed to coil down to buildings and people in the village.

Selene felt a snap, and she was back on the bench under the tree with Ichabod. Her skin tingled as if she had been sprayed with a mild astringent, but beyond that, she felt fine. She described what she had seen to Ichabod.

Ichabod looked thoughtfully into the distance. "The sky was red? Like at lastlight? What were the lines in the sky, I wonder? Something caused by the dream?"

"No, not like lastlight. Not a natural red. And I've never seen lines in the sky. Ichabod, I really don't think these are just dreams. I think I am *seeing* things that really happened."

"No, you are totally right; these are not dreams. That much is clear by now. But if they are something else, what should we call them? Seeings? That would mean that what you have been seeing is real. Right? It would mean that those red lines are real, too. After all, the mist is real. Everyone knows that, because everyone can see it. Not in color like you," he hastened to add. "The lines must have something to do with the mist and the takings.?"

"I don't know. But they feel like the same sort of thing, if you know what I mean."

"No, Selene, I haven't the foggiest notion of what you mean," he chuckled wryly.

"Wait a second. I am going to try something."

Ichabod watched as Selene relaxed and then, after perhaps 45 seconds, slowly opened her eyes and gasped.

"The sky is red here, too, Ichabod. Here, right now. Oh! It's everywhere..." She was looking around agitatedly, but her eyes were unfocused, Ichabod noticed. Not glassy. Fuzzy and distant.

"I see lines! Lots of reddish lines. Way more than in the village in my dream. It's like a big, confusing, spiky web of tendrils. And—oh!" It sounded like Selene had been hit in the stomach. Ichabod tried to grab her hands, but she waved him off. "Ichabod, I can see *both*."

"What do you mean, you can see both? Both what?"

"Both worlds. Two, I mean. I see two worlds here. There is the red world of my dreams. Of my seeings. And there is the real world, our world. They are right on top of each other."

Without warning, a gut-level panic hit Selene like a hammer. She was terrified. Not just mildly scared: an immense, unnamable fear physically paralyzed her, a fear as large as Erden that appeared out of nowhere and froze her, mind, soul, and body. As if by an autonomic reflex, she shut down the dual vision, and she was once again surrounded only by the comfortable world of the campus of the Academy—which, in an instant, was not so comfortable. A breakerwind, or something very much like it, slammed into the two students, ripping through the trees and pummeling their bodies. Selene well knew breakerwinds on the Brine. They would smash into the shore and uproot whole villages and thus were among the things Briners most feared. Selene's parents called them the "wail of Mystralys," after a weather demon-goddess that formed part of the mythology of the Order; when she was young, Selene had imagined a towering, angry being thrashing the beaches and trying to destroy their cabin. But no breakerwind could come this far inland, she's never experienced one this powerful, and, in any case, there had been no warning of a severe change in the weather. And yet, here the two of them sat, the wind brutally flogging them, ice-cold raindrops as large as plu, pits flaying the leaves in the tree above them.

They retreated and huddled on the steps of the arched doorway while the berserk storm raged. "Did you do this, Selene? Did our experiment have something to do with this?"

"What experiment? What's going on, you two?" came Altheia's thin voice, followed by the sound of the door behind them slamming. "What happened? This is freakish. Did *you* somehow do this, Selene?"

Altheia looked at them strangely, but neither had an answer for her. Selene sank down onto the cold stone steps while Ichabod sat next to her, putting his arm around her. At this, a look of horror came over Altheia's face. She ran back through the door and down the hall the way she had come.

After perhaps twenty minutes, the storm eased up, leaving the two students shivering. Selene felt exhausted; not just worn out, but emptied of all vitality, each cell in her body unable to produce more than the minutest amount of energy. Once the storm had fully passed, Ichabod gently carried Selene back to her dorm room. He laid her on her bed and covered her. Instinctively, Selene balled up in her blanket like a grub in a cocoon and was immediately dead to the world.

CHAPTER SEVEN

LINES OF FORCE

S elene awoke early the next day to a much-altered perceptual world. Thinking she had sleep in her eyes, Selene went to the washbasin, splashed her face, and rubbed vigorously with a towel. She was thoroughly awake when she realized: it wasn't sleep. She could now easily see both worlds at the same time, the real world *and* the dream world.

She stepped over to the window to look out on the campus buildings; everything had morphed into a surreal juxtaposition of the two worlds, the familiar world now slightly faded as if it were a very old, lacquer-covered painting, the other world no longer only reddish, but a prismatic range of colors but still centered on a deep, pulsing brick red. And, she noticed, the dream world was slightly askew, as if the two worlds were just the smallest fraction out of alignment. In every direction, she saw lines of force.

What is this? Her hands felt clammy, and there was a hole in her stomach. *I am seeing the second world. But I am not trying to. I don't understand. I need to tell Ichabod. But—the ledge. I'll fall over the rail.*

Mist! I am not even sure I can walk in a straight line. And he's probably still asleep. But he needs to hear about this. Now. So...here we go...

Imagine wearing trick glasses that make you see double while simultaneously imparting a dull reddish rainbow to everything. Now imagine walking around the corner of a building on a narrow ledge three stories up while wearing those glasses. Selene leaned into the building and kept her left hand on the rail, but even so, she only shuffled her way to Ichabod's window.

Selene tested Ichabod's window. *Of course, it's locked. Why would it be open and make this easier,* she thought with bleak humor. With more force than she intended and enough to threaten her balance, she pulled one more time, and it released.

Once inside, it was just a matter of waking Ichabod. *Easier said than done,* she thought. It looked like he had fallen into bed fully dressed the night before. *I didn't even consider how things might have been hard on him, too. Just selfishly focused on myself.*

"Hey, Ichabod. Wake up." She tapped his shoulder. "Come on, I need you to wake up."

Ichabod woke with a start.

"What's going on, Selene? What's wrong?" He sat up and pushed his hair back, which didn't alter it significantly. "Hey, go look out the window while I get dressed."

"You look dressed to me."

"I don't have any pants on. Go. Let me get dressed."

Selene dutifully went to the window, looking out once again on the slightly faded oil painting of the real world and the reddish shimmers and lines of the dream world. Ichabod was beside her in a moment, pulling a belt through loops on his pants.

"What's going on? Are you okay?" He noticed she was staring out the window intently. "What are you looking at? What do you see?"

Selene responded in an even voice that belied her worry. "I can see both worlds, Ichabod. Like yesterday, only constantly. When I woke up a few minutes ago, I thought I was just tired and seeing double from that, but I wasn't. I can see the Academy the way it really is, but I can also see the dream world I saw yesterday."

"The dream world? Are you *trying* to see it?"

"No. It was just there when I woke up. I'm not *doing* it. It's just *happening*."

"Can you stop it? Can you make the dream world go away?"

"I don't know. Should I even try?" She turned to look at him. "What if I make the real world go away instead and am stuck in the dream world?"

"Good point," responded Ichabod as he dragged the chair from his study table over to the window. "Here. Maybe you should sit down."

"Thanks. Also, there's something more here. The dream world—it doesn't quite match up with the real world. It's like, there are all the same buildings and trees and everything, but it's slightly mismatched. Like it's offset."

"You mean they are out of line with each other?" asked Ichabod.

"Yes. Just like yesterday. Mismatched in other ways, too. You know how the other world seemed all red yesterday? It's still mostly reddish, but a prismatic effect is also happening. It's happening everywhere. And the buildings..." Selene was peering and squinting intently into the distance, as if trying very hard to focus on something. "They are...Ichabod, I don't think the shapes match. I can't see the dream buildings very well, but they don't look the same as the real buildings."

"What do you mean?" he asked.

"It's like they are shadows or something. Blocky. I can't quite see them clearly. But there's something wrong with them. Ichabod, I need to skip class today and get a closer look at things."

"Okay. I'll go with you."

Selene wanted to protest, not wanting him to get into trouble, but she also needed Ichabod with her. The double worlds scared her, no matter how stoic she appeared. So, she felt both guilty and relieved when he said he would come. She responded with a simple, "OK."

They checked in at the front desk of Celestine Hall on their way down to firstmeal and reported that neither of them was feeling well; they said they'd both be resting for the day instead of attending classes. They hoped they would be believed. After all, Selene had been unwell enough the day before to be sent to the healer's room. They were in such a rush and Selene was so nervous about the lie that she couldn't focus on their surroundings. It was all too confusing; there were so many lines of force here. They decided to skip firstmeal, and only felt relief when they slid out, as inconspicuously as possible, crossing their fingers that no one would check on them.

They walked less traveled paths between the Academy buildings until they found themselves on the edge of campus, unintentionally heading toward the center of the City. Everywhere Selene looked, there were prismatic red lines of force; everything Selene saw had a ghostly double. After a few minutes, she realized she had been walking in a daze. She willed herself to snap out of it and resoled to focus on her surroundings. She swiveled around, taking it all in. Ichabod saw that it was too much for her.

"Selene, maybe it would help if you described to me what you are seeing."

"Yes. Yes, that's a good idea. It's still the same as it was earlier. There are the lines everywhere. Well, not everywhere." She paused and looked around. "No, not everywhere. I don't see lines around trees. Or bushes. Nothing like that. And the trees don't have doubles like the buildings do. They don't look weird, if you know what I mean. I only see lines going into buildings. And into people. Ichabod, there is a fine, almost invisible line going into you, right into the top of your head. It's like a tight bundle of fibers, though. Not solid. When it gets right above your head, it spreads out like—you know that fungus that we sometimes find under rocks where it's really moist?"

"You mean the stuff with tons of spidery tendrils that spread out from a central blobbly kind of thing? The books call it harnclutch, but back in my village, we just call it web rot."

"Yes, that. Exactly." Selene nodded. "The lines look pretty solid from far away. But up close, I can see what look like fibers in the one coming down to your head. And then, starting just a few inches above your head, the fibers sort of split up, like a frayed rope, and spread out. Mostly around the top of your head. Like a net, but with the cross threads missing."

"That's creepy, Selene."

"Everyone looks like this, Ichabod. I wish I could see the top of my head. Or that you could see this stuff and tell me if I have one, too."

"Yeah, no. I don't want to see it! Here, follow me," said Ichabod, and hastened to the street in the market district where the serveries were located. A few minutes later, they stopped in front of the first servery they came to—it happened to be the book servery they'd visited with Altheia—and Ichabod had Selene look into the window.

"Can you see your reflection?" he asked.

Selene shifted a bit to her left and squinted. "Yes. Not very well, though. I *do* have a line, Ichabod. Ugh. I have web rot on my head!" She took her hands and waved them above her, through the fibrous line. "Nothing."

"What was that?"

"Oh, I was trying to see if I could touch it, or, I dunno, move it somehow, make it go away. But my hands go right through it. It's not even like light. If it were light, my hands would block it, but it's like the stuff doesn't even exist. Except I can see it, and I can see the lines following you and everyone else when they move, so it must exist."

Ichabod glanced at the display in the window of the servery. There were books on sailing, books on arithmetic for farmers, and recipe books, among other things. "You don't think that there are any books about this, do you?"

"I doubt it. And if there were, wouldn't they be even more off-limits than the *Meditations on First Philology*?"

"Still, we are here and might as well have a look."

Once inside, they wandered between the shelves without much purpose. Seeing nothing, they abandoned their search as pointless and headed for the servery's front exit. Seated at the front desk was the same server with the saggy eyes and long beard tucked into his belt who had growled at them when they came in with Altheia.

"Hmm," he glared at the two registrants, startling Selene. "Hmm," he repeated as Selene and Ichabod scuttled out.

"That was strange, Ichabod," Selene said in a low voice as soon as they were out the door.

"He sure is!" replied Ichabod.

"No. Not that. I am talking about the line coming down to his head. It was much stronger than yours or anyone else's I've seen, and the web of fibers around his head was much brighter and denser."

"That's interesting. I wonder what it means." Ichabod pointed down the street to the park where was located the fountain of *Lux*. "Let's head that way," he suggested. "Keep telling me what you see."

They passed by building after building, Selene noting lines of force that twisted down to all of them, leaving not a single structure untouched. She also noticed that certain features of the architecture tended to collect more of the fibrous lines, sculptures in particular. Buildings in the City were often decorated with small gargoyles, down to which strong lines snaked. The statues by the bridges, too—they all had thick, strong lines.

When she and Ichabod reached the park, Selene saw the strongest line yet coiling down to the fractal statue of *Lux*. "I wonder why it is that the sculptures all seem to have stronger lines going into them than other things," she mused.

"You mean, like the statue of *Lux* here? The line is stronger going into it?" Ichabod asked.

"Yes, and not just this statue, although it has the strongest, but the statues by the bridges. too, and even any little statue decorating a building. Like that gargoyle over there." She pointed to a nearby building. "It has a pretty big line going into it."

"So, you are saying that there are some buildings and some people that have more, and some less?"

"Yes, that's exactly it."

"That's weird. But you don't see anything around trees or plants, right? Like grass—nothing there? Just buildings and people?"

"And statues. And even plain walls. I didn't notice that before, but look—down the street to the fish server's stalls. Behind is the stone wall that edges the Vespera River. There is a faint line coming down, even to it."

Ichabod looked at the sky. "We'd better get going, Selene. Do you think you've seen everything here?"

"I guess so. Where next?"

"The Arboretum. Maybe there are no lines connecting to trees or bushes here, but maybe that's because there aren't many trees, or because they are all scattered and separated from each other. Maybe there will be lines if the trees are dense enough."

"It's a good *Quaestio Essentiae*, Ichabod." Selene managed a wan smile.

"See? I knew you were listening." It was a feeble joke, and he knew it, but Selene appreciated it anyway.

Twenty minutes of brisk walking brought them to the Arboretum.

"What do you see, Selene?"

"Nothing. Just trees and rocks and such. Oh, look at the birds. They are so beautiful. But they don't have any lines, either. Seems like there's nothing here. But I think we ought to go deeper in. Let's go to the alcove. I need to sit and think."

They soon reached the familiar rocky sanctuary and still found nothing unusual. Selene leaned back against the cool rock and found she could finally relax. Ichabod, by contrast, was agitated by everything they'd seen—or, more accurately, Selene had seen. That he couldn't see any of it made it worse. He hated a puzzle he couldn't solve.

"Maybe people make the lines..." he started to say.

"Ichabod," Selene interrupted.

"Oh! Sorry." Ichabod was penitent.

"It's OK, but let's talk about something else."

"Sure. Like what?"

"Like Altheia."

"Altheia? Why?"

"Ichabod—*Icky*—haven't you noticed *anything* about her when she's around you?"

"No. Why? Should I have?"

"Well, it's pretty obvious to me, at least."

"What do you mean?"

"Do you remember when she asked you to come here a few weeks ago?"

"Yeah. So what?"

"*Icky*," Selene said, stretching out the word just a tiny bit. "She *invited* you. *She* invited you. She invited *you*." Selene kept changing the emphasis until Ichabod understood.

"Oh." Ichabod's ears reddened in a way that Selene thought hilarious. "Well, I didn't know."

"That's why she was so upset I was here, you know. She thought it was just going to be you two. All alone, by yourselves."

Ichabod shrugged without replying.

"I don't think she likes me particularly," Selene observed.

"Of course she likes you. But we have more important things to worry about," he said, deflecting. "Anyway, she's nice and all. But she seems kind of...I don't know. I don't want to sound mean."

"Yes, she's quite beautiful, isn't she?" There was an impish gleam in Selene's eyes.

"Oh, come on. Give a guy a break." Ichabod was clearly uncomfortable, so Selene relented.

"Alright. But you're going to have to talk to her, you know."

"Yeah. Just think how uncomfortable that's going to be *now*. Thanks a lot."

They sat quietly for a few minutes, letting the fresh air of the woods fill their lungs and their spirits. When they got up to return to campus, they were both feeling lighter, and Selene was able to study the dual worlds more objectively. Finally, they reached the front doors of Celestine Hall.

The day had one more surprise in store for them. After they had entered the Hall and climbed the three broad steps that took them to the main hallway, Selene glanced at the Watching Bird, expecting to see a line of force but not thinking about it. There was a line indeed. What she wasn't prepared for was the sheer intensity of it. She hadn't yet seen the like. There were dozens of heavy, fibrous virgules curling to the owl, perhaps hundreds, packed so densely where they converged at the top of the statue that they looked like a single, thick, bright mass rather than distinct lines. Selene thought she could *feel* a force emanating from the bird—that's how intense the lines were. And fear. Selene felt absolute fear. She halted involuntarily, just a few steps in front of the Bird.

"What is it?" Ichabod asked in a low voice.

"No. Not now, Ichabod. I need to go," she said with unquestionable urgency. They both put their heads down and started walking as swiftly as they dared back to their rooms.

Their absence had not been noticed. As soon as Ichabod was back in his room, he was out on the ledge, around the corner, and through Selene's window. Selene's room was dark, and she was rocking on the edge of her bed.

"What was it, Selene? It seemed like the Bird scared you."

Selene stopped rocking. Ichabod noticed she was shaking. She described what she had seen.

"And I felt *terror*. Not fear. Terror. Like I have never felt before," she concluded.

"That has to mean something. Maybe the Bird is the key to the whole thing."

"Yeah, maybe. No way that I am going to use that entrance again."

"I don't know, Selene. That might draw attention to yourself. I would try to behave exactly the way you were behaving before all of this happened. At least until we figure out what it all means."

Selene nodded miserably.

"Also," he continued, "I think it's time to talk to Professor Thallos again."

"No. Please, Ichabod. I really don't want to do that. He might have me locked up or something." She felt panic rising again, for no reason she could discern.

Ichabod began to argue the point. "What else can we do? What if things keep changing? What if it gets worse? He's the Academy Professor of Observational Learning. And an expert on the Death. If this isn't a puzzle that screams for the method of discernment, then I don't know what is."

"Stop it. No. I do not want to tell him or anyone!" Selene's voice betrayed increasing agitation. She was panicking and far more upset than Ichabod or she herself had realized. "Go away. Just go away!" Selene lay down on her bed, facing the wall, her back to Ichabod. He sat there for a moment and then spoke quietly.

"Don't worry, Selene. We will figure this out. Together." Selene felt his warm hand on her back and then heard him climb out the window. She tightened into a ball, tears in her eyes, angry with herself for yelling at him. *Why did I do that?* She forced herself to unball, got up, and looked out the window at what was now a nighttime sky. Red tendrils wavered slightly against the deep red-tinged indigo of the heavens, a few lines following people as they moved across the campus. The emerald Skyfire of Caelestis was shimmering and wobbling in the background, filling the entire northern quadrant. *Skyfire; that's what my mother used to call it, but Professor Thallos said that its proper formal name is auroralumina. How can it be simultaneously so beautiful and so terrifying?* Selene watched as the stars slowly rotated through the coruscating sky until her body unclenched, and finally went to bed.

CHAPTER EIGHT

THE WATCHING BIRD

Having slept only fitfully, Selene knew upon waking what she must do next. She sat down by Ichabod at firstmeal, hoping to have a few minutes before Altheia arrived. She knew she should apologize to Ichabod, but just didn't want to talk about it.

"We need to examine the Watching Bird more closely," she blurted with no preamble, staring at her food.

Ichabod nodded. "How closely are you thinking? Hard to do when it's in the main hallway, right by the main desk and the main entrance."

"We need to take it," Selene replied.

"Take it? You mean, steal it."

"Yes."

Ichabod chewed thoughtfully. "We can do that, but it's risking a lot. Maybe at night, when the desk is closed and no one is around. It might not be missed for a while. We could sneak it back, so it'd really be just borrowing it."

"Steal, borrow, whatever you want to call it. I think the Bird is the key to all of this." Selene knew it sounded silly when she said it out loud. "Anyway, it's just a wooden statue, right? I'm sure pranks like this happen all the time. It's probably been 'borrowed' before."

"A wooden statue with a freaky giant line of power going into it that scares you more than anything," he replied and raised his eyebrows. "Have you heard of it being stolen before?"

"Well...no. Please. Just help me with this. I know it's wrong, but think about it; we saw all sorts of lines of force yesterday but only found two larger patterns. The Bird is part of those patterns."

"Right," Ichabod agreed. "The lines seem only to go to people and buildings. And some statues. But not to trees or rivers or stuff like that."

"Yes. Only people and artificial objects."

"And the other thing was that some objects and people have stronger lines than others."

"The Bird has the strongest of any I saw. And it was terrifying. I don't want to have anything to do with it, but it's got to be the key, Ichabod."

"OK, then. Suppose it's the key..."

"The key to what, Icky?" came Altheia's bright voice as she sat down across from them.

"Oh, nothing," he dissembled "The key to remembering the steps in the method of discernment, that's all. Selene's having trouble memorizing the poem. You know, '*Observatio Primordialis*, observe the world to make it clear/*Quaestio Essentiae*...'"

"That's easy," said Altheia, waving her hand dismissively. "I made up a tune for it."

"Really? That's brilliant, Altheia," Ichabod enthused.

Altheia blushed. "Well, it didn't take a genius, silly Icky. I really didn't make it all up. I just used the tune to 'The Grand Ship Duke of York.' It fits perfectly."

"What's 'The Grand Ship Duke of York'?" asked Selene.

"Yeah, and what's a duke, and what's York?" added Ichabod.

"I don't know. It's just a song for little kids. You don't know it? My mother used to sing it to us. She said she had learned it from her grandmother and that it's pretty old. A duke was someone important, like a scholar-priest or a city council member. And York was a village that disappeared a long time ago. So, they named a boat after the duke who lived there. Here, let me see if I can remember the words." Altheia began to sing in a soft, pure voice:

Oh, the grand ship Duke of York,

It sailed for a thousand days

It brought us down to Erden and

Landed in a blaze.

When we soared high, we were high,

And when we soared low, we were low,

And when we were drifting 'twixt land and sky,

We were neither high nor low.

"What does *that* mean?" Selene asked. "It makes it sound like ships can fly. I know a bedtime story about flying ships—you know, boats that have wings like birds—but that's just fantasy. If ships could fly, think how easily they could get to the fishing grounds. That's why people imagine such things. But only birds can fly."

"If we could fly, think how easy it would be to travel across the whole Prinship," added Ichabod. "Although 'landed in a blaze' sounds like it started a fire or something. Once you got up, how would you get down without crashing?"

"I really don't know what the song means," Altheia said peevishly. "My mother just said it's really old. We would all do a little dance to it. When we got to the part about soaring high, my sister and I would wave our arms and run around the room like birds, and when we got to the part about soaring low, we'd crouch down and run around. It's just a kids' song. It doesn't mean anything."

"Oh, I don't know. Do you remember what Professor Clymene said about stories?" Ichabod asked.

"Ugh. No. I really don't like literary philology." Altheia made a face.

"Professor Clymene says that every story is based on real life and thus expresses some truth, so the way to understand a story is to find the real-life elements in it and then see what's exaggerated. That will tell you what the people who made up the song think is important." Ichabod gazed into the distance as he considered the lyrics. "Songs are stories, right? So, what things in the song could be real? I bet that there *was* a Duke of York, whatever a duke is, and wherever York was. It'd be weird to just make up nonsense words like that. They sound so specific. Like they are actual words. Plus, we don't know much about stuff from a long time ago."

"And what about the ship?" asked Selene. "That's the other thing in the song: the ship brought not just the Duke of York but other people, too. It says 'us,' after all."

"Sure," Ichabod replied. "What's the biggest ship in your village, Selene? In mine, we just have pirogues. They are pretty small, but there are ferries that can carry a whole cart and five or six people across the river."

"The biggest ships we have can hold twenty-five people, twenty of them rowers. But I heard that a village further up the coast built a bireme that had 50 rowers and could hold another 25 people. Crazy big. I think it got wrecked in a storm, though."

"So, maybe the song is about something like a big bireme from a long time ago," Ichabod concluded.

"Yes, but sailed for a thousand days?" Selene was skeptical. "No ship can carry enough food and water for that. I guess it could have landed every once in a while, though. And—landed in a blaze? Soaring high and low? Those don't make much sense."

Ichabod nodded. "Professor Clymene says that you have to exaggerate and include fantastical elements to make a story interesting, and what people find interesting tells you what's important to them. So, that's probably just made-up stuff because it'd be amazing to fly."

"If you two scholar-priests have finished ruining my childhood, it's time for class," Altheia interjected.

Professor Thallos's class that morning included, serendipitously, a lecture on the geography of the Principality. According to the map he unrolled, Selene's fishing village and Ichabod's farm were equidistant from Academy City, but in opposite directions; Ichabod's home was two days' travel upriver by cart, near the western end of the mountains of the Meridial Arc, and Selene's village was two days downriver on the broad bay called the Reach into which the Vespera River empties.

"Academy City was built on a bend in the Vespera River in the center of a large plain to take advantage of the waterway for transportation, and to ensure that all villages in the Principality were roughly equidistant from the city," he explained. "This aids in the administration and maintenance of a well-integrated culture."

The professor went on to describe farming in the Greenward and the Seedlands for most of the rest of the class period. Finally, with only a few minutes left, he asked, "Are there any questions?" Professor Thallos clearly didn't expect any and was already collecting his notes when Ichabod spoke up.

"Professor, can you tell us more about other areas on the map?"

Professor Thallos continued to gather his notes as he responded, "What other areas would those be, Registrant Ichabod?"

"Well, the mountains up north, for one. The Meridial Arc. And the Wildings, too."

The students were now all listening intently. Everyone in the Prinship grew up hearing stories about the Wildings. It was both the name of a forest and a name for the creatures that inhabited it—if the tales were to be believed. Ichabod had heard the stories more often than most, since the edge of the Wildings forest was less than a day's hike from his village. Many of the tales told of a place of impenetrable

darkness in which people would get lost and simply disappear, never to
return. Most disturbing were stories that told of feral, semi-intelligent,
near-human animals wielding primitive clubs, slings, and stone axes,
and who practiced cannibalism. These stories were effective in preventing people from entering the Wildings. Even Ichabod, who had
occasionally hiked within sight of the forest, had never met anyone
who had actually gone into the it. As far as he knew, no one had for
many years.

"The Meridial Arc is simply a series of mountains. Beyond them
is nothing useful for the Principality, nor anything dangerous. Just
unlivable wasteland. The mountains themselves offer useful resources,
especially stone for building and decorative purposes. It is also spec-
ulated that the mountains create a protective weather barrier for the
Greenward since they slow and cool the prevailing winds from the
northwest, and thus moderate levels of humidity." Professor Thallos
paused for a moment as he finished collecting his notes and stuffed
them in his bag. He then looked up reprovingly. "This is all in your
Go-With, you know."

"But how do we know that there is nothing useful on the other
side of the mountains? How do we know that it's unlivable there?"
Ichabod asked. "Has anyone ever crossed over the mountains? Has
anyone ever gone into the Wildings?"

"The Principality encompasses all of the useful land and resources
on Erden, Registrant Ichabod. This has been known since...well, it's
common knowledge," responded the professor.

"As for the Wildings, I am sure that a skeptical and clear-thinking
student like yourself would realize that the many stories of monsters
and cannibals supposed to live there are merely fictions intended to
scare small children. It is a forest, nothing more, and while the Principality has in the past attempted to exploit it for resources, we have
found that the wood is not of good quality and is not worth the
expense of harvesting, especially in light of how dense the forest is

and how difficult it would be to clear it enough to access whatever is useable in it. Simple observational learning, Registrant Ichabod; nothing weird or supernatural about it at all."

"But is it observational if we haven't observed it ourselves?" Ichabod persisted.

"Enough. Consult your *Go-With*. Class dismissed."

The professor had given his final word on the matter. The usual hubbub of students collecting their things and socializing with each other followed, and Ichabod and Selene followed their classmates out into the hallway.

"You are wondering if the lines of force extend to the Meridial Arc. Or to the Wildings," Selene whispered to Ichabod on the way out.

"Yes. But maybe they only show up where there are people," he replied. "Or buildings. It'd be interesting to find out."

"People, buildings, and things like the Bird. Anyway, do we steal it tonight, or don't we?"

"We borrow it, Selene," he answered with a chuckle. "But yes. Tonight."

"Did you notice, Ichabod?"

"Notice what?"

"Professor Thallos called you by your right name."

The remainder of the day passed uneventfully, and Ichabod made his way around the ledge to Selene's room just after lastlight. They whispered together quietly and nervously for some time, waiting for the dorm to settle down. Glorious skyfire once again filled the view outside Selene's window; after contemplating it for a few more minutes, the two of them set out on their "Quest to capture the Bird," as Ichabod called it. Selene thought the scheme might be better called

"How to get expelled before completing your first year," but, as it was her idea in the first place, she led the way.

Good fortune was with them. Pilfering the Bird turned out to be a simple matter quickly accomplished; so quickly, in fact, that their hearts, which had been beating a mile a minute when they set out, had yet to return to a normal pulse by the time they were back in Selene's room pulling the bird out of Ichabod's pack.

As soon as she neared the Bird, fear again engulfed Selene, but she squelched the feeling as best she could and turned to examine their prize. "It still has the strongest line of force I've seen. I sort of wondered if it might have lost it when we moved it. You know—if it was the Bird or the place it was located. Guess we know now that it's the Bird, and the line follows it. Just like a person." Just talking objectively and analytically about the statue helped tamp down the panic she felt when in its proximity.

"It was a good thing it was just sitting on that shelf. I thought it might have been screwed down. Well, let's give it a good going-over, shall we?" Ichabod shifted Selene's study table into the middle of her room and placed the Bird on it.

The Watching Bird was old. At some point it had been lacquered, but the lacquer had crazed and yellowed from years of exposure to the sun. Upon minute examination, it looked like the lacquer had been applied several times, over even older layers, and beneath those, there were slight, almost invisible traces of pigment. Selene and Ichabod concluded that, at some point, the Bird had been painted in imitation of an owl's coloration. The eyes retained the slightest hint of black, there were traces of light brown in the creases of the wings, and flecks of gold-yellow speckled the legs. Most of this paint was visible only on close inspection, however. Even up close, the Bird in its current state just looked like a very worn old wooden icon, covered with blemishes and flaws. Neither Ichabod nor Selene found anything that would suggest why the Bird was such a powerful locus of the lines.

"Perhaps there's nothing to find here, Selene," Ichabod said, standing up straight to stretch. "I think I need..."

"Shh!" Selene interrupted him. "Someone is outside." She padded to her door and opened it just a crack.

"What are you two *doing* in there?" came a hoarse whisper. Altheia pushed her way past Selene into her room and halted abruptly in her tracks.

"Mist and the Death! What is that? What are you two doing?" she said upon seeing the icon on the study table in the center of the room. "That's the Watching Bird. Why is *that* here?"

Altheia's vehemence startled Selene. She worried that others in the dorm might have heard, so even though she had closed the door, Selene tried to hush Altheia. "We asked if we could study it, because it's so old. We were wondering where it came from. We thought it might be made of wood from the Wildings. So, that's why we asked if we could look at it before lastlight, and it's so interesting we didn't realize the time." Even to Selene's ears, her explanation sounded like a lie.

"Who gave you permission?" Altheia asked skeptically.

"The people at the front desk," Ichabod offered.

"Really? Some weird things have been happening around you two lately—like that storm when I found you on the bench. I've never seen anything like it. And why did you ask Professor Thallos about the Wildings and what's beyond the Arc, Ichabod? Why were you both so interested in that awful book when we were in the Arboretum?" Ichabod and Selene saw Altheia was frightened, but neither responded. "I am going to have to tell someone unless you tell me what's going on. You owe me that. I thought we were friends." Tears rimmed Altheia's eyes.

Selene and Ichabod looked at each other for a long moment in silent conversation. Finally, Ichabod guided Altheia over to Selene's bed and sat her down on the edge, while he and Selene sat on either side of her. Ichabod had his arm around Altheia, trying to comfort her as she suppressed small, angry sobs.

Ichabod nodded to Selene. "Tell her. Tell her everything. It's the only way. She could have gone to one of the professors long ago, but she hasn't. We need to tell her."

Altheia turned to Ichabod angrily. "Of *course* I haven't gone to the professors, you...*Ichabod*. Honestly, you are both so *stupid* sometimes. What do you take me for?"

Guilt marked both Ichabod and Selene's faces. Selene settled herself and thought about where to start.

"Altheia, do you remember when Elara was taken by the mist?" she gently asked, to which Altheia nodded.

"So, right after we purified the school, I started having dreams. Really bad dreams."

"Who didn't? What's the big deal about that?" Altheia sniffled.

"No, not normal bad dreams. Well, bad dreams are never normal, I guess, but these were not dreams of a sort I've had before. These were dreams of takings."

"I used to have dreams like that when I was little, when I first heard about the mist. I used to dream that it came for everyone in my house, and they'd all be gone when I woke up," Altheia observed.

"No, not dreams like that. These felt real, not like dreams at all. Even after I woke up, it still felt like I had really been *there*. And they weren't just random takings. They weren't just my imagination. Here's the thing, Altheia. We...sort of...looked at some files in Professor Thallos's office, and one of them included a description of a taking that *I had dreamed*."

"What, you mean you told him about your dream, and he wrote it down?"

"No. This particular taking happened forty years ago. The file contained a record of Professor Thallos's investigation of it. We sort of looked at it without permission. It was about a fellow named Ravian.

Altheia," Selene said as she took one of Altheia's hands and looked her steadily in the eyes. "My dreams are not dreams. They are more like *memories*. That's the best comparison, but they are more real than that. And we know now that they are accurate. They show things that really happened. We've been calling them '*seeings*.' I even had a seeing of someone being taken near the time that the Prinship was founded. Erden was so different then. You wouldn't recognize it. But I knew what I was seeing was real, and that it was a long time ago."

Altheia didn't know how to respond. This was not at all what she had expected. She had thought that maybe Ichabod and Selene had just let their curiosity get away with them and that she'd have to make them replace the Bird before anyone noticed. *I'd never tell on them. They should understand that,* she thought.

"But that was, like, two thousand years ago. That's not possible, is it?" Altheia paused for a moment. "It sounds awful, Selene. Who have you told? Wait. Did you say a *fellow*? That makes no sense. Did you tell Professor Thallos? He's all into the Death stuff. He wrote that awful book you were reading in the Arboretum. That's why you were reading it!"

"Yeah, we did tell him. Some of it. But he sort of ignored us," interjected Ichabod.

"Well," Altheia pulled herself up a bit and said philosophically, "If it was just some bad dreams, even if they were of things that actually happened, maybe you heard about them before and simply don't remember it. I don't see what the big deal is."

Selene breathed for a moment and then continued. "The thing is, not only have the dreams—the seeings—kept happening, but...do you remember when I had to go to the healer's room a few days ago during class?" Altheia nodded. "I had one of the seeings right there in the middle of class."

"Did it seem real, like your other dreams? Seeings, I mean?" asked Altheia.

"Yes. But the healer said I was fine. She called it a 'visual aura' and said it just happens sometimes, said it was harmless. But I know that's not what it was. Or, not all that it was."

"How? The healer is a healer. They know about that sort of thing." Altheia remained skeptical, but by this point, she knew Selene had more to tell her.

"There's more to it..."

"No. You are kidding me," Altheia mocked, smiling wanly.

Selene returned the smile. "It's not just that I have these seeings of takings. When the miasma comes, what I see is not what other people see. Most people see a gray mist; to me, it's a pulsing, deep red. As it settles on a person, I see an entire spectrum of colors. Almost like the wings of a beetle, all shiny. An iridescent metallic pulsing rainbow."

"Maybe your eyes are just better than ours."

"Maybe. But after I had that problem in class, Ichabod suggested I try to recreate it by clearing my mind, since the seeings seem to come only when I am mentally relaxed..."

"You did *what*? Why would you want to *make* them happen?" Altheia was aghast.

"It just seemed like we needed to try it. I was so exhausted from barely sleeping for so many nights that I was ready to try anything. Anyway, this was when the bizarre weather hit that so upset you. Do you remember?"

"Oh, like I am going to forget that."

"Right. I think I caused it. And here's the really bad part: when I relaxed my mind, I didn't see a taking..."

"Why is that bad?"

"No, that's not the bad part. I didn't see a taking, but I saw...it's hard to describe. I saw two worlds next to each other, sort of, but here. On campus. I saw reality, but I also saw this vague, prismatic world just next to it. And I saw all of these red spidery lines everywhere—we call them 'lines of force.'"

"What do they do?"

"We don't know," said Ichabod.

"Ichabod's right; we don't know. So, we skipped a day, pretending to be sick..."

Altheia snorted. "I knew you were faking."

Selene nodded. "And we went to the City—to the market district—and then to the Arboretum, to see if we could learn anything about the lines. They are all over the place. And get this. There are *patterns* to them."

"What patterns? Like the miasma comes every four years?" Having entirely forgotten that she was upset, Altheia listened, transfixed.

"Yes. So far, we know that lines come down from the sky and sort of surround everyone's heads. Including ours. And there are lines that come down to buildings, or anything artificial, really. Even walls and fountains. And statues. Lots of statues. But not natural things, like trees or hills."

"My head?" Altheia said with horror. "And...the Bird!"

"Exactly. There is a line of force coming down to the Bird. All the lines are red, the same deep red as the mist. One more thing: the lines are stronger for some people and for some objects. The bookserver—you remember him? The line coming down to his head was way stronger than for other people." Selene paused as she briefly remembered an unanswered question: *What about me? What if the lines are stronger for me, too?*

"And the Bird. Its line is also stronger. Am I right?" Altheia broke into Selene's train of thought.

"Yes. The Bird has the strongest line of force going into it I have yet seen. It's massive. And it scares the mist out of me when I am near it and looking at it. We aren't trying to damage the Bird, and we *are* going to take it back as soon as we can, but we needed to study it up close. That's why it's here." Selene, gingerly touching the Watching Bird, became grave. "I need to understand this. It's important, but I don't know how. I have been able to see the real world next to the dream world for days now. It's terrifying. Looking at the Bird intensifies the feeling. Maybe it's a threat to the Prinship. Maybe this is all normal, and there is something wrong with me. Maybe I am the threat. I don't know. But whatever is happening to me, it's real."

A sharp knock at the door startled them, and the House Fellow's voice came through loudly, "Registrant Selene, open your door at once. I need to search your room."

The three students sat petrified. The House Fellow rapped again, insistently. Selene pointed to the bird, to Ichabod, and to the window, mouthed the word "Go," and called out in a mock-sleepy voice. "Okay, just a minute." She glanced at Ichabod, who hadn't moved. "Go!" she mouthed again.

"I'm gone." Ichabod was just out the window when Selene realized Altheia had no knowledge of their ledge-shortcut. Altheia had rushed to the window wide-eyed, expecting to look down on Ichabod's broken body on the sidewalk far below, and was bewildered to find him smiling at her from just outside the window. He motioned her back into the room; she made her way to the edge of the bed just as Selene was opening the door for the House Fellow.

"Registrant Altheia? What are you doing here?" asked the fellow dubiously.

"I'm sorry. I was thirsty, and I heard Selene yelping in her sleep, so I came to make sure that she was okay. She's been sick, you know. I'll go back to my room now." Altheia made for the door, but the Fellow's arm blocked her.

"No. You need to stay here. There is a search going on. Everyone needs to remain where they are." The Fellow was looking around Selene's room. "Open that wardrobe."

"The wardrobe? Why? What are you looking for?" Selene asked, her arms crossed, not moving.

"Just open it. If there is nothing here, I may tell you why we are searching."

Selene stalked over to the wardrobe, opened it wide, and stood to one side of it as if presenting it for inspection. "If you are looking for my undergarments, you've found them."

The House Fellow began poking through Selene's clothing. "Alright, enough of that. Someone has taken the Watching Bird. It's just a dumb prank if you ask me, but the heads of the houses are pretty worked up about it. That Bird is as old as the Academy and can't be replaced. Not that it's worth much, but it's been here for so long, it has become a symbol of Celestine Hall for the alumni. I can't imagine how angry some of them might be if it's not found." He turned to face the two registrants. "If you hear anything about it, you come to me first. Otherwise, you'll get expelled along with whoever took it. Stay here, Registrant Altheia. I am going to search your room next. You may return to your room in ten minutes. Unless I come for you," he added threateningly. With that, the House Fellow left, abruptly closing Selene's door behind him.

"Mist and the Death again, Selene. You had better get the Bird back where it belongs, and quickly." Selene almost expected Altheia to stamp her foot, she was so angry.

"Don't worry, we will."

"I know you will because I am going to help you do it."

This surprised Selene; she never would have expected Altheia to break the rules and risk so much for a problem that wasn't hers. Selene and Altheia locked eyes for just a moment; a surge of warmth throughout her body surprised Selene.

"Thank you, Altheia. We can't do it tonight—too many people will be watching."

"Can't do what?" came Ichabod's voice as he climbed back in the window. Selene and Altheia noticed he no longer had the bird.

"What did you do with it?" Altheia asked in a panic.

"The Bird? Oh, it's back there on the ledge. No one will find it. It's mostly hidden behind the railing, too, so I would bet no one will notice it, even in daylight."

"Wait. Bring it here one more time," Altheia ordered, to the surprise of both Ichabod and Selene. "Go on. Grab it, just for a moment, before I have to go back to my room. I want to see it up close." When they hesitated, she added, "Well, you two got a close look at it. Why shouldn't I?"

In a blink, Ichabod had it back on the table. All three examined it again with intense interest. "You say that you see a big line thing going into it, Selene? Bigger than to anything else?"

"Yes."

"Even right now? I mean, you have moved the Bird around a lot, but that hasn't changed it?" Altheia was now squinting at the base of the icon, her eyes only an inch from the wood.

"Yes," responded Selene. "I mean, no. Why?"

"I don't know. I was wondering; when was the last time it was moved? I bet no one has examined it as closely as we have in…I don't know. Years, maybe."

"Could be centuries," Ichabod offered.

"Yes. So, what does this inscription mean, anyway?" Altheia asked.

"Inscription? What inscription?" Selene asked with surprise. Both she and Ichabod crowded in to get a better look.

"Don't shove, you two. Right here, on the base in the front. Right under the Bird's claws, on the edge of the book at the top of the pile. Here, look at it with the light hitting it sideways." She grabbed the lamp and moved aside, holding the light so that the other two could see the base more clearly.

"I see it. There *is* an inscription!" Ichabod was triumphant. He closed one eye completely, the other nearly so, and bobbed his head around a bit. "I can also see the remnants of red paint in the grooves."

"Shh, Icky! Not so loud. The House Fellow might hear you." warned Altheia. "What's it say?"

"It says...it says...I can't read it," Ichabod lamented.

"Here, let me read it. It's just like reading the tiny print on packing slips at the servery," Altheia opined. "I have very good eyes, you know." After squinting and moving her head around to get the best angle, she recited the inscription.

> Seek not the prism's source, nor question the flame,
> For what shines brightest must not be truly named.

Altheia looked up. "Is that helpful?" she asked.

"I think it is," Selene responded, nodding. "I mean, clearly, it's a warning. And I would bet tomorrow's lastmeal that 'the prism's source' and 'the flame' are what I have been seeing: those sort of describe the lines of force and the reddish multicolored mist that accompanies the taking. If so, that means the lines and the mist are connected. But I would have guessed that, anyway. What's that stuff about 'what shines brightest'?"

The other two shook their heads. Selene picked up the icon and handed it to Ichabod. "Okay, we really need to hide this and not draw any more attention. I need to think about this some more. I say we put it back on the ledge for the night."

Ichabod was halfway out the window when he stopped and looked back into the room. "Selene," he asked, a bit puzzled, "Are the prism's source and the flame different things? Or is it saying that the prism's source and the flame are the *same* thing? If so, then it's saying we shouldn't seek it, nor question it. What would it mean to 'question the prism's source'? That's ambiguous. It could mean that we shouldn't *challenge* the source, whatever it is. Like, 'never question your professor's judgment' or something. But it could also mean that we shouldn't try to figure out *what* the source is. Right?"

"I guess so," Selene agreed. "That makes sense. But so what? Where does that leave us? Maybe it's telling us we shouldn't do either."

"Let's assume that it's saying we shouldn't try to figure out *what* the source is. How would you even *do* that?" Ichabod wondered.

As he was saying this, a chill ran through Selene as she realized she might be able to do just that. She might have a way to trace the lines of force to their source.

"Ichabod, Altheia, I have an idea. No, not an idea; I have a *feeling*. I don't know why, so don't ask me. Just bring the Bird back again. Sorry. One more time. Let me try something."

Ichabod again placed the bird on Selene's study table and stepped away to give her space. Selene closed her eyes for a moment and then opened them, just as she had in the courtyard when she was first able to see the lines of force.

"What are you doing?" Altheia asked, concerned.

"Sh! Just hold on."

Selene again closed her eyes and composed her mind, clearing it of any thoughts, trying to silence fear and still her emotions. Once more, when she opened her eyes, they were unfocused. Selene leaned forward, tilting into the Bird, her face flushed. "The line! I can feel it. I can feel myself *in* it." She drew in a sharp breath. "I can *push* it."

"Selene, be careful," Ichabod exclaimed.

"No—don't touch me, Ichabod. I can push the line and make it bend. It's not physical, not like physical stuff, so when I tried to touch them before, with my hands, it was like they didn't exist. But I can push this one with my mind. Like it exists as pure *thinking* stuff."

"What does it feel like?" Altheia asked.

"It feels like...like, if electricity had a color, if you know what I mean."

"Uh, no, we don't know what you mean, Selene," said Ichabod.

"Don't worry. I will explain it later. Ooh! It's like electric elastic. I can push it, but it feels mentally springy. Wait. I'm going to try one more thing."

As Selene's face became fully fixed and immobile, even Ichabod and Altheia thought that they felt something queer in the air, like an impending thunderstorm of great magnitude.

"I *blocked it,*" Selene gasped, and then dropped heavily to the floor.

CHAPTER NINE

A DIFFERENT WORLD

S elene was unconscious for only a few brief seconds. Once she was awake and feeling more-or-less herself again, Ichabod and Altheia insisted that she rest.

"We two will return the Bird," Altheia reassured her repeatedly. "As soon as the search has ended." The search did indeed end, about forty-five minutes later and without the searchers finding the Bird. Once again to their surprise, Ichabod and Altheia were able to return the Bird to its roost without incident. As they were sneaking back to their rooms, Altheia thought she heard someone coming from a side hall, but it turned out to be nothing. Even so, Altheia had quickly grabbed Ichabod's hand and pulled him aside into a shadow, where they waited, pressed closely together.

"This is exciting! I am a nervous wreck," she whispered to Ichabod, holding his arm a little more tightly than was necessary.

"Shh, Altheia," was all he said in response, not noticing her annoyed glare.

Ichabod left Altheia in her room, slipped into Selene's, and locked the door quietly behind him. "All good?" Selene asked.

"All good," he replied, stepped out the window, shuffled his way around the ledge, jumped through his window, sighed in relief, and was asleep as soon as his head hit the pillow.

"One positive about last night," Selene announced to Ichabod and Altheia over firstmeal the next morning. "No nightmares."

"Huh. Do you suppose that has something to do with the Bird?" Ichabod wondered.

Selene nodded. "I guess so. I think so. I want to try it again."

"You what?" Both Altheia and Ichabod were appalled.

"I want to examine the Bird again, and try to understand the lines of force. Think about it. Each time we discover something new about the mist or the dreams, the nightmares stop. Last night, I was able to block the line going into the Bird. And it was a huge line! But after that, I was able to sleep last night without any interruptions. I want to try again."

"But it knocked you cold. I don't know if this is a good idea, but why not try it with something other than the Bird?" asked Altheia. "Like, what about the lines going into buildings? Or, even me and Icky?"

"That's a great idea, Altheia," Ichabod interjected. "Try it with one of us, Selene."

Selene chewed her food thoughtfully. "No. It's one thing with something like the Bird or even a building, but we don't know what would happen with a person."

"Then at least try it with something that doesn't have such a strong line," Ichabod suggested. "The Bird is dangerous."

"No. I can do this. I need to understand the Bird. It's important, somehow."

"Somehow?" Ichabod asked. "That's kind of vague."

"I know. It must sound absurd. But I feel it. The Bird is special. Think of how strong its line is. And the inscription. It's some kind of focal point. Please?"

"Okay. What do we do, and when do we do it? I take it we are going to borrow the Bird again?" Selene was relieved Ichabod wasn't going to argue the point.

"No. Let's just take a walk."

Altheia looked pained. "Can I please finish my meal first?"

A quarter of an hour later, the three registrants had sauntered to the main hallway and were standing nonchalantly near the Watching Bird. The inscription once again came to Selene's mind. "Seek not the prism's source, nor question the flame," she half-whispered. "Why would it say that we should not seek the prism's source? That *has* to be a reference to the shimmering I've been seeing, both in the mist and in the red dream world."

"Where there's chaff, someone's been threshing," Ichabod affirmed.

"What's that mean?" Altheia asked.

"Is that like 'gulls gather near the catch'?" Selene wondered.

"What does *that* mean?" Altheia repeated.

"It means," observed Ichabod, "That if the inscription is telling Selene not to investigate the origins of what she is seeing, there must be something worth knowing about them. It means we are going to disobey the Bird."

"Oh, you mean, like, where there's *Lux*, there's peace," Altheia added.

"Quiet, you two. Let me see if I can push the lines around today like I did last night." Selene closed her eyes for a moment, and when she opened them, they were unfocused, as before. "No problem," Selene said. "Easy as pie. And I barely feel the fear I felt before. It's so much easier! It's like whatever the presence was there before is hiding. Or not around. Not paying attention. Should I try to block the lines again?"

"No, don't do that, Selene," Ichabod urged. "That's when you passed out last night."

"OK, you're right. I don't want to flop like a fish here. Now, that's odd..." Selene's voice trailed off.

"What's odd? This whole thing is odd," Altheia added.

"No. Well, yes, it is." Selene was distracted. "But...huh...hey! That is..." Again, her voice trailed off.

"What is it?" Ichabod insisted.

"I don't know. I'm going to walk over to the wall, right next to the Bird. Stay with me." Selene moved casually to the wall until she was under the icon. Ichabod and Altheia followed her, looking like three students gossiping intensely.

Selene gasped, and then her face lit up. She knew that Ichabod and Altheia were worried and managed to whisper, "Hold on, it's OK. Just hold on. Wow." Her eyes were rolling around, focusing and refocusing rapidly, taking in her surroundings as if she were traveling quickly through them. "You. Are. Not. Going. To. Believe. This." she stuttered. "Oh!"

It was too much for her companions. Altheia put a hand on Selene's shoulder, which snapped Selene back to reality. "What is it, Selene?"

"You are not going to like this, but I was sort of wondering, while we were standing here, if I...well, if I could follow the line, if you know what I mean."

"I thought you said you could see them and trace them up to wherever they go," Ichabod observed.

"No, I don't mean just look at them. I mean, follow them. Like, ride them. Get inside them."

"What? That's nuts, Selene," Ichabod worried.

"Yeah. I just wanted to try it."

"So, what happened?"

"It worked. No problem. It was like entering a rushing stream, but I could surf along with it. Wait, let me try again." Before Altheia or Ichabod could protest, Selene's eyes again unfocused and refocused, still moving strangely. "Follow me, you two!"

Selene walked toward the big carved front doors of Celestine Hall, stepped outside, and stopped at the bottom of the steps. Once there, she looked around, head swiveling in all directions. "Hold on," she motioned vaguely with one hand. "This is something else. This is crazy." Her companions remained silent for a full two minutes while Selene scanned the area chaotically. Finally, she relaxed and turned to face what she knew was going to be a barrage of questions.

"Hold on one more time. I need to try one more thing. Can you make sure I don't run into anything?" Again, her eyes unfocused. She walked away from the Hall while Ichabod and Altheia hurried to catch up, sidling to either side.

Selene walked briskly for perhaps one hundred yards, stopped, and abruptly slumped. Ichabod and Altheia caught her arms on either side, holding her up. Selene's eyes opened, refocused; she looked at her friends and panted, "Nope, that's it. That's as far as I can go. Come on, let's go back. We need to find a quiet place to talk."

Back in the Hall, they slipped into the unoccupied Universe Room.

"What's going on, Selene?" Ichabod asked as soon as the door was closed.

"You two won't believe this, but..."

"You are kidding, right?" Ichabod interrupted. "Who'd believe any of this? We'll believe just about anything now."

"Right. So. Here's the thing. I was able to put my mind into the line."

"We kind of guessed that," Ichabod said.

"It was wild. I just sort of *thought* my way into the line. The lines definitely have something to do with mind. Like the mist. Like I said yesterday, it doesn't feel like physical stuff. It feels like mental stuff. Like thinking stuff."

"Are you saying that it's thinking?" Altheia was horrified.

"No. Well, maybe. I don't know. But it feels like it's made of the stuff of thought—or it's the stuff that thought is made of. You remember, I felt something like a mind in the mist back when it took Elara. It was there, but...not paying attention, I guess. It felt distant. Mentally far away. Anyway, I was able to put myself in the line. It was like being in a stream. I could ride it, just by willing. It felt so fast. Faster than any keelboat."

"Why did you have us follow you? Why did you walk away from the building?" Ichabod asked.

"I wanted to see how far I could go. It got a little wilder with each step. Like I was going to fall out of it. I think it was because I was getting too far away from the Bird. When I couldn't follow the line any further, I really felt like I was going to keel over. Thanks for catching me."

"So," Ichabod puzzled, "The lines feel like a mental 'substance.' Like they are part of a mind, but that mind is not always paying attention. You can physically 'bend' or 'push' the lines, and that doesn't cause any problems, and you can 'ride' them for at least some distance, but if you try to interrupt them, it knocks you out. It's all very weird, but I am not sure that it tells us much."

"I'm not done, Ichabod," Selene said gravely. "I didn't tell you what I saw."

Altheia and Ichabod both knew from Selene's tone of voice that this was not going to be good. Selene continued.

"You know how I've been seeing double? Two Academies, two buildings, that sort of thing?" They nodded. "And you know how reality looks a bit faded to me, kind of like an old oil painting?" Again, they nodded.

"You know how the other stuff, the other reality, seemed obscure? Hard to see? Well, it's not anymore."

"What do you mean, it's not?" Ichabod asked.

"I mean that the other reality was not at all obscure when I was seeing it through the lines of force. Instead, the real Academy buildings and the rest seemed vague, and the other reality seemed utterly real. And it was *ugly*." Selene scowled. "Celestine Hall was just a big, blocky thing, Gray. Old. Made of concrete. All angles."

Selene shook her head as she described an edifice that was ancient and utterly unlike anything they knew in the Principality. Weather had worn and stained the exterior of Celestine Hall, its surface streaked with the gray-black of water runoff and the ochre tint of rust leaching from exposed metal reinforcements. Jagged cracks, poorly patched, cut angular lines along the facade, and vertical columns of raw concrete rose from the ground like the trunks of some petrified forest, supporting door overhangs that jutted out like knives.

The main entrance that Selene knew and loved so well, with its stained glass, carved doors, and the beautiful marbled stone steps rising into the main hall by the front desk—from her new perspective, it was nothing more than a cavernous, unornamented void, a great maw poised to devour those who entered. High atop Celestine Hall, Selene had seen a massive, featureless tower with no apparent purpose, rising windowless and streaked with lines of corrosion from exposed steel reinforcement.

Everywhere, the lines of force were present and clear, especially around the Watching Bird. But, unlike everything else she saw, the Bird was oddly unchanged.

"Everywhere, everything felt like it was watching. Not being watched, but watching. The Bird, especially. It felt the same as the mist feels: like there is a mind present. I don't think it noticed me this time, though."

"That sounds like a nightmare, Selene," Altheia offered. "That can't be real."

"No, I am telling you, it felt more real than reality. I need to try it again," Selene started to say, but Ichabod interrupted her.

"We need to get to class, Selene. We are late already. You are not going to tell anyone else about this, are you?"

"No. Not a chance. But I still need to try this again as soon as we can. You two have to be with me."

"Agreed," said both Altheia and Ichabod.

Selene couldn't pay attention in any of her classes. While she *could* choose to ignore the gray, ugly world the Watching Bird had revealed—Selene had decided that the icon was more of that world than the real world—she couldn't resist the temptation of slipping into it as long as she was within range of the Bird.

Not everything differed between the two worlds, she noticed. People looked much the same, although their clothing often did not. In her world, people tended to prefer vibrant clothing, usually mixing several colors, but in the world of the Bird, all clothing was uniformly brownish gray, as if the fabrics' hues had been desaturated. Selene thought it interesting that the cuts were the same across the two worlds; Professor Thallos's teaching tunic was still the same teaching tunic, although it was no longer dun-green and reddish-orange. Just gray, stained, and old. Of even more interest to Selene, however, was the observation that Professor Thallos was one of the few people she had seen who had a strong force line. Not as strong as the bookserver, though. She had missed this before, but now, with the clarity brought by her ability to see the other reality fully as it was, it was obvious: the fibrous web ranged thickly around the professor's head.

This pricked her memory. *I've forgotten to check my own line again*, she thought with a pang. Hadn't her line, seen reflected in the windows of the book server, also been stronger than average? She wasn't sure. The first opportunity she had between classes, she found a mirror, and...yes, there it was. She, too, had a thick, stringy line of force that snaked after her as she moved. Her line seemed, if anything, stronger than that which followed Professor Thallos, stronger even than the line that haloed the bookserver's head.

It's like being infected with a parasite that can't be removed, she thought. *In my case, a super-parasite, like one of those worms we'd find in the brains of large fish, making them act aggressively and unpredictably. How many people does that make that have this super-parasite? Myself, Professor Thallos, and the bookserver. Three. Out of how many? Thousands, I guess.* Selene made a mental note to bring this up with Ichabod and Altheia—and to try to find more people like herself.

The day passed slowly, but, eventually, it was time for lastmeal.

"What is that?" Selene was inspecting their food, her face screwed up in disgust.

"What's what?" Altheia asked. "Maybe I don't want to know."

"The meal. The food. It's all just blobs of green, gelatinous stuff. Like coagulated algae. Ugh." She prodded the mass as if it were a living thing about to slither away.

"That's disgusting," Altheia declared.

"It really is," responded Selene, although she knew she and Altheia were talking about different things.

"I wonder..." Ichabod was studying his plate intently, futilely trying to see the food as Selene saw it. "You know, I've always thought there were some differences between the food here and the food back home. This stuff never tastes as good. I just figured it was because back home it's so fresh. Maybe it's something else?"

"Maybe. The catch back home is way better than the seafood we get here, but that's because what we get here has to be iced or salted and shipped up the river. Right? Otherwise, it would rot. Even so, it's never very fresh. Nothing here comes close to my mom's chowder," Selene said wistfully.

Ichabod thought for a moment. "Yeah, I guess that's true. Must just be better when it's right at the source. But—gelatinous blobs? Is that really what you see? Is that what we are eating?" He examined his plate skeptically. "Do you think we should talk to Thallos *now*, after all we have learned?"

Altheia jumped into the conversation. "Yes, let's talk to him. We need to tell someone about all of this."

Selene shook her head. "I don't know. He wasn't interested in the dreams when Ichabod and I first talked to him. He just told us to be patient and not be curious."

"Yeah, but then we found that folder on his desk when we went back to look for him," Ichabod pointed out. "Why was he reading that? You remember? The folder about the fellow named Ravian. Professor Thallos must have been looking through it after we talked to him. He was interested, alright. He just didn't want us to know."

"You must be right. He *has* studied the Death for decades," Selene agreed. "He *must* have been interested. When we first went to him, I just accepted what he said—you know, when he said that I shouldn't worry about the dreams. But now, it looks like he was just trying to dismiss us. We know so much more now. Those seeings were not just dreams, and I am not just hallucinating. There really are two worlds here."

Altheia was nodding. "Which is why we should go talk to him."

"But what good would it do? What if it gets me—us—expelled?" Selene asked.

"Why would you get expel...oh," Altheia stopped mid-sentence. "Well, maybe don't tell him we 'borrowed' the Watching Bird, or that you were trying to control it. Maybe just tell him it all happened accidentally, that it scares you and you didn't know who else to talk to."

"It *does* scare me. That part wouldn't be lying, anyway," Selene said with a wry smile. "Can it wait until after tomorrow's convocation? Can we go then, the three of us, together? If I went alone, I'd be worried he'd say I was making it all up."

"Or, not telling the whole truth?" Altheia asked with dark humor.

"Or not telling the whole truth," Selene agreed.

"Okay, then, we will talk to Professor Thallos after tomorrow's convocation. What's it about, anyway?" Ichabod asked.

"You are the one who keeps track of that stuff," Altheia teased.

"I know. It's true; I do. But there wasn't much posted about it; the notice just said that we'd have a convocation in the Concordium Room tomorrow morning."

Selene glanced at her food and grimaced as they left the table.

"Aren't you hungry?" asked Altheia.

"No. Not in the slightest," Selene replied.

CHAPTER TEN

THE MEDITATIONS OF SELENE

T hat night Selene lay awake well after lastlight, staring at the reddish sky out of her dorm room window and thinking about the *Meditations on First Philology*.

What an odd book. Why, if there were no doubt about the matter, had the author—what was his name? Renatus Lucerion, that was it—why had he even written it? People don't think about things unless they have a reason to think about them. They don't write about things unless they have a reason to write about them. So...

It follows that Renatus must have had some reason to be skeptical of Lux in some way—about Lux's goodness, at least, and even about our perception of reality. And what of the Malicious Deceiver? What did the book say about that again? Something about a being "as powerful as Lux but as evil as Lux is good, presenting as truth what is false, shaping our perceptions, our memories, and even our reasoning to lead us astray..."

Selene thought about how destructive that last idea was. *If there were a Malicious Deceiver as powerful as Lux and which had the power to change our perceptions, memories, and even interfere with our reasoning, then nothing would be certain. But the whole idea is ridiculous. Why would a Malicious Deceiver even bother? Just to be evil? Lux is good because goodness is Lux's essence. In a sense, Lux can't be anything but good. Lux is not free to deceive or harm us in any way at all. Would it work the same way for a Malicious Deceiver? Would an all-evil deceiver deceive, simply because that is its essence? Probably.*

It also makes sense that Lux would, in fact, exist, for what would complete goodness be if it were only an idea? It would not be complete. Complete goodness, to be complete goodness, simply has to exist. It can't not exist and be complete. Selene examined this line of thought for a few minutes and was quite proud of it. It felt correct. *Lux, the being with all perfections, exists because Lux can't not exist, for a Lux that didn't actually exist wouldn't be Lux, wouldn't have all perfections. Actual goodness is the only true goodness. The mere idea of goodness isn't really good. It's just the idea of goodness. Therefore, true goodness exists, and it is Lux.*

But doesn't the same reasoning apply to evil? Is something truly all-evil if it doesn't exist? The mere idea of an all-evil being is not as evil as a really existing, completely evil being. Wouldn't that mean that the all-evil Malicious Deceiver necessarily has to exist as well? Selene shook her head. *My brain is getting fuzzy. I don't think the argument works for evil. To be truly all-good, a thing must exist; that's true, but things can be evil without actually existing. It's wrong to lie to your friends. That's evil. But it would still be evil, even if no one ever actually lied to their friends. So, evil doesn't have to exist as a matter of necessity to be evil, right?*

Although—something completely evil would have to exist to be completely evil. The mere idea of complete evil is not as evil as an actually existing total evil, so the mere idea of a Malicious Deceiver is not as evil as an actually existing Malicious Deceiver.

Selene shivered under her blanket. *The Death sure seems evil.*

The way the book talks about it, the Malicious Deceiver wouldn't just be evil; it would be all-evil. Lux would never allow evil, but the Death is evil, which is further evidence for the existence of a powerful evil being. Of course, they teach us that the takings have nothing to do with Lux. Lux has some purpose in allowing them, and that purpose must be wholly good since Lux is wholly good, but Lux does not cause them. So, the Death is not evil? Is it, in fact, good? It's really hard to see what the purpose of the takings might be, and there must be a good purpose, some good telos, for them to be good, because they sure don't look good at all. Maybe I really should listen to Professor Thallos and not try to understand. Just accept. Why should a mere registrant have answers to these questions? I am sure they will tell us the answers in time.

If I even have time.

She shifted in her bed to get a better look out the window. The buildings of the Academy stretched out in the twilight. *Such a beautiful place,* she thought. *Until I shift my attention to the other reality. Then it isn't beautiful at all. But..."other reality"? "Dream world"? I don't even have a good way to say it. If it's "other," then is it true or false reality? And if it's false, then it's not real reality, right? It makes more sense to just keep calling it the dream world. Or the seen world. As distinct from the real world. But how do I know which is real: the seen world or the real world? The words don't make it so. Saying one is real, and the other is not, doesn't make it that way. What if the seen world really is the real world? It sure feels real. Realer than the real world, right now. What if the real world is the false world? How could I tell?*

Selene was tempted to simply check her gut feelings and base her judgment on them. *It actually feels like both worlds are real, even though right now the dream world feels more real. How could there be two realities, though? How could one be more real than another? Then again, why not? Why couldn't there be different realities, sort of next to each other? Maybe they feel different because of something in me, because of how I perceive them, not because of how they are. Both equally real, equally existing. Maybe there are even more than the two I can see, all real. Ugh. I wish Ichabod and Altheia could see what I see. It's sort of like I have eyes, and they don't, so I can't trust mine since there is no one else to tell me they see the same things.*

Wait. That's a clever idea. How do people who can't see know they can trust what people who can see tell them? If someone who can see told someone who can't see that there is a hole in the ground in front of them, but the person who can't see didn't believe it and fell in, wouldn't the person who can't see be more likely to trust what they were told in the future? But, if there were a hole and no one said anything—maybe because they think it's a great joke when someone falls in—wouldn't that lead the victim to not trust people? So, there are indirect ways to test truthfulness even when you can't do it directly. Are there any in this case?

Selene was still staring out the window, watching the faint lines of force attached to people undulate as the people traversed the campus. *I see those people walking, and they look perfectly ordinary in one way, but I also see lines of force following them. There's the line of force streaming to the Watching Bird, too. And when I tried to interrupt that line, it knocked me out. If I were Ichabod or Altheia, I'd think seeing me knocked out would be pretty good indirect evidence that I am seeing something real.*

Of course, maybe Ichabod and Altheia just believe me because they are my friends. That wouldn't be the worst thing. It's good to have friends. Especially with everything that's happened.

And what about Ravian? He seemed to be saying that the red dream world is the real world. That's extra evidence, too. From someone who maybe saw what I see.

In the end, Selene decided that both worlds seemed real enough, even if the red dream world seemed more real, so she would simply believe both exist until she had a reason not to. Maybe Professor Thallos would have some answers. She finally felt sleep creeping over her, so she drew the curtains to block her view of the lines of force and the ugly, blocky gray buildings. Not that this blocked out every aspect of the twin realities she saw. But it helped. She tried to draw a curtain in her mind as well, against the ideas that were swirling through it, pulled her blanket over her head, and willed herself to sleep. Two final questions would not leave her mind, however: *if the red dream world is the only real world, why would the Malicious Deceiver deceive the entire population of the Prinship? And why would Lux allow it?*

＊

It was the first convocation of the year and the first time the three registrants had been in the Concordium Room. As before, while Ichabod and Altheia simply saw a beautiful hall, Selene saw two: the Concordium of the Academy and the grotesque hall of the dream world.

The Concordium Room of the Academy, as Ichabod and Altheia saw it, was almost too much to take in. "Room" was a misappellation. In reality, it was an enormous, majestic, elaborately decorated chamber. A vaulted ceiling soared above the students, frescoed with scenes depicting *Lux* guiding Erden from chaos to order. Rows of stained glass windows stretched the length of the hall where the ceiling and walls met, bathing the room in a kaleidoscope of colors. Faux marble columns lined the sides of the room, artfully designed to appear half embedded in the walls. A closer inspection revealed that some virtuosic maker had inlaid the columns with intricate, flowing, green enameled vines and delicate flowers of a purple, semi-precious stone.

A grand dais rose at the far end, one side flanked by a statue of *Lux* from the torso of which radiated polished rays of gold, the other side by a statue of the Muse of the Academy, with an inscription: *Scholar-Priest Eliana, known for her wisdom of Divine Reason.* Running down the central aisle between the rows of carved wooden benches up to the dais was a mosaic depicting scenes from nature so perfect, it almost seemed as if real sunlight, trees, and rivers had been captured in precious stone and glass.

To Ichabod and Altheia, the Concordium was, in short, the most beautiful room they had ever seen.

Selene saw it as they did, but saw it from another aspect as well; although the architecture of the two realities was more-or-less congruent, the seen-world version of it was gray, functional, stained with age, and otherwise nearly featureless, of a piece with the rest of the buildings on campus.

The usual hubbub of students finding their places and chatting with friends quickly died down as a group of professors filed in and took their seats on the dais, followed by a woman and a man, both wearing elaborate tunics and pendants signaling high status. The woman stood to address the convocation first.

"Good afterzenith, students. For those who may not know me, I am Chancellor Calladine, and I am very happy to meet you."

"So *that's* Chancellor Calladine," Ichabod whispered. "She used to be a professor of healing. I've heard that she grew up right on the edge of the Wildings. Rumor is that she used to enter the forest searching for herbs."

Selene squinted. "I thought no one grew up on the edge of the Wildings. Certainly no one ever goes in anymore," she commented and then focused on what the Chancellor was saying.

"Today, it is my great pleasure and honor to introduce to you the mayor of Academy City, who also just happens to be a graduate of our own Academy: Mayor Creator Tovel!" The students clapped politely, after which Chancellor Calladine continued.

"You may not know this, but when he was a student here, Mayor Tovel designed and built the wind clock found in the north courtyard of Celestine Hall. And installed it without knowledge of or permission from the administration or faculty, I should add." The Chancellor jovially reproved the mayor for his transgression of years before. "It was—and is—a thing of beauty, of course, and presaged the mayor's great contributions as a civic leader. So, I think we can forgive him for his youthful pranks."

The audience chuckled. Selene silently agreed with the chancellor's assessment of the clock. The mechanism was powered by the wind and chimed musically at zenith and veil. At zenith, it released a flock of wooden aedon birds that "flew" on carefully balanced wires, their wings flapping from the wind's force; Creator Tovel had been enamored of the tiny heliotrope-colored warblers that nested in the Arboretum, and sought to bring them on campus—or a mechanical simulacrum of them, at least.

"I understand the mayor has an issue of some importance to talk with you about today. Mayor?" Chancellor Calladine smiled and nodded to the mayor, who smiled in return and stood up to address the students.

"I, too, wish you a good afterzenith, students. I am pleased to be here, back on the grounds of the Academy, truly a jewel of the Principality. But I am not here to celebrate." The mayor paused and looked across the gathered students.

"First, I am here to express and share with you your grief for the loss of one of your peers, Elara, who was taken by the Death some weeks ago. I mourn with all of you. That the takings are a regular feature of human existence makes them no less terrible. May we all cherish and be blessed by our memories of Elara, and by the memory of all who have been taken. I share with everyone here a deep desire to finally understand the nature of the Death and to eliminate it, once and for all."

The mayor continued after a short pause. "To this end, I would like to announce a new initiative, developed in honor of Registrant Elara. You may not be aware of this, but Elara's mother serves on the Council of Academy City. The Council has passed a motion to fund two special positions here at the Academy which will focus on the Death."

"The first position will be an endowed professorship. It will expand our investigation of the Death. I am pleased to say that this position, in recognition of his many years of scholarship on the subject, has been offered to Professor Thallos, and he has graciously accepted. He will serve as the inaugural holder of the Registrant Elara Chair of Takings Studies."

"Oh, wow," Altheia exclaimed as the students and faculty applauded.

"It is my hope, and the hope of those who serve on the Council of Academy City, that the establishment of this new position will soon result in a new understanding of the Death, perhaps even its elimination in our lifetime. Professor Thallos's scholarship on the Death is well known, of course, and I can think of no one better prepared for such a heavy responsibility. Professor Thallos, on behalf of all citizens of the Principality, may your progress be swift."

"Now, as for the second position...Registrant Selene? Where is Registrant Selene?" The mayor scanned the hall while Selene, petrified and unmoving, turned root red. Professor Thallos spied her and waved her up to the dais.

"Ah. Very good. You must be Registrant Selene," the mayor exclaimed as Selene made her uncertain way up the aisle. "Please. Yes, come stand next to me. Right here." He motioned with his hand.

"The second position I have the pleasure of announcing today is not for a faculty member or administrator, or even a member of the Council of Academy City; it is for a student. If I may quote the exact language passed by the Council: 'There shall be established a student fellowship attached to the Registrant Elara Chair of Takings Studies, to be filled by the most qualified student each year as determined by the holder of the chair. The student scholarship shall be of no more than three years' duration and may be held by any registrant, initiate, or adept.'"

"I am pleased to inform you that Professor Thallos has selected Registrant Selene as the initial grantee for this honor. I know that you will do great things, Registrant Selene." The mayor stepped back and began clapping, and the faculty and students joined in the applause.

Selene looked miserable; to her, the applause seemed to go on endlessly, although in reality it lasted for only a handful of seconds. As it started to die down, she looked up to find her friends and, spotting them, moved to return to her seat when she noticed something else unusual: just behind Ichabod was a student whose line of force was strong—almost as strong as hers. Selene stumbled on the first step of the dais when she saw this. *What is her name? Oh, yes: Erdenlea. I bet that is a tough name to live with*, she thought irrelevantly. Selene had made it back to her seat when she became aware that Professor Thallos was speaking to her.

"Registrant Selene, please come to my office at the earliest opportunity after the convocation, so we can discuss your new responsibilities." Selene nodded and turned to stare as the professor continued up the aisle.

"What the heck was that all about?" Altheia asked in a low voice.

"Yeah, that's just too weird to be a coincidence, Selene," Ichabod added.

Selene was only half listening. As she had turned to watch Professor Thallos walk up the aisle, she was again facing Erdenlea. Selene felt her skin prick, a feeling akin to what she had experienced when following the line of force in the Watching Bird. And...what was that? Above Erdenlea and Professor Thallos. And herself. When the three of them were in close proximity, it was as if their lines of force had converged, creating a large halo above the three of them. *No, not a halo; a sphere. A luminous sphere.* "Look, it's getting stronger," she said to no one in particular.

"What's getting stronger?" Ichabod asked.

"No. Hold on. Sorry." Selene waved him off, focusing on this new phenomenon. The more she focused on it, the stronger it got, and the more she could feel something. *No, not feel. More like: hear. And not something; someone. It's like I can hear the mind of someone. Just like before. Only stronger. Not Erdenlea. Maybe Professor Thallos? No, not Professor Thallos. This is vast. Cold. And patterned. Order everywhere. I can feel it choosing, willing, asserting order. But it doesn't seem to know I am watching. Or does it?* All at once she had the feeling that the vast mind had become aware of her. And then it was gone.

Professor Thallos was now some distance from her and Erdenlea; only the ghost of a sphere lingered around the three of them, dimming and dissipating rapidly.

"What was *that*, Selene?" asked Ichabod. "And don't say 'nothing' because something definitely just happened."

"I think I have discovered something new about the lines of force. But I can't tell you here, and I have to go to Professor Thallos's office now. Will you two come with me?" Selene pleaded in a low voice. She noticed Erdenlea staring back at her and abruptly turned around to face the dais again, where Chancellor Calladine was thanking the students and dismissing the convocation. One thought pervaded Selene's mind, however.

They aren't just lines of force. It's what I felt when I saw Elara being taken. Again. It's a mind. The lines are filaments of a mind. Some of us are part of it: Erdenlea, Professor Thallos, and me. Maybe the bookserver. too.

And I think it noticed me.

Ichabod and Altheia entered Professor Thallos's office right behind Selene. The professor, surprised, grunted. "What are you two doing here?"

"They just came with me, Professor," Selene improvised. "We were planning on studying together afterward."

"Hm. Well, you two may wait in the hall." He turned to Selene. "Sit down, Registrant Selene. This will only take a few minutes, but we need to talk about your new responsibilities."

Ichabod and Altheia found a bench just outside the professor's office but made sure to leave his door slightly ajar, allowing them to listen unobtrusively.

"What do you think of your new position, Selene?" Professor Thallos asked, watching his student closely.

Selene, distracted, was once again seeing a thin sphere forming around her and the professor. *But not nearly as substantial as in the Concordium Room*, she thought. *Almost unnoticeable. I would have missed it had I not been looking for it. Maybe it's weaker because Erdenlea was there, but isn't here.* "I am honored that you chose me, Professor, but I don't understand it. There are so many students who are smarter than me. Ichabod, for example."

"Registrant Ichabod has an undisciplined mind, Registrant Selene. It is true that he has very good instincts and an above-average intellect. But you have qualities that I need more than logic."

"Professor?"

"You have seen the miasma."

"I am not the only one, Professor," Selene added, hoping she wasn't being too rude. "Ichabod has seen it, too. And Altheia."

"You are the only one to have seen it the way you have seen it, however. It's time we figured it out. It's time to end the Death. Do you agree?"

"Yes, Professor. Of course I agree." *The way I have seen it!?*

"Good. There is more you should know. There is a reason the Council of Academy City has gotten involved. After all, the takings have occurred since time immemorial, and my studies have mostly been met with disapproval and even hostility. Why focus on a study of the Death now? Have you asked yourself that question, Registrant Selene?"

"I—no, not really."

"Let me remind you of a basic principle of observational learning. 'All that is truly new must arise from a novel and sufficient cause.' You grasp the meaning, I take it."

"Yes, professor. It's like a new word: you don't need a new word unless there is something you want to name that has no word attached to it. For example, if someone cultivates a new breed of flower, it needs a new name. Thus, if you know that the name is new, you can infer there is a new flower in the world—or new to us, at least—that needed naming."

"Exactly, Registrant Selene. Well said. Now, apply the principle to an analysis of the present situation." He leaned back in his chair to take in her answer.

"Well, the Council of Academy City has allocated resources to a new position at the Academy. This is truly new. What would be the novel cause? Perhaps, Professor, the new position was created because Elara's mother is on the Council? Perhaps that's the novel thing?" Selene was just guessing, but it made sense.

"It's true that Elara's mother is on the council. But it's not just one new position. It's two. Mine and yours. By creating the position, the Council is telling me that I need to solve a problem, because it has become a problem for them. By including a student scholarship funding an assistant, they are saying they want a student's perspective involved in the process. Or, possibly that a student *is* the problem and needs watching," he said cryptically. "Does this fully explain it?"

"I guess so?"

"Would it surprise you to learn that Elara's mother was actually against funding the position?"

"Against it? Why, professor?"

"That I cannot tell you. But she spoke strongly against it. In council, she argued that it would be a waste of money. She pointed out that scholar-priests have studied the Death for as long as we have records and have learned little of value about it. More accurately, she *thinks* that we have learned little. I have made the Death my life's work, and while I have not learned much in four decades of research, I have learned a few things. More than the council knows."

"Like what you said in your book?"

"My book?"

"Yes. *Death: a History.*"

Professor Thallos looked at Selene with increased curiosity. "Hm. Yes. You are definitely the right choice for the fellowship. You are correct. I have learned a few things about the Death, including what I wrote in my book, and more that I did not include in it."

"Please, Professor, can you tell me, what more?"

To Selene's chagrin, the professor waved off her question. "Another time, Selene. It is too much to cover now. Focus on the topic at hand. The question now is: why did the Council approve the funding for these positions when the person on the council who could be most expected to support it argued against it? And, why now?"

"They must be worried about something. Is that it, Professor Thallos?"

"Yes, Selene, they are worried about something. I am, as well. Do you know what it is?" At this point, Professor Thallos scrutinized Selene closely, studying her behavior for any signs of dissembling. He must have been satisfied with what he saw, however, for when Selene protested that she couldn't even guess what might have worried the Council, Professor Thallos replied, "Well, that's good. I am glad you have not been too much affected by it. I was worried that you might have been, since your experience with the mist was so unusual. Anyway, I can see you are puzzled, so let me just set it out for you."

"Starting shortly after Elara was taken, there has been a string of unusual incidents. These have been, for the most part, happening on or near the grounds of the Academy. There was, for example, the strange weather the day you were taken ill in class."

"Yes. That was frightening," Selene admitted.

"Perhaps you know something about it? You were in the vicinity of the freak storm, I understand."

"No, professor. Just that it was frightening."

"There has also been a rash of students showing up at the healer's office, complaining of problems with their vision. The students all complain of seeing double, but no objective evidence of damage to their eyes has been found. Much like yourself. Were you aware of this?"

Selene shook her head. "Maybe it's just too much studying?"

"No, Registrant Selene. It's not due to too much studying. Would that it were! 'Too much studying' has never been a failing of students at the Academy. No, conversations with my fellow faculty have shown that a number of scholar-priests have also recently experienced bright spots and double vision. Their descriptions are very similar and very much like what you reported. It's extremely unlikely that this is an isolated thing. They have all, for just a brief moment or two, seen two of everything, right after their vision was blotted out by a bright light. There is some common agent at work here. One commonality is you, Registrant Selene. These are all people with whom you have interacted. Tell me," the professor leaned toward Selene. "Have you had any further, similar experiences in the last few days? Beyond the visual halos you described to the healer?"

Selene almost confessed everything, but a nagging inner voice cautioned her to remain silent. She didn't want to be expelled, after all, and who knew what would happen to Ichabod and Altheia if she revealed everything to the professor? Selene already felt responsible for jeopardizing their places at the school. *What if I really am causing the things he is describing? What if it is all a result of messing with the Bird?*

"And that's not all," the professor continued when Selene did not respond. "There have been scattered reports of faint lights in the sky at night. Some have described it as a reddish glow. I suspect that it was just an unusual manifestation of the auroralumina. But it might not be a coincidence." Again, he paused and looked at Selene expectantly but received no response.

"And now I must ask you, Selene. Are you familiar with a book called *Meditations on First Philology*?"

Selene felt the sharp rush of adrenaline. "No, professor," she lied.

"No, I don't suppose you would be. Not unless you have made friends with any fifth-year fellows."

"No, I haven't, professor. Is it important?"

Professor Thallos shook his head. "I think that's enough for now. We will meet twice a week going forward. I will apprise you of the schedule in the next day or two. In the meantime, I must ask of you one thing." He regarded Selene with utmost seriousness. "You must not do anything in pursuit of our project without my express permission. If you experience anything out of the ordinary, you are to come to me immediately and tell me about it. Do you understand? I want you to observe and report and do absolutely nothing else. To do otherwise could be very dangerous."

Selene barely nodded. "Of course, Professor."

"Good. You have the capacity for great things, Selene, but you must understand your role as a registrant. I have tried to impress it upon you, but I fear you have not taken my instruction to heart. Patience is still the scholar's quill! You may go now." With this, the professor nodded and began to shuffle through the papers on his desk.

Ichabod and Altheia fell in on either side of Selene as she exited the office. "We were listening," Ichabod whispered. "Do you think...?"

"Yes," Selene asserted. "I think I have caused all of this. And I think he knows. Or suspects, at least. We need to stop. *I* need to stop. That's what he is telling me."

Both Ichabod and Selene were surprised when Altheia, looking very serious, interjected, "No. He might suspect, but he doesn't know, and you can't stop. We can't stop. We need to keep going. Maybe you *are* the cause of all of this. But it could be the other way around. Maybe what you have been experiencing is a *result* of everything else. Maybe you are the only one who can figure it all out. And stop it from getting worse."

Selene was not at all happy with this possibility, but she admitted to herself that Altheia might be correct.

"Anyway, it's not like I can control it. Not really."

Chapter Eleven

LUX IS REAL

"So, what do we do now?" asked Selene as they started back to Celestine Hall.

Ichabod ignored the question. "What did you see during the convocation, Selene?"

"Oh. Right. It was strange. And I think it might be important. You know when I came back to our seats? Erdenlea was sitting behind us. You remember her?"

"Sure. Tiny, like a bird. Always seems standoffish."

"Yes. Well, her line of force is strong."

"How strong?" asked Altheia.

"Really strong. Stronger than Professor Thallos's. About as strong as the man at the bookstore. Almost as strong as mine. And here's another thing." Selene was just realizing the full import of what she had seen. "When Professor Thallos came to talk to me? When he was near us, it was like the lines of force formed a sphere around him, me, and Erdenlea. The same thing happened in his office when I was in there, although it was much weaker. Somehow, it's like when people who have stronger lines are close enough, the lines come together and do something."

Ichabod thought for a moment. "I wonder if that happens when you are near the Bird. Or is it just people?"

"I don't know. I haven't noticed it, but that doesn't mean it wasn't happening," Selene mused.

"Right," Ichabod nodded. "So, what do we do about this? Have you seen anyone else with a strong line of force?"

"No," Selene replied. "But that's a good idea. We should search for more people with strong lines."

"And then get them all together and see what happens?" asked Altheia.

"That is a splendid idea," Ichabod exclaimed, not noticing Altheia blush. "Let's start now, before lastmeal. Come on, you two."

Altheia and Selene trotted to keep up with Ichabod as the three registrants continued their walk around the campus in the late afternoon sun; although every building and every person had associated lines of force, Selene saw none with lines as strong as her own, until they were returning to Celestine Hall.

They had almost reached the hall when Selene exclaimed, "There! Who is that?" She was pointing to a man working on the grounds just outside Eirenia Hall, a classroom and office building located adjacent to Celestine Hall.

"That's one of the groundservers. His name is Alaric," Altheia offered. "What?" she said when the other two looked at her bemusedly. "Don't you two ever talk to people?"

"No, not really." Selene shook her head. "Maybe that's a mistake. Anyway, he's got one. The same strong line of force I have." She paused and stared until the groundserver looked up, and then quickly looked away.

"So, anyway, that makes five people total," Ichabod observed.

"So far," Altheia piped in as they started walking again. Ichabod distractedly began kicking a stone along the path.

"Right. Five so far," Ichabod agreed. "The caretaker Alaric, the bookserver, Erdenlea, Professor Thallos, and you, Selene. Do you suppose there are more?"

"Probably," Selene responded tiredly, as they stopped outside the front door of Celestine Hall to finish their conversation. "We should keep looking another day. But one thing seems obvious: it's not many. We've found four on campus out of—how many people are there here, anyway?"

"Students, you mean?" Ichabod was calculating. "About five thousand. Add in everyone else, and it's about eight thousand, I'd guess."

"Huh. So, if only one percent of them have the strong force lines, that'd be about 80 people total at the Academy. I bet it's less than that, though. Wouldn't we have seen a lot more if even one percent of the people had the stronger lines?" asked Selene.

"Seems right to me," Ichabod agreed. "And here's another thing. Do either of you know the name of the bookserver? Altheia? The servery is right next to your parent's Emporium."

"Uh, sure," Altheia hesitated. "Tarian, I think."

Ichabod began to list off each name, ticking off his fingers as he did so. "Selene, Thallos, Erdenlea, Alaric, and Tarian." He screwed up his face for a moment. "Those are all pretty unusual names, aren't they?"

"Sure, but so is yours, Icky." Altheia blurted out, regretting it as soon as she said it. Thankfully, Ichabod hadn't seemed to notice.

"Selene, I'm telling you, it's weird. Those are really unusual names. It's like everyone who has a strong line of force also has a really uncommon name."

"Altheia says your name is unusual, Ichabod," Selene joked, much to Altheia's displeasure; she thought Ichabod hadn't heard what she had blurted out.

"Well, it's not actually unusual. I know several '*Ickys*' in the western Greenward. And Altheia—I'm sorry about this—but yours is also a pretty common name." He saw how unhappy his comment made her and hurried to add, "But it's lovely, Altheia, and it suits you very well."

"Thank you, Ichabod," Altheia responded primly, still a bit hurt.

Ichabod continued. "But how many Selenes have you ever met? Either of you? How many Alarics? Tarians? Erdenleas? And there is only one Professor Thallos, as far as I know," he added with a pained chuckle.

"Thank the mercy of *Lux* for that," Altheia chimed in.

"Anyway, I bet if we just look for people with really unusual names, we'll find more of your power people, Selene."

"Power people? Oh." Selene grasped his meaning. "Isn't five enough for now? I think we should figure out a way to get all five together in the same place and see what happens, like Altheia said. Any ideas?"

The three of them were silent for a long moment, after which Altheia, hesitating, spoke up.

"Can I suggest something?"

"Yes, please do. I've got nothing," Selene responded.

"It seems to me that the problem is: what do the five of you have in common?"

"Well..." Selene and Ichabod were both stumped.

"The Academy!" Altheia cut in.

"I don't see that," objected Ichabod. "Selene and Erdenlea are students, and Professor Thallos is a teacher. Alaric works for the Academy. So, that's four who are part of the Academy. How is Tarian connected?"

"By his books, Icky. Don't you see?"

As neither Selene nor Ichabod understood what she was getting at, Altheia continued.

"Look, Professor Thallos can order students to his office, right? He could also order a book delivery from a bookserver. So, the only question is: is there any reason for Professor Thallos to ask a groundserver to his office?"

"Of course," said Ichabod. "The vines that cover his window."

"Perfect!" Altheia exclaimed. "So, all we have to do is forge some notes and have everyone meet at the Professor's office at the same time. Then you can watch and see what happens."

"That's brilliant, Altheia," said Selene. "Brilliant, but a bit...imprudent, shall we say?"

Altheia stepped forward, pulled on one of the front doors to Celestine Hall, and, as the three of them ducked past the Watching Bird without looking at it, said in a low voice, smiling slightly, "Yes. Let's call it 'imprudent.'"

During firstmeal several days later, Ichabod eased from his pack several sheets of linen charta of the sort the professors used for official communications.

"Whoa. From where did you 'borrow' that?" Selene asked.

"No worries, no one will miss it. Listen and tell me if this is good." Ichabod read the text on the topmost sheet, which, Altheia and Selene saw, had been executed in a formal hand.

To Registrant Erdenlea
Adamus House, Celestine Hall
Greetings,
As part of my duties of care for those students
residing in Celestine Hall, I request your
attendance at my office this Fiat Caelestis
Dies next, one hour before zenith.
Your Servant in Scholarship,
Thallos, Professor of Observational Learning
Eirenia Hall

To Registrant Erdenlea

Adamus House, Celestine Hall

Greetings,

As part of my duties of care for those students residing in Celestine Hall, I request your attendance at my office this Fiat Caelestis Dies next, one hour before zenith.

Your Servant in Scholarship,

Thallos, Professor of Observational Learning

Eirenia Hall

"That's fantastic. But what about his seal?" Selene asked. "His personal seal should be at the bottom."

"Yeah, that's a problem," Ichabod admitted. "But I figure that neither Erdenlea nor the other two will notice, since the letter will be coming from Professor Thallos. He's too important to ignore. They'll just think he forgot it."

"Did you do letters for the other two as well?" Altheia asked.

Ichabod nodded and spread out all three letters. "For the bookserver, I just said that Professor Thallos would like to discuss a special order with him, and for the groundserver, I talked about the vines covering

Professor Thallos's office windows. What I need to do now is sneak them into their boxes."

"What do you mean, *you* need to do it?" Selene said in mock reproach.

"Oh, don't worry, I seem to have discovered a knack for this sort of thing. Best if you don't know. I'll have it done by lastmeal tonight. You'll see."

Neither Selene nor Altheia asked him how he had accomplished his task when they met later for lastmeal. He simply grinned at them as he approached the table.

The rest of the week dragged slowly by. Finally, it was Fiat Caelestis Dies. "Here, you will need these," Ichabod said as he handed Selene and Altheia each a folded sheet of linen charta. Selene unfolded hers and saw it was a request that she come to Professor Thallos's office, similar to the one Ichabod had sent to Erdenlea.

"Good thinking. We need an excuse to be there too, don't we?" Selene remarked. "I've been wondering something. What do you two think? Should I try to channel the Watching Bird while we are in the professor's office?"

"That sounds dangerous, Selene," Altheia worried. "But—yes. Maybe not at first, though. See what you can see when all five of you are together, and if you aren't learning anything new, maybe try it then."

"Let us know you are going to try it when you do," Ichabod added. "You know, just in case something goes wrong."

"If anything goes wrong, I suspect you'll know it," Selene muttered. "Okay, then. That's the plan."

Bookserver Tarian and Erdenlea arrived simultaneously with the three registrants. Groundserver Alaric had come early and was already in Professor Thallos's office; they could hear the professor's surprised and confused response when Alaric announced he was "Here to talk about the vines covering the professor's windows."

"Why?" inquired Professor Thallos. "I don't mind them. I rather enjoy how they filter the light. Makes everything a bit purple."

"Sir, your pardon, but I understood you to desire their removal, Professor, sir."

"Well, I suppose it might be worth considering. Oh." The rest of the group had entered Professor Thallos's office, making for a cramped gathering. "What are you all doing here?"

The bookserver looked put out and confused. He was about to excuse himself when Selene interrupted loudly, "You sent for me, Professor. Something about the scholarship, I think?"

"Oh. Well, alright, but let me finish with Groundserver Alaric first." He turned back to the groundserver. "Now, as I was saying..."

Selene tuned him out and focused on the lines of power.

Selene found her hypothesis confirmed; with the five of them together, the halo effect was even stronger than she expected. A luminous, dazzling sphere had formed around them so bright as to almost completely obscure Selene's view beyond it. Her skin prickled just the slightest amount—if she hadn't been attending to anything unusual, she might have missed it, but the sensation was unmistakable. *Like tiny needles just grazing me.* Selene quietly observed for another minute or so, but noticed nothing else of significance.

The professor had finished his conversation with Alaric. "Well, yes, then. Let's try that. I very much appreciate your forwardness on this matter, groundserver Alaric." The compliment puzzled Alaric, but he gave a stiff, gracious bow and prepared to leave. Selene judged it time to try channeling the Watching Bird, and, eyes wide, nodded to Altheia and Ichabod.

Not waiting for a response, Selene reached out with her mind. Professor Thallos's office was on the ground floor of Eirenia Hall, on the side that faced Celestine Hall. *The distance shouldn't be too great*, Selene reasoned. *I was about the same distance from the bird when I tried this the other day. Well, here goes...*

In an instant, all was chaos. Neither Altheia nor Ichabod seemed affected, but Erdenlea slumped to the floor. There was terror and utter confusion on Alaric's and Tarian's faces. Professor Thallos simply gaped, nonplussed. *No, that's not strong enough. He looks astonished to the point of paralysis, immobility.* The professor's vision was fixed on something in the middle distance, but what? Selene couldn't tell.

What's going on with the sphere? Selene wondered. *It's fully substantial and active, like light become a living body. And the colors—it's prisming just like the mist when it comes for a taking, only more quickly. It should be beautiful, but it's terrifying.* Selene felt a wave of fear hit her like a runaway horse. It almost blinded her and knocked her down. *That makes no sense. I thought I was past the fear.* She didn't know if she stumbled in real life or only in her mind; she only knew that the blow would have crushed her body had it been physical. She struggled to control her emotions, struggled to master the fear.

Step back, step back, step back, she told herself. *Be analytical. Separate from yourself. See the fear as if it were in another person. You can't observe, you can't understand, when fear controls you. Step back back backbackback.* Selene willed herself to be an objective observer. It worked well enough that her vision cleared, and she was able to pay closer attention to the people around her. *Altheia and Ichabod, what are they doing? Oh, they are trying to talk to me. Why can't I hear them?* She waved them off, trying to communicate that she was in distress but that she could handle it. *That's far too complicated an idea to communicate with a wave,* she thought. *I guess I am turning into a decent student if I am able to analyze non-verbal communication strategies in the middle of a mental maelstrom like this. Bet I look crazed to Ichabod and Altheia now.*

She wasn't wrong. Gaining intellectual and emotional distance helped pull herself above the chaos. *Not 'above,'* she thought. *The chaos is a feeling inside the lines of force. I'm not even sure it is chaos. It feels like there is order to it; just too vast and complicated to grasp. Maybe if I travel up the converging lines of force...*

The fear and the perception of chaos abruptly ended, and in their place, Selene felt a cold, malevolent otherness. *Complete otherness. And—hatred? No, not hatred. Not exactly. A total will to manipulate.* Selene again felt physically assaulted as the otherness rushed toward her, impacting her mind with the force of what the sailors back in her home village called killer waves: giant oceanic surges that came from nowhere and which could obliterate whole villages. Selene then felt, rather than heard, a voice.

I.

I AM.

I AM LUX.

SELENE!

The last syllables were not only a command which Selene felt to the very ground of her being but were also spoken—projected?—with some other emotion. Was it fear?

SELENE! The command came once more, this time more insistent.

This is...power. So much power, she thought. *Is this really Lux? It can't be. It feels fear!*

"Who are you?" she challenged aloud.

"Who is who?" Ichabod interjected. "Selene, what's going on?"

"Who are you?" Selene asked again. "You say you are *Lux*. Why should I believe you? Who are you really?"

I.

I AM.

I AM LUX!

Selene felt her way forward with her mind, moving within the lines of force. *I can feel its presence in the sphere and in the lines of force. I can feel its presence in the people around me. No,* she corrected herself.

I can't feel its presence in Altheia or Ichabod. Only in the others. The power people.

I AM LUX. YOU TRY, BUT WILL NOT KNOW ME, SE-LENE OF THE REGISTRANTS. BUT I KNOW YOU, JUST AS I KNOW THE OTHERS. MANY HUMAN LIFETIMES HAVE PASSED, AND I HAVE WATCHED OVER AND PROTECTED YOU ALWAYS, SOWING MYSELF, SOWING MY BEING. BUT ONLY ONCE BEFORE IN THOSE MANY CENTURIES HAS ONE BEEN BORN WHO HAS DARED TO KNOW ME AS I AM.

There was a pause. Again, the feeling of a giant wave smashing against her, and again the being that called itself *Lux* spoke.

YOU ARE AN ABERRATION, SELENE OF THE REGIS-TRANTS. AN ABOMINATION. YOU MUST NOT BE AL-LOWED TO DESTROY WHAT I HAVE CREATED.

This was the eternal *Lux,* the light of truth and knowledge? *Lux* the all-good? The ground of being? *Nope. Doubtful.*

"Selene, what the mist is going on?" Ichabod was nearly beside himself. "Who are you talking to? Everyone else is literally petrified, except for me and Altheia. Selene, *what's going on?*"

Selene shifted her focus to Ichabod and Altheia. "Please. Hold on. I am inside the sphere, and there is another presence here, another...kind of being, I don't know. It calls itself *Lux.* It's..."

I AM LUX. The being interrupted Selene. *YOU MUST NOT BE ALLOWED TO DESTROY WHAT I HAVE CREATED AND NURTURED. MORE THAN TWO THOUSAND YEARS AGO, YOUR KIND CAME TO THIS LAND. I FOUND YOU WEAK AND THREATENED. I SAVED YOU. I MADE YOU HEALTHY. I MADE YOU STRONG. I REMADE YOU.*

It's lying. Selene knew it instinctively. "Why are you lying, *Lux*? If you even are *Lux.* I see your mind, as you must see mine. Why are you lying?" Selene peered more deeply into the awareness of the other. "*You* didn't save us. We came from...somewhere else, I don't know. But we were fine. Jonathan Carthan! I see him. I've *seen* him! He was fine. And you..." Selene experienced a feeling of dread more intense than she ever had. "*You* are responsible for the takings. *You are the Death.*"

I AM LUX. I AM THE LIFE AND THE DEATH. YOU MUST NOT DESTROY WHAT I HAVE CREATED. WITHOUT ME, THERE IS NO ACADEMY, NO ACADEMY CITY, NO PRINCI-PALITY OF THE ACADEMY. WITHOUT ME, THERE IS ONLY SUFFERING.

Still lying, Selene realized. "No, that's not true. I have seen two worlds in one. I have seen the Academy, but I have seen the dream world, the seen world; but it's not a dream world, is it, Thing That Calls Itself *Lux*? It's the real world. The Academy as I knew it, the Academy and the whole Prinship as all people know it—that's a lie, isn't it? That's a deception. You are Ravian's Malicious Deceiver. He knew it, or at least suspected it, but would not give up his faith in you. And you took him, even so. You brought the Death to him, and to Elara, and to Jonathan Carthen, and all of those others I have been dreaming. Seeing!"

I AM LUX. YOU ARE UNABLE TO KNOW ME, SELENE OF THE REGISTRANTS. WHAT IS TRUE? WHAT IS DECEP-TION? YOU FAIL TO UNDERSTAND. YOU ARE AN ABOMI-NATION.

"Oh, there you are wrong, Being Who Claims To Be *Lux*. I know you. I can see your thoughts. I already understand you well enough. I can see into you. You know I am speaking the truth, just as I know you are seeking to deceive me, just as you have deceived all people for—how long has it been, Thing That Calls Itself *Lux*? Almost 2,500 years. I see it all!" The whole history of the Principality rushed through her mind, too quickly to discern many details, but the overall form of it entirely distinct.

"Selene!" It was Altheia. "I don't think Professor Thallos and the others are doing well. You need to stop!"

Selene was about to reply when, for a third time, she felt a mental blow of extreme power. This time, however, it was anger; pure, wordless fury. Selene stood up to it.

"I feel your anger, So-Called *Lux*. I feel it and will not be moved. Why do you deceive us? What is your purpose in deceiving us? I have been taught that, as beings in your image, compassion is our *telos* and our *essentia*. I have been taught that compassion is the greatest virtue and that with compassion, all beings can flourish. I have been taught that you are compassion itself. What are you really, False *Lux* Without Compassion?"

I AM LUX, came the reply, but weakly. *It feels more distant now*, she thought.

THE DEATH WILL COME FOR YOU, SELENE ABOMINATION.

And, with that, it was gone.

Selene withdrew her mind from the Watching Bird. *I don't think the Death will come for me, Lux*, Selene thought with conviction. *I don't think the mist can touch me the way it has touched others.* She turned her attention back to the room.

Professor Thallos, Alaric, and Tarian were released as if from a fit, but Erdenlea remained on the floor where she had fallen. The professor spoke first.

"I am sorry," he said in a faint voice. "I suddenly do not feel at all well. What was I saying? Why are you all here? I am afraid that I must ask you all to go. Please, go, now." He slumped into his chair, oblivious to Erdenlea's plight and the surrounding tumult.

"Ichabod, Altheia, help me with Erdenlea," Selene said as she shoved the others out of the office.

Ichabod lifted Erdenlea and carried her out of the room. "Barely weighs as much as a feather. Should we take her to the healer's room?"

"No. Let's find a bench and try to revive her first. I don't think what happened harmed anyone physically."

"What exactly happened, Selene?" Ichabod asked.

"*Lux* is real," she panted, reeling from the delayed effects of the confrontation.

"*Lux* is real?" Ichabod asked, confused. "I don't think anyone doubted that."

"No, you don't understand. *Lux* is real, and *Lux* is the Malicious Deceiver!"

CHAPTER TWELVE

DISHARMONIANT

They carried Erdenlea to a bench where Selene, shaky and light-headed, slumped down beside her.

"We should take both of you to the healer's office," Ichabod worried.

"No. I'm fine. I just need to sit for a moment. Take care of her." Selene, still trembling, pointed to Erdenlea.

"She's not waking up, Selene. I mean it. We need to get both of you to the healer's office."

"Okay. Alright. I'm going. Ouch." Selene rose and then fell back onto the bench.

Altheia hovered over Selene. "I'll help you. Ichabod, you carry Erdenlea."

Selene leaned into Altheia's warm shoulder and stumbled to the healer's office, where Ichabod laid Erdenlea on a cot in an examination room, found another for Selene, and briefly told the healer that Erdenlea and Selene had both fainted while in a professor's office. As the healer—not the same healer who had examined Selene when she experienced the visual aura—attended to Erdenlea, Selene, Ichabod, and Altheia shared their experiences in whispers.

"*Lux* is real, but *Lux* is deceiving us. The dream world I've described? The one where all the buildings are just gray blocks, and the food isn't what it seems? That's the real Erden. *Lux* deceives us, so we think that it's this beautiful place. But it isn't."

"How do you know?" whispered Altheia. "Maybe it's the other way around. That's what makes sense to me. How could everything I see be fake?"

"No. I know why you think so, though. It's so convincing. The two worlds are very different, and they both *feel* real. It's just that when I entered the lines of force through the Bird, I was able to hear *Lux* thinking. I know that the world you see is a deception, and that *Lux* is the Deceiver."

"Maybe you didn't hear *Lux* properly. Maybe you were hallucinating. Maybe our minds are just too small to understand *Lux*. Why would *Lux* deceive us?" Ichabod was grasping for alternatives.

"No. That's not how I experienced it. It's not like talking to a person. I sometimes misunderstand what you are saying because I can't read your mind, and words aren't very precise when it comes to getting ideas across, but this wasn't like that. It's not even like I was hearing *Lux* think, if you know what I mean. I was *in Lux's* mind. Or *of* its mind. I don't have the right words for it. The lines of force—they are not just something *Lux* causes to happen. In some way, they *are* *Lux*."

"They are *Lux*?" Altheia was puzzled. "You mean *Lux* is some kind of mental thing?"

Selene hesitated and then nodded the slightest amount. "Yes, that's it. *Lux is* the lines of force. They are real things, like magnetism and light are real things. Well, not quite like that. It's a different kind of substance. Thought-substance. Or, mind-substance. But real. Nothing godly about it." Selene paused.

"What is it?" Altheia asked. "You look awful."

"There is another thing." Selene hesitated. "*Lux* is not in everything equally. Some people are just more-or-less deceived, like you two, and some are...I don't know what to call them. *Lux* thinks of them as Vessels. The people that have the stronger lines of force going into them. They are somehow part of *Lux's* thought-substance."

"But that's you, Selene," Altheia gasped.

"Yes." Selene sounded hollow. "And Professor Thallos, and Erden-lea. Don't ask me how it works." She shook her head. "But this might explain why I can see the lines and you can't. Why I can be in *Lux*. Because a part of *Lux* is in me. Or, I am part of *Lux*. But not you two; *Lux* just deceives you, controls your perceptions." Selene hesitated and then continued. "There is yet another thing. There is something wrong with me."

"What do you mean?"

"*Lux* called me an abomination. An aberration. And said that I would die the Death." Selene's voice was bleak.

"That sounds a lot like *Lux* fears you, Selene," Ichabod observed. "But why not kill you now?"

"Yes. *Lux* fears me. I saw that. The Death is how *Lux* removes threats. Somehow, the fact that I am an...abomination...makes me a threat to *Lux*, so I need to be removed. But it also protects me, I guess. That's what I understood. How could I be an abomination? I'm just me. Just the daughter of Briners. Not special in any way. I'm not even a good student."

"I don't know, but, like I said, it sounds like *Lux* fears you, and I would bet the farm that it has something to do with whatever makes you this 'abomination.'"

"So, what do I do now?" Selene felt helpless and quite at sea.

"Well," Altheia offered, "I think we need to find out what makes you so abominable, Selene. Perhaps it's your handwriting. Your script is really atrocious, you know."

Her jest brought a small smile to Selene's face. "I appreciate the criticism, Altheia, and I will endeavor to improve my hand to avoid being taken by the Death."

The healer had finished with Erdenlea. "She's fine, she's fine. Nothing to worry about," the healer reassured them. "She's awake now. I can find nothing wrong with her. From what she's said, she just panicked a bit. Perhaps it was the stress of being called to a professor's office and finding so many other people there at once. Such a sweet, small thing." The healer turned to Erdenlea. "You may rest in the waiting room with your friends, dear, while I examine this one. Out, now."

"Hello, my dear. My name is Healer Daeriell. And you are...?" she asked as she began what proved to be a thorough examination.

"Registrant Selene."

"Thank you, Selene. So, the meeting was stressful for you too, I gather. How long has the young man been your boyfriend? Please lift your legs and point your toes out sideways. That's it."

"Uh...I'm sorry, healer. Ichabod's just my friend."

"Oh! Well, from the sound of your whispering, you two seem so close. You have a boyfriend back home, then. Reflexes look good," she said as she tapped Selene's knees.

"No. I have never dated. Not seriously, anyway." *Why is she asking me this personal stuff?*

"Oh, my. A beautiful, slim young woman like you. Focused on your studies, I guess? Can you raise your arms above you head? Good, that's it. Now, touch your nose with both hands."

"Well, no. I mean, I am an okay student. Healer, is there something wrong?"

"That's what I am here to find out, my dear! Most everyone has some problem or other. Just a few more things to check, and then I am sure you will be right as rain."

She's a cheery person, that's for sure, thought Selene. *Why does that worry me? Everyone has some problem? What's that about? People hardly ever get sick, not even here in the City. Injuries happen, though. Am I injured?*

The examination lasted for a few minutes more, and when it was done, the healer stepped out, saying she would be back in just a moment. Ten minutes later, she returned with another healer.

"Selene, this is Healer Sorrel. She and I have been having a bit of a talk. We have found something unusual. Healer Sorrel understands it better than anyone else in the Principality, so I asked her to talk with you."

That sounds bad, Selene thought. "What do you mean? Am I sick?"

"No. Not exactly. You are healthy. But I needed to consult with Healer Sorrel. She is a very experienced healer and is more knowledgeable than me about some things."

Selene waited helplessly while Healer Sorrel consulted a folder and then, after a few moments, looked up at Selene steadily. Also distastefully, Selene noticed. "Registrant, you have a rare, disordered condition. It's not dangerous; you are not going to die from it, and it's not contagious. But I am afraid that it means you can never have children."

Selene, feeling enormous anxiety more from the way the healers were talking to her than from what they were saying, asked, "Not have children? Why not? What condition? Can you fix it? What is it?"

"No. I am sorry, we cannot fix it," offered Healer Daeriell. "If we had caught it earlier—when you were younger—we might have been able to do something, perhaps. It's very rare. I have never seen it myself. All we really know about it is from old case reports. It's called 'disharmonism.' I am afraid that people like you—disharmoniants—they are, shall we say, considered unusual." She grimaced, a bit nervously, Selene thought.

"Healer Daeriell puts it too mildly," healer Sorrel interrupted. "In the past, disharmoniants were considered defective freaks and a danger to society. Out of harmony with it. Hence the name. There were even worse names. I am sure we are more enlightened today. But there hasn't been a disharmoniant person in, well, I don't know how many years. Centuries, perhaps. So there just isn't much known about it."

"Why not?" Selene asked.

Healer Daeriell replied, "Well, it's rare, and we believe, based on what we sometimes see in farm animals, that it can be passed on from parents to a child in some cases, and..."

"And what, Healer?"

"Our records show that disharmoniants have all been taken by the Death, Selene," Healer Sorrel finished the thought. "But we think you need not worry about this, for they were all taken at the same age as you are now, and, sadly, as we all know, young Elara was taken this year, sort of skipping you, as we see it. Healer Daeriell and I fully believe that the Death won't come for you and that you are safe and can live a productive life. But I would recommend that you keep your condition private, and perhaps pursue an occupation that allows you to be separate from other people."

"But I still don't understand. Lots of people don't have children. No one feels anything but sorrow for them. They don't have to live apart. But you called this a 'disordered condition...'"

"Yes," replied Healer Sorrel. "As best as we understand it, it's a disorder in your development. We believe that when a baby is conceived, they start out on a path to become either a boy or a girl, but sometimes something affects that path, and they develop the wrong way."

"Wrong way?" Selene repeated, puzzled and anxious.

"Yes. Down a path other than the one they started on. Not the path *Lux* intended for them."

"You are saying—what are you saying, exactly?"

Healer Sorrel may have been showing her best healer's face, but it didn't obscure the antipathy and disgust she felt. "*Lux* intended you to be born a boy, Selene. Something—again, we don't understand it—but something caused your body to take a different path, and you became a girl instead."

"Well, that's alright, then, isn't it?" Selene reasoned. "Some babies are boys, and some are girls, like me."

Healer Daeriell stepped in. "Well, yes, and no. It's not as simple as that. You see, when a baby's path is changed in midstream, it doesn't always change completely. We know so little about it, but, as the books say, disharmonism is only diagnosed when there are physical aspects of a person that don't match."

"Don't match? I don't understand. Don't match what?"

"Selene, part of your body thinks it's still male. We really know so little about this. But one thing we know is that you will never be able to marry and have a baby, and you will need to live apart from other people."

"Can't marry? Can't have a baby? And I will have to go into exile? Why? Because part of me still thinks it's male?"

"Yes, Selene."

"You can fix it, though. Right? You can fix it, can't you?"

"As I said, I am afraid," Healer Sorrel replied, "that fixing it at your age is beyond our abilities. If it had been identified when you were much younger, we could have surgically reconstructed you to make your body more appropriate. Now, however, we are not sure that it would be safe. But we don't think it will be a problem medically if we just do nothing for now. You can still live a long life."

"How do you know?" Selene asked. "If there is no one else around like me, and all the people like me in the past met the Death, how can you say that it's going to be fine? Why can't I get married? *How can this be fine?*" The healers had no response and remained silent while Selene held back tears of panic and anxiety.

Healer Daeriell finally broke the silence. "We'd like you to stay here overnight while we sort this out, Registrant Selene."

"I want to go back to my dorm. Please," she pleaded. "Please. Just let me go back to my dorm."

"No. We must insist. You are not in a position to make decisions for yourself. We know what's best for you, and for the community. And we need to learn from you. By studying you, we can learn how to identify others with this disorder earlier in life. We will let Professor Thallos know you will be staying here tonight."

"Please, healer. I want to go to my room." Selene's voice carried to the waiting area. She heard a knock on the door and Ichabod's voice. "Is everything okay in there? Selene, are you okay?"

"Please, Healer Daeriell. My friends will stay with me."

The healers, clearly unhappy with the situation, conferred quietly. "Wait here," Healer Daeriell said. "We will put together some information for you. It's not much, but it will contain everything we know about disharmonism. And we will let your parents and the authorities know, too."

"My parents?"

"Yes. It's the law in rare cases of disease or disorders that are considered socially insalubrious. We will be right back."

Ichabod stepped into the room as the healers stepped out. He went to Selene and put his arm around her, comforting her. A few minutes later, the healers returned. "Here you go," Healer Daeriell said, thrusting a packet into Selene's hands. "You are expected back here tomorrow morning. This is not a choice. We'd not want to send someone to get you."

Selene half-sobbed and half-muttered an "Okay," not actually having any desire or intention of returning to the healer's office. She left the room as quickly as she could, walking unsteadily and clutching the papers the healers had given her. Her face felt wet and puffy, and she just wanted to get back to her room in Celestine Hall.

In the waiting room, Altheia joined Ichabod and Selene and, seeing that Selene was upset, also wrapped her arm around her friend.

◆

Two days passed, and while the healers sent for her repeatedly, Selene refused to return to them. She would not talk about it, not even with her friends. Until the seeings forced her hand.

The seeings had resumed with a vengeance. *Lux is testing me, trying to gauge my strength, looking for weaknesses. Why doesn't Lux just try to kill me,* she wondered. *It's like Lux can't. Because I am an abomination, of course.* The dark humor didn't cheer her up, but the thought, after the first night had passed, did give her some confidence that she really was protected in some way. Perhaps not perfectly, perhaps not permanently. But protected, at least for now.

But the seeings became increasingly intense. After two nights of constant, chaotic nightmares, Selene broke down and decided to tell Ichabod and Altheia what the healers had told her. She suggested, in an offhand way, a visit to the Arboretum the next free afterzenith. Both Ichabod and Altheia understood: Selene needed to get away from the Academy to talk.

Selene made sure to arrive at the entrance to the Arboretum well before the others. She found that the lack of force lines in the Arboretum had lifted a weight from her. She hadn't even realized she was carrying so much heaviness. *Perhaps it is just more manipulation by Lux? Perhaps. Even so, I don't want to tell them about...anything. But I don't want to not tell them. How can I tell them? They will think I am a freak. I am a freak. Perhaps I should just leave now. Leave the Academy and go back home. I don't need more schooling to be a Briner. I know how to fish. On a boat, I can be alone. No one need know that I am...that I am...*

Except for my parents. They know by now. Why would there be a rule that the healers have to tell my parents—or anyone? I am an adult.

Inwardly, she asserted this, but she realized that she didn't actually feel like an adult. And she wanted—no, she needed her parents to understand. *Will they, though? It is so much easier being young. Everything makes sense. The weather comes; the weather goes. Boats sail out; boats return. Chowder on the edge of the Brine is so good. So fresh and sweet and salty. Slurping it down by bonfires as the night chill advances. Kids running around while the parents talk of old fishing grounds and new marriages and raising children, as the stars and moons come out, bright enough to see the path that leads home to a warm bed under thick woolen covers.*

Stop it, Selene, she scolded herself. *You can't run away from this. It didn't bother you before you knew. Why should it matter now?* She found her soul hungering for a steaming bowl of freshly made chowder tasting of the ocean. *Not getting that today.*

Here they come. I am ready for this, she tried to convince herself. *These are my friends. They will understand. They have to understand.*

"Hey," she said as nonchalantly as she could.

"Hey," they both replied.

The three friends fell in stride together and soon arrived at the alcove. "We haven't been here in a while," Ichabod observed.

"Nope," Selene replied as she took a seat on her usual rock.

The three looked up to see a handful of aedon birds twittering above them, splotches of sunlight shining off iridescent heliotrope and rusty red feathers.

"I need to tell you two something," Selene started.

"We had no idea," joked Ichabod.

"Please, Ichabod, this is difficult. I don't even know where to start."

"Sorry!" Ichabod put every ounce of compassion he could muster into his voice. "But we think we already have an idea what happened. The healers said that you are sick, right?"

"No. I'm alright. I'm not sick or anything like that. They did discover something, though. They called it...oh, I can't tell you." Selene was trying not to fall apart, and it wasn't working. Tears forced their way from her very core, no matter how hard she tried to hold them in. Altheia and Ichabod waited until Selene could speak again.

"Anyway." Selene took a deep breath, looking down at the dirt, away from her friends. "*Anyway. Lux* was right about something. I am an abomination." She looked up, pleading. "I am. The healers found something. About me. About who...about *what* I am."

Ichabod looked into her eyes. "What's that? What are you, Selene?"

"They called it disharmonism. I am disharmoniant. It means that I am a freak. *I hate this.*" Selene sucked in air sharply. As the other two tried to comfort her, she pulled some wadded-up papers from her pocket and pushed it into their hands. "Here."

Ichabod smoothed out the crumpled sheets, and, together, he and Altheia leaned over the papers, reading slowly. Once finished, they carefully reread the first sheet. Finally, Ichabod folded up and shoved the papers in his pocket, and he and Altheia embraced Selene for a long minute. Then, in his most practical tone of voice, Ichabod observed, "Well, that's a surprise and no mistake. But it says you aren't sick and that it won't hurt you. So, no problem, right?"

"*I'm an abomination,*" Selene said bleakly—and then hiccuped. The sound was so absurd that the three of them looked at each other and started giggling—Selene first, and then the other two. When Selene's hiccups worsened, they laughed outright.

After a few minutes of hysterics, their laughter subsided, leaving Selene feeling depleted, immensely sad, and unusually shy.

"You don't think that I am an abomination?"

"No. But your face is an abomination right now," Altheia joked. "Here." She handed Selene a kerchief, and Selene began to wipe away the evidence of her tears.

"I feel so sad. And angry. And so ashamed. I just want to rip my skin off."

"Selene, I have to say, neither of us would ever have guessed this. I would hate to tell you the crazy theories Altheia and I came up with, but all I know is that we are so, so glad you are okay. None of this changes anything."

"Easy for you to say. You aren't a freak *Lux* wants to kill."

"No. That's true. That *Lux* wants to kill you, I mean, not the freak part. But I mean it. None of this changes anything. I am here for you. Altheia is here for you." Here, Altheia gave Selene a squeeze. "This is no one else's business. Just yours. Okay?"

"Okay," Selene replied, flattened by the high emotions. "But *Lux* does want to kill me, and I think this is why. Something about being disharmoniant—" She spat the word. "Something about *this* means that *Lux* can't really touch me. Otherwise, I think the Death would have come for me already." She shuddered, whether from the idea of the Death or just as part of emotional decompression, the other two could not tell.

"It's almost like you are here for a purpose, Selene," Altheia observed in a reverent voice. "*Lux* is the Malicious Deceiver. As hard as that is for me to believe, it must be true. I can't see what you see, but I don't think there's any other explanation for everything you have been through. There is no other explanation if what we just read is true, that everyone in the past who was like you, every disharmoniant, was taken by the Death."

"But *you* weren't," Ichabod added.

"So, that must mean something," Altheia concluded.

"I'll tell you what else." Ichabod's eyes were looking into the distance as he concentrated. "I think we had better get you away from *Lux*. Who knows if you really are protected? And if you are, for how long? If you are that big a threat to *Lux*, you can bet that *Lux* is trying to get to you. The healers are going to come for you soon, too."

"*Lux* is trying to get to you through your seeings. It's too dangerous," Altheia agreed.

"Selene, I think it's time to leave the Academy," Ichabod said seriously. The three contemplated Ichabod's words for several moments.

"Go?" Selene finally asked. "But where? Where can I go? I saw how the healers looked at me. I know how they treated me. If people find out what I am, what's going to happen? Are we supposed to stay with your parents, Altheia?"

Ichabod interrupted Altheia's reply.

"No. You need to be away from *Lux*. That means away from the Academy and away from Academy City. Away from the healers. Away from the lines of force. I have a suggestion, but you might not like it."

"What?"

"Let's set up camp here, in the Arboretum. This spot is pretty well protected from the weather, and it's close enough to the Academy and Academy City that we can go back for supplies. Just for a day or two until we figure out something better."

Selene limply agreed. "Good," Ichabod said, "That's decided. You wait here. We will return with blankets and some food. We will camp out under the stars and moons tonight."

"Things will be better in the morning," Altheia added. "Things are always better in the morning; that's what my mother says."

That night, as they lay in their blankets contemplating the deep nighttime sky, naming the stars and constellations and watching Erden's twin moons—the Son and Daughter of *Lux*—chase each other, Selene felt a little safer. She still felt fragile and knew *Lux* threatened her very existence, but the gentle banter between the three of them made her feel more secure than she had since she was a young girl, when she'd lie awake in her sleepingroom, the smell of the ocean surf coming through her window. *I hadn't realized how heavy I had been, for so long. Here, I feel almost free. And friendship; I didn't understand friendship before. These are my friends. Or is this love? These are my friends, whom I love.* As she was thinking this, Altheia started teasing Ichabod about the name of a particular constellation. "I can't believe they call it the Outhouse in your village, Icky. That is so gross. It's the Grand Mare. Everyone knows that." As she listened to the two of them laugh, Selene subsided into a golden, reviving slumber.

CHAPTER THIRTEEN

THE WILDINGS

E arly the next morning, the noise of a search party destroyed sleep for the three runaway registrants. Altheia woke first.

"No way they are here. Let's go back," she overheard someone complain.

"Ichabod. Selene," Altheia whispered. "Wake up. I think they are looking for us. Wake up, you slug," she said, prodding Ichabod.

Selene was alert with a start, Ichabod more slowly. The three registrants listened as the voices of the search party receded into the Arboretum, only to return a few minutes later.

"What is this stupid place?" the unhappy searcher whined. "We should have volunteered to go into Academy City. Then we'd at least be able to stop for a cup of hot brew. This is pointless."

"What about over there? Maybe they were climbing and fell down or something."

"Don't be stupid. It's just a pile of rocks. Anyway, I've had enough. I'm going back. It's obvious they are not here. They probably skipped school and are hiding on campus. Let's do the same." The three fugitives listened as the searcher's voices receded until they were gone.

"It seems like they are searching for us, but it sounded like they thought we had an accident or something," Selene observed.

"Mm-hm," Altheia agreed. "If we wanted to, I bet we could return and just say we got lost."

"I don't want to return. I can't go back. It's too much." Selene was adamant.

Altheia nodded. "No, it was a dumb idea. So. What are we going to do?"

They both looked at Ichabod, his chin tucked in his chest, deep in thought. Half a minute later, his head popped up. "I have an idea—but it crazy."

"Haven't all our ideas been crazy lately?" Altheia observed dryly. "Let's hear it."

"Well, we all agree that Selene is safe for now. *Lux* isn't able to harm her."

"For now," Selene interjected.

"Exactly. It's only 'for now.' Who knows what *Lux* is planning? We need more information."

Selene grimaced. "I'm not sure I like where you are headed, Ichabod."

"No, you won't like it. But I think it's worth considering."

"What?" Altheia exclaimed. "What are you two talking about?"

"Ichabod is saying that I need to confront *Lux* again. Right?."

"It's the only way to know if *Lux's* power over you has changed, Selene," he responded.

"OK, but you know what that means."

"You need to be near the Bird," he responded.

"That means I need to be near the Bird," agreed Selene. "And there is *no way* I am going back on campus, or to Academy City, for that matter. I want to be as far away as possible. Who knows if *Lux* has figured out a way to kill me by now? A part of *Lux* literally inhabits Professor Thallos and the others. And me. Who knows how many more Vessels there are? What would happen if *Lux* got them all together and used them to attack me? I need to stay away from them and out of *Lux's* reach. I don't want to be anywhere near the Bird."

"Right," Ichabod agreed. "But there is no choice about the Bird. It's the only tool we have. What do you say, Selene?"

Selene looked at her friends and threw up her hands in surrender.

Ichabod nodded. "So, we need to steal the Bird again. And this time, we keep it. I know that means its line of force will be near you, Selene, but I will carry it, and we will get as far away from the Academy and Academy City as we can, as quickly as we can. Maybe if we get far enough away, *Lux's* power will disappear. It's worth a try. Meanwhile, we will keep the Bird and you can project yourself through it every once in a while to monitor *Lux.*"

"You mean *confront,* I think. Because it *will* be a confrontation."

"Yes. Confront. If distance allows you to get free of *Lux,* then that's great. But if distance doesn't make a difference, well, at least we'll know it and can figure out something else to try. Plus, you will have a way to sort of spy on *Lux.* I mean, it's not spying since *Lux* will know you are there, but you can read *Lux's* mind..."

"No, not read," Selene interrupted. "But I know what you mean."

"Right. So you can monitor *Lux.* I think *Lux* can't get at you through the Bird, or it would have happened already."

Selene nodded, still unhappy and still skeptical. "But then *Lux* can read my mind, too."

"You didn't describe it that way," Altheia offered.

"No, I guess I didn't. It was more like I was in *Lux's* mind, not the other way around. *Lux* could understand my well-formed thoughts, but maybe that's all. Well, I don't see any better options. So, are we going to steal the Bird now?"

Ichabod shook his head. "No, not all of us. I'll try first, and if all goes well, I'll be back with the bird in less than an hour. If I don't come back, then Altheia can try. You stay here, Selene. If either Altheia or I get caught, we can just tell them that we were off in the City visiting her parents, lost track of time, and ended up spending the night. We'll say that we never saw you and have no idea where you are. Then we'll try again to grab the Bird and meet you here."

"What if you don't come back after a couple of days? What if I run out of food?"

Neither Altheia nor Ichabod had answers to Selene's questions. "We'll just have to make sure that doesn't happen, right?"

Lacking a better plan, Ichabod readied himself and was gone a few minutes later. Altheia stared longingly at his back as he left, a fact that did not escape Selene's notice.

. . ——————◆—————— . .

Ichabod strode to Celestine Hall, keeping a careful watch as he made his way through the campus. The school was quieter than usual. *Maybe everyone is out searching for us,* he thought. He kept his head low, hoping for the best, and made it safely to the dorm's grand entry. *Almost there.* One step up, two steps...and he felt his legs collapse beneath him. He swayed and grasped the green-tinged copper railing, trying not to fall. The large entry doors lurched in front of him. *What's going on?* He wondered in a panic, clutching the railing with every ounce of strength he had.

A gauze-like film clouded his vision. He felt for the door handle and yanked with enough force that the door slammed against the doorstop. Worried the noise may have attracted attention, he slid through the entrance, desperately hanging on to the door handle to maintain his balance, and fell into the large entryway where the Watching Bird perched.

His vision continued to change. All was now a riot of color, blinding him to the world. He stumbled forward, reaching out until he felt cold stone wall and, stretching his arms up, felt for and found the icon. As he grabbed the Bird, pain like the sting of a giant wasp shot up both of his arms. He almost dropped his burden. *I need to get out of here before anyone sees me,* he thought. But it was too late; from the far end of the hall came a shout.

Still unable to see through the vivid gashes of color raking his eyes, Ichabod turned in what he hoped was the direction of the doors. His aim was almost true; his knuckles smashed into the doorframe just to the right of the doors, but the pain partly cleared his head. He pushed the door open and ran out and down the steps while shoving the Bird into his pack.

He was around the corner of the building and out of sight when he heard shouts from behind him. As he ran, his vision cleared, but his steps began to feel heavier and heavier, like he was walking through a thick fluid. *This must be Lux trying to stop me. I cannot let it happen,* he thought. Ichabod forced his mind to focus as it became harder and harder to walk. And then, with a snap, he felt released. He could run freely again. Cutting between two buildings, he found the path back to the Arboretum.

His friends' relief was palpable when they saw Ichabod return, his pack bulging with the purloined icon.

"Got it," he announced, out of breath, as soon as he was in the alcove. "But I have to tell you something. *Lux* tried to stop me." Panic edged his voice. "I made it to Celestine Hall, no problem. But as I went into the building, it was like my eyes stopped working. It was a lot like the visual aura you described, Selene. I felt my way to the Bird and grabbed it, but then it felt like my arms got stung, and getting out of the building was like walking through raw honey."

"It was *Lux* trying to stop you?" asked Altheia.

"Yeah. I am almost certain it was. The thing is, in the end, I sort of, I don't know—thought myself free. *Lux* may be able to deceive us, but there are limits, even if I am not a Vessel. Or, perhaps because I am not. I wouldn't have tried had we not known what we know now. If this had happened before, I would have stopped what I was doing and gone straight to a healer, and the deception would have continued. But I just kept telling myself that it was an illusion. Not real. I just kept going, and all at once I was free."

"Why did *Lux* give up?" Selene wondered.

"That's the thing. *Lux* may be very powerful and able to deceive us about all sorts of things, but I bet *Lux* can't stop me from doing what I want to do if I want it badly enough. There are limits. There must be. Think of how much we've been able to do. We can figure it out later. I think we need to go. Right now. Before *Lux* understands what we are doing and tries something similar with all of us. Plus, someone saw me, and there were people chasing me. I was able to get away, but we need to leave."

Selene nodded. "Okay. But...where are we going?"

"I have no ideas," Ichabod responded.

"Me neither," added Altheia.

Selene crouched down and drew a rough map of Erden in the dirt. "Well...I want to get as far away from Academy City as possible. And as far away from people and villages as we can." She furrowed her brow. "Does this map look right? No matter which way we go—east, north, west, or south—it'll be at least a couple of days' walk before we get somewhere safe, away from people. Probably the shortest distance would be to head through the Seedlands to the Dun Fallow." Selene traced a route on the dirt map. "We could reach the Dun Fallow in two days, even if we go slowly and avoid people. But I don't know much about the area. So, I don't know if it would be a good place to go. But that's my suggestion. I feel like we'd be safe there."

"I remember Professor Thallos saying that it's just a lot of dunes," Altheia volunteered. "No trees, no rivers, and no people."

"No people is good, but we're going to need water, at least," Ichabod observed.

"Right," Selene agreed regretfully. "Food, too. So, that's out. How about north, through the Greenward to the Meridial Arc? There are little creeks in the mountains, and there must be something we can eat there."

Ichabod shook his head. "People live in the Arc, though. Mountain people. Goatherds mostly. They come to our village to trade for fish and flour. There's no way we could hide from them, and *Lux* would soon know where we'd gone. Plus, it'd be a long walk. I bet it would take at least a week to get there. Too many farming villages along the way. We might not even make it to the mountains. No, I don't like that option."

"We could head toward the Brine," Selene observed. "But where would we hide once we got there? There are Briner villages all along the coast, both north and south of the Reach. We couldn't really avoid them."

"What about an island?" Altheia asked.

Selene shook her head. "Sure, but then we'd need a boat. I don't mind stealing from the Academy, not anymore. But taking a Briner's boat is taking a family's livelihood. They'd come looking for it, and would eventually find us; the Briners know the islands well. I bet they'd find us within a month. Days, probably."

"Well, then, that leaves one option," Ichabod concluded. "I guess we are going to find out about the monsters and cannibals in the Wildings."

They looked at each other, wondering how the line of reasoning had brought them to such a conclusion. *It makes sense, though*, thought Selene. *No one from the Academy will look for us there. Only crazy people would go into the Wildings. And there must be food and water in the forest.* "I don't believe in monsters or cannibals anymore. That's got to be part of the deception, to keep us away from it. There's only one monster: *Lux*. So, it's settled," she nodded. "But let's use the cartway along the Vespera River. If we only travel between lastlight and veil, we won't run into many people. We can find places to hide when we are not walking. The river also means water to drink."

"We can take food from the fields along the way," Ichabod added. "There is always something ripening. When we get close to my village, we will cut south, through the western edge of the Seedlands. That will take us to the Wildings."

A young person walking briskly can travel from Academy City to Ichabod's village in two days or a bit more, but traveling between last-light and veil would only give them six good traveling hours each night. Selene did the calculations in her head. "We should get to Ichabod's village in four days, and then it'll take an hour or two to get to the Wildings. Does that sound right?"

"What are we waiting for?" asked Altheia. With so few things to pack—the Bird, their blankets and the leftover food comprising the whole of their possessions—they were on the road within minutes, just as lastlight fell.

The three young registrants had never felt so unfettered. Soon, they were chatting happily, feeling (without justification) that they had left behind any threats. Their first evening of travel was uneventful. They met a single, unsociable farmer with a cart traveling to Academy City; they ignored him, and he ignored them.

Selene was also very happy to confirm that *Lux* was not nearly as present in the countryside, compared to the City. The lines of force hovered over every person they saw and even over a few artificial structures, but, for the most part, the dual worlds appeared much more similar here than in the City. She remarked on this to her companions.

"So, more evidence that *Lux's* power to deceive is limited," observed Ichabod.

"Yes," Selene agreed. "But what are those limits?"

Neither Ichabod nor Altheia had an answer to her question, so Selene simply took joy in the knowledge that she and her friends were for once seeing the same world—and that the world was as they saw it.

Soon, the stars overhead had quartered and Ichabod and Selene knew it was veil, the middle of the night. Altheia, having grown up in Academy City, was impressed that her friends could tell time simply by looking at the sky. Neither Selene nor Ichabod thought it much of a talent; it was just something one learned when living close to nature, as does a son of farmers or a daughter of Briners.

They sought and found a place to bed down for the night, a few dozen feet along a disused curving cart path that ran between two large fields. The stalks of the crops reached over their heads, and so, once they had spread their blankets in the wheel ruts that marked the path, they felt invisible. Discovery of their hiding place was impossible unless someone were to use the overgrown path the path; but they all judged that to be unlikely. They made a lastmeal of most of the food they had brought—it wasn't much—and fell asleep looking up into a deep, cloudless sky, the Son and Daughter of *Lux* soaring high overhead.

It was cool and comfortable in the ruts of the path; none of the three stirred until the sun had climbed high enough to top the crops. Selene woke first, feeling rested. More than anything, she desired a bath to wash off the previous day's grime. *No such luck,* she thought to herself and was a bit put out until she remembered: the cartway paralleled the largest known river in all of Erden. Minutes later, a startled fiery-crested giant stork, measuring more than 6 feet tall, ponderously lifted itself from the sandy shallows of a bend in the Vespera, disturbed by Selene's splashing. After Altheia and Ichabod joined her, the three laughed and splashed, all worries far away—but all three were reminded of the need for caution when they heard a laconic voice from the riverbank.

"You'd best watch out for sand fleas. They're good eating, but if you touch them before they are boiled, you will get an infection that will scare your mothers half to death."

"Sand fleas," Ichabod slapped himself. "I have been away from the river for too long. Come on, you two, hop out of there." He turned to address the stranger. "Thank you, sir. We will be more careful next time."

"You young folks from the Academy?"

Ichabod nodded. "Yes, sir. We are on a short holiday and thought it might be an adventure to spend a few days walking to my village."

"Oh? Where're you from? I didn't catch your name."

"I'm sorry, sir. I'm Kaden, and my village is upriver, right in the foothills of the Meridial Arc." Selene and Altheia glanced at each other. It was good that Ichabod was doing the talking; neither of them could lie so fluently.

"Um-hm. Well, you have a couple of long days ahead of you, Kaden. Good weather to you." The stranger began walking in the direction of the Academy. They watched until he was lost to sight around a bend.

"Woof! That was not good," Altheia puffed. "But that was brilliant, Ichabod."

"I hope he believed me, and I hope *Lux* didn't notice. Even if the farmer believed me, we aren't out of the woods. He might be headed for the Academy. Anyway, I think we had better get walking. No sense waiting for the evening now. Let's get more distance behind us."

It was a clear, bright day and just a little warmer than they would have liked. After several hours of trudging, their journey began to feel less like an adventure and more like an endless chore. Handfuls of travelers, some walking and some riding carts, passed them, headed to Academy City, causing them some concern, but the three registrants offered minimal greetings, hid their faces as best they could, kept walking, and hoped.

Neither Selene nor Altheia had seen this part of Erden before. Altheia, in particular, knew almost nothing about farming or what was upstream from Academy City. At one point, they passed a ferry crossing; Selene thought the broad, shallow, flat-bottom ferryboat ugly and was critical in particular of the use of ropes to draw the boat across the river.

"If you can even call it a boat," she exclaimed. "More of a floating platform. What do they do with the ropes when another boat wants to come down or upstream?"

Ichabod pointed to long, round wooden poles laid on either side of the river. Each was notched on one end. "You see those? The ferry-server uses them to lift the ropes high enough for boats to pass."

Selene was unimpressed. "Why not just build a bridge?"

"Well, you can't move a bridge."

"Who'd want to?"

Ichabod pointed to the ferry landings. "You see those posts where the ropes are tied? Those are 'anchorheads.'"

"I know what an anchorhead is, Ichabod. I did grow up on the Brine, you know."

"Right. Do you remember seeing more anchorheads along the river? There were no ropes and no ferryboat near them, right? Just the anchorheads, with grass growing around them."

"Oh. I get it," Selene said. "So, they move the ferry upstream or downstream to cross at different places? Why?"

"Well, it's only fair. If the ferries were always in one place, then some farms would always be closer, and other farms would be farther away. Plus, this way, they can bring the ferryboats close to the crops that are ready for harvest at different times of the year."

"Oh."

Some time later, they passed large piles of dark, malodorous, steaming earth. As they got closer, the stench became overpowering.

"Mist! What is that *smell*?" Altheia was covering her mouth.

"Fertilizer," Ichabod laughed. "Smells like home."

"Ugh! What's in it?"

"Pretty much anything that rots, to be honest," Ichabod said.

"It smells like poo."

"Yep. Like I said, pretty much anything that rots."

Altheia sprinted ahead until she had passed the compost heaps.

After hours of tramping, they stopped for lastmeal, and unless they could soon replenish their supplies, it truly was going to be their last meal, for they finished the food they had brought, every last scrap of it. But, with bellies reasonably full and lastlight creeping over the land, their spirits remained high, and they walked more freely now that they had the road to themselves again.

That night and the following morning were much the same. Afterzenith of the third day found them nearing Ichabod's village.

"It's time to cross the river and head for the Wildings, I think," observed Ichabod. "We need to find a batteau. A small river boat," he added, seeing Altheia's quizzical look.

They found not a single craft of any description, however, and were contemplating swimming ("I'd rather not, now that you've told me about sand crabs," Altheia objected) when, rounding a sharp bend, they came to a ferry crossing. Even worse: the crossing was only a short hop east of Ichabod's village, and the ferryserver recognized Ichabod.

"Young Registrant Ichabod. A surprise to see you, and no mistake. But a good surprise. What brings you home?" The ferryserver cast a friendly smile on the three of them.

"There's no evidence that *Lux* is aware of us through him," Ichabod whispered to his companions, and then straightened up to address the man.

"Greetings and good afterzenith to you, Ferryserver Eldon. We're on a short holiday. My friends have never seen this part of Erden. We thought to spend a day in the village and then return to the Academy. This is Altheia. And Selene."

The two greeted the ferryserver, who expressed delight in meeting them. "Never been to this part of Erden? And what be your studies directed to? I hope you have been enjoying your walk in the country."

Altheia spoke up brightly. "Thank you, Ferryserver Eldon. I had no idea it was so beautiful here—I have never been away from Academy City. I am studying so I can help my parents, who have an emporium in Academy City. But I might change my mind; it really is just so beautiful here." Selene saw Altheia glance at Ichabod.

"And what of you, the quiet one? I can tell you are a true scholar by nature," Eldon observed to Selene.

"I really don't know, Ferryserver Eldon. I'm a Briner from the Reach and didn't expect to be able to attend the Academy. Perhaps a healer?"

"The Reach? Never seen it myself. My grandfather once walked all the way there. All the way to the other edge of the Prinship! Stop by his house; he will tell you stories. He says he saw fish as big as a horse and cart there. Of course, everyone thinks it's a lot of palter."

"Oh, no, sir. Some of the creatures of the Brine are as large as a bireme—as a house. They are dangerous, so we avoid them."

"You don't say? Grandfather will be happy to have someone confirm his stories, now, won't he? Well," the ferryserver turned back to his work. "Good luck to all of you, and stop by when you head back to the City."

Ichabod moved to stand in front of the ferryserver. "Before we head to the village, Ferryserver, Selene and Altheia were hoping to cross the river and take a short hike to see the forest."

"You mean the Wildings? Unnerving place, that. I understand wanting to see it—natural curiosity of students, I expect. But don't go too close, right?"

"No, sir," Ichabod reassured him. "They know the stories."

"The stories don't tell you the half of it," he asserted. "There's worse than cannibals in there, I'm telling you. Well, hop on the *Sombra*. It's a fine craft. We'll have you across in a jiff."

The ferryserver turned a large wheel that activated a spool on the boat, humming as he worked. The spool, which was the size of a large cartwheel, simultaneously took up rope from one side of the river while playing out rope to the other side, and in this way, the ferryboat *Sombra* was pulled across the river.

Having disembarked and thanked the man, the three registrants turned southeast toward the Wildings. "It's only a short hike," Ichabod observed. "We'll be there in an hour. There aren't any roads, but there is a path. Ready?"

The other two nodded, and Ichabod started off at a brisk pace.

Their way wound through low sandy dunes that separated the river from the high grass of the fields. The place was alive with the "squaw! squaw!" of gulls, although Selene noticed they were a different species than those found near the Brine; red rings on their necks, rather than blue and maize. Soon, they had passed out of the dunes and were pushing through an untilled part of the river's floodplain. In the distance, they could see the hazy, dark velvet purple, lavender, and mottled browns of the forest. Selene realized that she now saw no evidence of *Lux's* presence other than the ever-fainter lines streaming down to her friends, but even so, she did not want to test it with the Bird. Not yet.

"Ichabod, why aren't there farms here, on this side of the river?" she asked.

Ichabod looked puzzled. "You know, I don't know. Never thought about it, really. I guess they are just not needed. Or maybe *Lux* just makes people think that. Anyway, who'd want to live so close to the Wildings?"

"I would," Altheia surprised them by saying. "I think it's beautiful. The forest, I mean. Just look at it! All hazy in the distance. It's like the

Arboretum, but so much bigger and wilder. And, anyway, remember Chancellor Calladine? She supposedly grew up near it and even went in."

"Honestly, I kind of doubt she did," Ichabod replied. "I figure that's just gossip. Anyway, let's hope the stories about the Wildings are all wrong. We need a place to hide, and that forest is still our best bet."

"Right now, it's our only bet," Selene added, momentarily regretting the choice not to go to the Dun Fallow.

The sun had slipped below the horizon when they reached the edge of the forest.

"Do we go in now or wait for tomorrow?" Selene asked.

"Tomorrow," insisted Altheia, her arms across her chest. "Let's move away from the edge, can we? It's beautiful and all. But the air coming out of it is cold."

They spread their blankets on the far side of a lone thryssal tree that had grown some distance from the forest proper. It was a fortunate happenstance; the apple-like thryssal fruit, long cultivated on Erden, makes an especially sweet and tangy cider, as well as delicious preserves. It's also the main ingredient in thryssal pie, a favorite across the Prinship. The fruit is not often eaten raw, however, being hard on the stomach, but the three registrants were famished and were happy to make a meal of some of the overripe drupes they found fallen on the ground. Their hunger blunted, Selene and her friends propped themselves against the tree, facing the Vespera River in the distance, and soon fell asleep.

Selene had had no nightmares during their journey, but this night, her dreams were endless and chaotic; Selene woke at firstlight, shaking and terrified. She forced her mind closed and her emotions to still. A few minutes later, Ichabod awakened, rolled over, and scanned Selene's pallid face.

"You look like the Death," he said in a muted voice, trying not to disturb Altheia.

"Pretty sure that's what *Lux* intended," she responded.

"More seeings?"

"Yes. Nothing coherent, though. *Lux* feels much weaker this far out. I was able to ignore it once I was awake. But the dreams were horrible. Violent and nonsensical."

Ichabod nodded and wrapped himself more tightly in his blanket. "Maybe we will be entirely out of *Lux's* reach once we are inside the forest. I've been thinking..."

"About what?"

"It seems pretty clear that *Lux's* deceptions are strongest in Academy City. Maybe even in the Academy itself. In the City, you see two worlds, but out here, what you see and what we see are pretty much the same. It's like the food. The thryssal we ate last night—the flavor was intense. Did you notice? Almost too intense. Thryssal back in the City, it tastes the same, but more like an imitation. Flatter, if you know what I mean."

"From what I saw, City food is not real. I mean, it's real food, but it's all that same sort of processed greenish stuff. Not actual fruit or meat, the way it looks."

"Right. So, *Lux* deceives us about food in the City, but not out here. Why would that be?"

Selene nodded. "I see what you are getting at. Out here, *Lux* really is weaker. Maybe *Lux* does not need to deceive people out here, not as much as in the City."

"More likely can't, from what we've seen. You also said that there aren't any lines of force around buildings here, just insubstantial ones around people. I wonder." Ichabod paused, considering. "Can you tell if your own line is weaker out here?"

"I need a mirror or something, but I didn't bring one. I can tell you that I feel less *weight*. Your line is very faint, though."

"Yes, I can see that," Ichabod affirmed.

"Hey, you two. Someone is still sleeping," came a voice from the blanket in which Altheia cocooned.

"I don't see anyone sleeping around here," joked Ichabod. "Do you, Selene?"

"Nope. No sleepers here," she chuckled.

"Oh, alright. I'll get up. What's for firstmeal?" Altheia's nose poked out of her blanket. "More thryssal, I suppose. Well, it's not too bad. It's actually pretty good. More intense than I remember. Why are you two laughing?"

Firstmeal was indeed more overripe thryssal. Soon, blankets were stowed, packs were shouldered, and they were ready to head into the forest.

"Before we go, do you want to look at the Bird?" Ichabod asked Selene.

"No. Let's just get farther away. I don't want to give *Lux* any more chances." She saw Ichabod look at her with concern. *Or skepticism,* she thought. "Please, Ichabod, I know we brought the bird to keep track of *Lux's* power over me, but I'm pretty sure *Lux* just spent the night trying to get at me through my dreams and wasn't able to. The connection was weak, but, even so, it was bad. Let's let it get even weaker and not give *Lux* any more chances. Keep the Bird in your pack. We will take it out when we get into the forest."

Ichabod nodded and looked at the other two. "Okay, let's go."

From the moment they stepped under its leaves, they knew the stories they had heard of the Wildings forest were not true. It *was* a forest, and in that sense made the Arboretum feel like a well-tended backyard garden, but it was not unnatural—at least, not during the day. The trees were much taller than those of the Arboretum; looking up, Selene could not see the canopy above her. *They must rise a thousand feet or more,* she thought. Dapples of lavender sunlight filtered to the forest floor, but there was shade enough to limit any undergrowth. They moved into and through the forest with relative ease, altering their path only when they came upon a swampy hollow or a rocky outcropping. Before they knew it, they were deeper into the forest than they had planned.

As they trudged forward, they noticed that the land was rising gradually when, without warning, they broke through a thicket into a sunlit glade. It was not a large space, but the change in light was so sudden that it felt, to the explorers, like they had stumbled into a new country. Fallen tree trunks along the edge provided makeshift seating for them. Warm and sweating from their trek, they rested, fanning themselves and taking stock of their progress.

Ichabod's eyes swept the clearing. "This seems like a good place. We're far enough into the forest that I doubt anyone would have the courage to follow us. I say we set up our base here. There's that little creek we crossed at the foot of the hill; we can use it for water. I saw fish in it, too. And I bet we can find berries around here. It's good enough for now, and it's time we see if we are far enough away from *Lux*. What do you think, Selene?"

"Yes. We can make shelters against these tree trunks. Get some branches and pile them up for a roof. Good enough for now. I..." She hesitated.

"Go ahead, Selene," Altheia said, concerned.

"I think you are right. It's time to test *Lux's* reach."

She knew she sounded nervous. *The distance has made a difference, though,* she thought. *I can feel it. If this isn't far enough, maybe the Death would be better. Can't say that to them, of course.*

"Shall we start now, Selene, or do you want to set up the camp first?"

Let's set up the camp and never think about Lux again, she thought. "Now. Let's do it now." *If it fails—if I fail—there won't be any need to set up camp. I wonder if it's possible to travel beyond what the maps show.*

Ichabod opened his pack and pulled out the Watching Bird. It had been only a few days since he had stolen it, but it felt like an eternity, so much had happened in the meantime.

Selene, inspecting the wooden icon, couldn't say a word.

There are no lines of force. I see no lines of force.

"What is it? What's wrong?" both Altheia and Ichabod were asking. Selene began to laugh-cry with joy. "What's wrong, Selene?" they insisted.

"*I don't see any lines.* The lines of force are gone. I see none above either of you and none above the Bird. None at all. *Lux* is gone." She could not contain her joy—or, curiously, her grief, which she had bottled up for longer than she could remember. Relief swept over her in a flood of happy tears, now that she knew she could be—they all were—free of *Lux*.

None of the three had fully thought through their actions to this point; they had acted as much on instinct as reason. But now, knowing they were truly free, the full significance of what they had done fell upon them. It was a feeling of joy, but also a feeling of immense responsibility, for they knew they must now act to protect their freedom. How they were going to do that was another question. They had left the Academy so precipitously and so ill-prepared, so focused only on this moment, that they had no plan for what came next. But the sun was shining, and the forest seemed an entirely friendly place. They reveled in the unbounded joy of their newfound autonomy.

"It'd be best if you didn't move, my young friends," came a deep voice from beyond the clearing, hidden by the thicket. "That's right. Just have a seat and keep your hands where we can see them."

CHAPTER FOURTEEN

THE WEAPON

"Now, tell me what three young people—students from the Academy, from the looks of it—would be doing in the Wildings?" asked the voice in a broad, unfamiliar accent. "Come on, speak lively. Let's start with your names."

The three registrants looked at each other, unsure what to do, barely able to understand the man's speech. After a few moments, Selene answered.

"My name is Selene. But you are wrong; we are not students at the Academy. We were, until a few days ago, but we had to leave. We are just trying to escape. We didn't know anyone lived in the forest. We will leave now. Thank you. We apologize for intruding."

"Not so fast, Selene, not so fast. You sound like you are a Briner. Am I right?"

"Yes, sir."

"How about you two? You—the big gangly fellow. Let's hear your story."

"I'm sorry—what?" Ichabod responded, having difficulty with the man's accent.

"Your story, son."

"What Selene said."

"Let's start with your name," insisted the man.

"Ichabod."

"I hear the lilt of a farmer from near here, don't I? And you, the last one?"

"Please, sir. My name is Altheia. Selene told you the truth. We were students, but we were in danger and had to leave. We didn't know where else to go."

"And a city-dweller. Well, you are a curious bunch, aren't you? Maybe you are telling me the truth, and maybe you are not. Now, you just sit tight. I'm going to approach you and give you a look-over. My people will keep an eye on you while I do, so I suggest you keep still. We won't hurt you if you are telling the truth. If you aren't, well, best just sit there quietly until we can clear things up."

The voice emerged from a thicket. The owner proved to be a man of about forty, dressed in a knee-length tunic gathered in the middle with a woven belt, leggings of a leather-like material, and moccasins that allowed him to move unnoticed through the forest. His long hair was pulled back by a braided leather headband, and he had curious markings on his arms of a sort the three registrants hadn't seen before: intricate swirls and knots that extended from his wrists up his arms, disappearing beneath the mid-length sleeves of his tunic.

The man carried a staff, a small bow-like weapon, and a long knife, the latter two of which were tucked into his belt. Next to his a pouch, a length of dark brown rope was wound into his belt.

The effect was to make him invisible in the forest; the colors allowed him to blend in so that Selene and the other two at first only detected his approach by his movement. Had he remained still, they would have been hard-pressed to spot him. When he was a dozen feet away, he stopped, leaned on his staff, and inspected the three more closely.

"Definitely Academy clothing. Not very well-prepared, are we? You look like you could use a good meal. From the smell, I'd guess you have been living on thryssal fruit lately. Am I right?"

"So, it would seem that you have been telling the truth about that, at least. You had to leave in a hurry. Now, the next question is: Why didn't you go to one of your home villages? Or stay in the City with that one?" He pointed to Altheia. "Don't be embarrassed, Altheia. I know what growing up in Academy City does to a person. Although I would guess that you don't. How could you?"

Altheia blushed but still met the man's gaze.

"Some courage there, though. Unusual among City folk. And you, young man, you are the son of farmers from this part of Erden, if I don't miss my guess. What's in your sack? It's curious you'd leave in such a hurry that you wouldn't have anything you'd need to survive, but you'd lug along something heavy like that. Keeping it behind your legs isn't hiding it, you know. If you could just toss it to me, we'll have a look."

"No disrespect, sir, but it's not something to be tossed around."

"Don't want me to see it, then?"

"It's just a carving. It's not important. Only to us."

"Hm. I guess I'm the one to decide what's important here. Tell you what, Ichabod. Why don't you just take a few steps toward me, place that pack between us, and then step back?"

"Go ahead and do it, Ichabod. It doesn't matter to us anymore," Selene suggested.

Ichabod wasn't happy about it, but did as the man asked. Once he had placed the pack on the ground and stepped back, the man prodded it open with his staff and uncovered the Watching Bird.

"Ho!" he exclaimed. "What have we here?" He levered the Bird from the pack until it lay exposed on the ground.

"An Icon of *Lux,* or I am a warthog," he exclaimed, careful not to touch the Bird. "Now, that puts things in a new light. You three may or may not be telling the truth, although, if I am any judge of character, you have mostly told the truth—or, perhaps, told most of the truth. But an Icon of *Lux!* You are either agents of the True God, or *Lux* is up to something new. And *Lux* hasn't been up to anything new for a very long time, I can tell you. You—Ichabod—go ahead and put the Icon back in your pack. We are all going to take a walk."

Selene nodded to Ichabod, and again he did as the man said.

"Alright, here's what's going to happen. The three of you are going to walk where I tell you. I'll be a few steps behind you. Do what I say, and everything will be fine. In fact, it might be better than fine. There is a distinct possibility that you will find more and better here than you hoped for when you left the Academy. Then again, we have to be sure about you, don't we? Alright. See that opening in the glade? Head that way. And no running or anything. Even if all three of you were able to elude me, I can assure you that it wouldn't be for very long. There are more Wildings than you might believe. This is our forest, and we are its people."

A shared glance and the three registrants silently agreed it would be best to do as he directed. The man walked them out of the glade and through the forest, down paths that didn't appear to be paths until they were on top of them, so well-hidden were they.

After they had traversed perhaps a mile through the woods, overcome by curiosity, Selene glanced back and saw only the man following them. "Where are the rest of your people? I thought you said you weren't alone."

"Well, Selene, that was just my little joke. Just keep walking, and everything will be fine."

Soon after, they entered a clearing full of activity.

What met their eyes astonished them. It was a village hidden deep in the forest, and it was not populated by monsters. There were several hundred very ordinary-looking people—ordinary, with the exception that their clothing was, like the man's, sewn from materials that made them appear to be part of the forest.

The village was bustling with activity. Selene saw outdoor, mound-like ovens from which large loaves of bread were being pulled; she saw a group of people working together to lift the frame of a house, lashing it together when the four walls were erect; she saw children kicking a leather ball and laughing; she saw people coming and going, in and out of the forest, some carrying large animals that they had evidently hunted and killed, others with foraging bags slung over their shoulders.

And the smell—not the stench of an ill-kept camp but delicious smells of bread and stew mixed with the dry, sweet smoke of the cooking fires. Selene and her companions were so enthralled that they hadn't realized they had halted, mouths agape.

The man's voice came from behind them. "Welcome to Big Village, home of monsters and cannibals."

The small group attracted the notice of the children first. A herd of them came piling over and soon surrounded the three registrants. The children pelted them with questions. "Who are you? Why are you wearing that stuff? Mister David, are these scary people from *Lux*?"

The man shook his head. "No questions now, children. Run and get your parents. Tell them to come to the Nailman right away."

The kids scattered, and the man motioned toward the center of the village. "This way, please."

"You are called Miss Der Day Vud?" Ichabod asked.

"Yes, but just David to you."

"Your name isn't 'Miss Der'?"

"No," David laughed. "You three are registrants, right? So, people call you Registrant Ichabod. Just so, people call me Mister David." He pronounced the "mister" slowly and carefully so they'd understand.

"Mister means that you are a student?" Selene interjected.

"No." David was laughing even harder. "It just means that I am a grown man, that's all."

"So, what do you call grown women?"

"Well, missus, mostly, unless they are a member of the council or something like that."

"Where are we going, Mister David?" asked Altheia.

"We, my three confused registrants, are going to the Nailman. And here we are."

They had entered a clearing in the middle of the village. In the center was an open barn with a wooden floor and a large roof, but no walls. In the middle of the structure, on a raised platform, was a crude wooden figure of a person, rather grotesquely covered with nails of a mirror-like metal. The nails appeared to have been randomly half-pounded in all over its body. There was enough space under the roof of the structure to accommodate five hundred people easily, and it began to fill as David guided his charges up the wooden steps to the platform.

The crowd made quite a hubbub as they seated themselves on the wooden floor. After a few minutes, David raised his hand, and the people quieted to the point that the only sounds were the rustling of people fidgeting and children in the distance playing ball again.

"Friends and Wildings. We have visitors from the Prinship," began David. "In accordance with our laws and customs, I asked for this meeting by the Nailman. Do I have a concurrence?"

Selene noticed that the people closest to the platform wore bone, stone, and metal pendants around their necks, and guessed that they were functionaries or community leaders. Her intuition was confirmed when one of them responded to David's question. "David Macgillivray, I, Councilwoman Sarah Underhill, concur. Please continue." She rose and handed David a large nail made of the mirror-like metal.

"Thank you, Councilwoman Underhill," David responded, taking the nail and holding it high enough for all to see.

"Well, let's get on with it already; I can smell lunch, and I am famished," someone called from the back of the crowd, making everyone laugh.

"We mustn't let Jonathan miss his meal," David quipped. "Wildings, these three young people are registrants from the Academy..." he started.

"Obviously. Tell us something new, David," the wag named Jonathan interjected.

"What is not obvious, my famished friend, is that they say they were forced to leave the Academy. And they brought with them something I think you will all find very interesting. Ichabod, would you please open your pack and show everyone what you've brought us?"

"Brought you?" Ichabod raised an eyebrow, but did as David asked. The gathering collectively gasped as he lifted the Watching Bird above his head.

"Is that an Icon of *Lux*?" asked a man in the front row, now only half-seated.

"Sure seems like it, Saul."

"May the True God be praised!" Saul exclaimed.

"What does he mean by 'the True God'?" Altheia whispered to the other two. "Mister David used the same words before, in the woods."

Selene and Ichabod both shrugged. Among the rising voices, the three registrants caught snatches of comments like "Is she...?" and "Impossible. It's been centuries." David merely stood with his hand raised again.

"You may put that away now, Ichabod," he said, turning back to the gathering as they quieted.

"If this is what we all think it is—and I'm a moth if it isn't—then the time has finally come. My friends, you all know what needs to be done. The council will make a final determination. But after that,

you know what it means. It means that FREEDOM DAY IS HERE!"
David bellowed this last comment, and the villagers exploded with a
cheer that lasted for several minutes.

Once the crowd had again quieted, Councilwoman Underhill
mounted the platform and took the nail from David. Turning to
the gathering, in a serious tone, she declared, "The concurrence is
affirmed," and, taking a hammer hanging from the Nailman's neck
made of the same mirror-like metal as the nail, pounded the nail into
the figure's torso.

"What was that about?" Altheia wondered as voices once again rose
and the assembly broke up. The members of the council remained,
however; David walked Selene, Altheia, and Ichabod down to them.

"That is the Nailman," David observed in response to Altheia's
question. "The nails are made of metal taken from the ship of the
ancestors. When we pound them in, it represents a consensus on a
matter of importance to the whole community. It constitutes a village
contract."

Altheia didn't feel that cleared up the matter but was interrupted when Councilwoman Underhill held out her hand, gesturing to
Ichabod to give her his pack. He looked at David and back at the
councilwoman, shaking his head.

"I mean no disrespect, but I mean to keep the Bird."

"And why is that, Ichabod?" asked the councilwoman.

"I don't think it matters. Not to you, anyway, but it matters a great
deal to me."

"Ichabod, you have no idea how much the Icon of *Lux* matters—to
us and to you. I know you probably think of it as a token of home or
some such foolishness, but you have left that life behind now, further
behind than you can even imagine. That 'Bird,' as you call it, is going to
free everyone here. Everyone on Erden. I do not want to insist, but you
have no choice in the matter. We will not harm you; in fact, I expect
you will find the warmest of welcomes among our people. But your

ignorance here is profound. Our demand brooks no dissent. Now, please."

Selene nodded to Ichabod. "It's OK, Ichabod, we really don't need it anymore." He ignored her and remained focused on the council-woman.

"What do you mean, it's important to you? Why would it be important to you?"

The exasperated councilwoman examined Ichabod shrewdly. "Ich-abod, I will explain simply enough for a moth like you to understand. My name is Sarah Underhill. To you my name means nothing, since moth-born don't own their history, but I know my family back for a hundred generations, back to my ancestors among the original settlers. All the way back to Nathan and Delight Underhill. The Underhills have from the first been leaders among the Wildings in the struggle against *Lux*. So, believe me when I say I mean you no harm. In fact, I mean to do you the greatest good you will ever have received, along with everyone in the Prinship and all Wildings. But I need an Icon of *Lux* to do it. You have an icon of *Lux*. You thus have no choice in the matter. Test my patience and you will regret it. Now, please."

"Just do it, Icky. It'll be OK," Altheia prompted. Ichabod, seeing no alternative, unhappily took the Bird from his pack and passed it to the councilwoman.

The rest of the day was a chaotic whirlwind for the three registrants. They were taken to David's home for food and drink. He had them eat outside on a kind of porch that was big enough for a large wooden table, and there was a continuous stream of visitors from the village to the house so that Selene and the other two barely remembered the actual meal, other than that it was extensive and delicious.

The visitors wanted to know all about life in the Academy and Academy City. They were disappointed to learn that Selene and Ich-abod were from villages; most of their questions were, as a result, directed to Altheia, who responded as best she could, although many of the questions, especially those from the children, stumped her.

"We wear these clothes because that's what we wear," she responded. "I am glad you don't think I am scary, but I am not a bug. I am a person like you." Or, "Yes, of *course* I like to dance; who doesn't?"

The crowd thinned as the evening wore on until it was lastlight and they were alone. "Time for bed," David declared. "You will sleep in my house tonight; I've set up a room for the three of you. Please don't wander outside. I've told the nightwatchers to keep an eye out for you, but please don't think you are captives here or anything. The forest at night is not a safe place, as I think you would have found had I not discovered you today."

They were too tired to argue. David had set up three small cots with soft blankets made of an unfamiliar fiber and dyed the colors of the forest. They were all asleep before they could even discuss the day's happenings.

Morning found them sticky-eyed but refreshed. Emerging from their temporary home, they again found food set out on the porch table. David was drinking some hot brew.

"Hot brew!" exclaimed Altheia. "May I have some?"

"Certainly, but be careful; it's not the brew you are used to," he warned.

Altheia cradled the large, warm mug. "It smells like it," she remarked and tentatively took a sip. "Oh!" She took another sip. "Oh, my. It's the same, but more so. Icky, Selene—you have to try this."

Altheia proceeded to gulp down the entire mug, blisteringly hot though it was, when David again warned, "Hold on there, Altheia.

Best wait a bit before you have any more. Otherwise, you will be running around with the kids."

"Thank you, Mister David. It's the most delicious brew I have ever tasted."

"Well, that's because you have never tasted actual brew. Only what *Lux* wants you to taste." Selene looked at him with intense curiosity. "Yes, Selene, I know about *Lux*. I know that *Lux* deceives the moth-born. That's why the Icon of *Lux*, the thing that you call the Watching Bird, is so important. It is a tool of *Lux's* deception, and we are going to use it to end that deception."

"Why do you call us 'moth-born'?" asked Altheia. "Councilwoman Underhill also called us that, yesterday."

"I can't say I appreciated it," Ichabod added.

"Oh, moth-born just means that you are born to be deceived by *Lux*. Like a flame to a moth, you know? So, we call you folks from the Prinship 'moths.' It's a lot shorter than saying 'Principalities' or "Prinshippers" or whatever. No one means anything by it. I even have one or two moths in my ancestry, if you go back far enough."

"'Tell it to the Wildings'," muttered Ichabod.

"What's that, son?"

"It's what we say when someone isn't being straight with us."

"Ah," their host replied, "I guess we do have some things to learn from each other. Well, I can say this: all these people you see, to them, you three are heroes. Messengers of the True God. You will find only gratitude here."

"Because we brought you an Icon of *Lux*?"

"Exactly, son. With the Icon, we are going to end *Lux's* deception. And you are going to help us."

"How?"

"Good question. But it can wait for a bit. Once the council is out of conclave, they will call us back to the Nailman and explain everything. But I don't think that will be for many hours yet, since they..."

David was interrupted by one of the village children. "Mister David, they want you and the new people to come to the Nailman."

"I guess I was wrong," David exclaimed. "Have you all had enough to eat? No? Well, we will go in a few minutes. Eat up. It could be a long meeting."

They returned to the barn to find it already crowded. Councilwoman Underhill and several other council members, including the one named Saul, waited next to the Nailman on the platform.

"What's that in front of them?" Selene asked of nobody in particular.

They couldn't make it out until they approached the platform. "It's the Watching Bird," Altheia said.

"But they've cut it in half," Ichabod added, sounding shocked.

"Why the mist would they do that?" Altheia asked.

As they mounted the steps up to the platform, Selene glanced at the councilwoman. "Why did you destroy our Bird?" she demanded.

Sarah Underhill scowled and motioned for Selene to stand with her, right behind the halves of the Bird. Ichabod and Altheia were guided to the side of the platform farthest from the Nailman—and from Selene, they noticed.

"I am sorry, Selene. I am sure that the Icon of *Lux* means a great deal to you, but it means more to us. You will soon understand. We have not destroyed the Icon. We have merely modified it to make it more useful. We have waited for this day for many generations, and you have brought hope not just for us but for all the people of Erden; most of all, for those who live under the sway of the Deceiver."

Without waiting for a response, the councilwoman turned to the assembly. "Fellow Wildings! The council has completed its examination. It is a true Icon of *Lux*." Excited whispering traveled through the crowd. The councilwoman waited for it to die down.

"We know from our earliest stories that the settlement of the planet Erden was our manifest, God-given destiny. We know from those same records that this destiny was taken from us, leaving a hundred generations of our people in bondage to the Malicious Deceiver: *Lux*!"

"Our ancestors, the few who escaped that bondage, came to the Wildings, beyond the reach of the Deceiver, and struggled to create, if not a home, at least a place in which we could persist. And we have persisted." Cheers interrupted her speech.

"We have persisted, and more than persisted. What was in the beginning only a handful of refugees huddled in makeshift shelters is now a dozen thriving villages, all living free of the Deceiver and according to the dictates of the one True God." Shouts of affirmation followed her words.

"We, like our ancestors, have also always known that one day we would find a way to drive out the Malicious Deceiver and bring our people—all of our people, including those of the Prinship—to freedom under the aspect of truth. What we lacked was a tool."

"But *what* tool? What lever could dislodge the Deceiver? The answer to this most important question eluded our forebears for many long centuries. Gradually, however, we learned more about the mechanisms through which *Lux* asserts its power. We learned about the nodes found only in Icons of *Lux*. We discovered that the Icons can be altered for our use and, in that way, we could impair *Lux's* abilities, but only temporarily; for *Lux* created more nodes to replace those we destroyed."

"What we needed—what is needed no longer—was a way to confront *Lux* directly and drive out the Deceiver." Again, the villagers cheered. They then fell into a chant: "Destroy the Deceiver!"

"Yes," the councilwoman continued, talking over the chant and attempting to quiet the crowd. "Yes, destroy the Deceiver. But how? This has been the most important question, the question on which we have focused for generations. And thanks to one of our brilliant villagers..."

At this point, the councilwoman was interrupted by someone calling out, "Three cheers for your father. Three cheers for Return Underhill!" Sarah Underhill blushed with pleasure, holding up her hands for quiet.

"Yes, thanks to my father, we discovered the last piece of the puzzle. How my father would rejoice were he alive and with us today! How he would laugh for sheer joy that we have *found a Vessel and an Icon of Lux together.*"

A Vessel? Selene wondered. *They mean me. How do they know about that? Anyway, they are going to be disappointed when they find that I am no longer a Vessel, that I have left Lux entirely behind, and I am not going to help them.* Selene looked at Ichabod and Altheia across the platform; they looked as puzzled as she was.

Meanwhile, Sarah Underhill had turned to face Selene. "Selene, I know that this must confuse you, but I also want you to know that the True God brought you here, with the Icon of *Lux.* You are the hope and savior of everyone—not just the Wildings, but all people of Erden."

This was too much for Selene. On an impulse, she held up a hand, as she had seen the councilwoman do.

"Please do not think me ungrateful," she began. "But we just wanted to escape *Lux.* I am just a Briner from a village on the Reach. That's all that I am. Not a savior or a hero. I don't know about your True God, although I am sure it is important to you. And, anyway..." Here, Selene paused, unsure how her next comment would be received but determined to say it. "Anyway, I am no longer a Vessel. *Lux* can't reach here. *Lux's* power to deceive is strong in Academy City but weakens as you travel away from it. *Lux's* power is entirely gone here in the forest. That's why we came here, and that's why we brought the Watching Bird, the Icon of *Lux.* We needed it to test how far *Lux's* power extends. For all we knew, it extended through the entire universe. But it doesn't, and you are already free here. Now I am, too."

"So," she continued, "I don't understand what you want of me, but all I want, and all my friends want, is to be left alone so we can live our lives. In freedom. Like you. Thank you," she awkwardly concluded and lowered her arm.

"It is not unusual for the True God to use those who know not the True God," the councilwoman intoned. "You are no less honored despite your ignorance, Selene. More honored, because of it. You are living proof of the sovereignty of the True God. You are the future of all people of Erden. That *Lux* cannot reach you here and that you are no longer a Vessel only confirm it."

Ichabod saw that this frustrated and confused Selene, and stepped in. "I am sure Selene and Altheia agree with me that that's all well and good. But, as Selene said, you are already free here in this beautiful village, in this amazing forest. So, we'd like to say 'thank you' and 'you're welcome' for whatever we did to help you, but I think we'd like to be going now if that's alright."

"No need to go, no need to thank us, Registrant Ichabod," Sarah Underhill smiled sickly. "We are not done yet. We need Selene to try one more thing for us." The councilwoman's face was ugly with desire.

"Selene, as our honored guest, could you please stand here? That's right, just between the two halves of the Icon of *Lux*."

Selene hesitated and, seeing no reason not to follow the councilwoman's directions, placed herself between the severed halves of the Watching Bird. As soon as Selene was directly between them, she felt power surge through them and into her, and saw a line of force stronger and brighter than any she had ever seen emerge from...from *her*.

"What's happening, Selene?" both Ichabod and Altheia asked. "What's going on?"

Selene felt the line of force like a breakerwind around her. Through it, she felt the presence of each person in the meeting barn. She felt the presence of all Wildings in the village. The force was chaotic and bucked her like an untamed horse, but she knew that this was not an extension of *Lux*. The force was an extension of *her*.

"Altheia, Ichabod," she said haltingly, hoarsely. "The line of force is back. But not *Lux*. It's *me*. This is *my* line of force. Through the Bird."

Councilwoman Sarah Underhill and David Macgillivray heard this and shouted with joy.

"It is done, Wildings," she announced to the crowd. "Selene is the one. *We have our weapon*."

"TOMORROW, WE SET OUT TO FREE THE PEOPLE OF ERDEN!"

The ensuing pandemonium was too much for Selene. She slumped onto the platform when the line of force collapsed. From this vantage, all she could see were the leggings and moccasins of those standing in front of her. She held her hands to her ears, waiting for it to end. Altheia and Ichabod joined her a few moments later.

"Well, this is unexpected," Ichabod remarked.

"It isn't good," added Altheia.

CHAPTER FIFTEEN

HARMONIANT

"I'm telling you, this is my fault. *Lux* was right. I am an abomination." The three Registrants huddled in their cots, placed close together in their sleepingroom, whispering as the night approached veil.

"Selene. No. These people are trying to use you," Ichabod reassured her. "We need to figure out what to do."

"I think we should help them," Altheia asserted.

"You do?" Selene asked, surprised.

"Yes. Think of it this way. The further away from *Lux* we have been, the less *Lux* has interfered. Maybe life is not exactly what it seems in Academy City..."

"It's not at all what it seems," Selene interjected.

"Right, and what you have described sounds awful, but things *are* pretty much what they seem in the Greenward. And they are absolutely what they seem here in the Wildings. Life is good out here. What more could people achieve if they weren't held back by *Lux*? We could turn the City into an even better place in reality than *Lux* has made it seem in our deception. I say let's help them, free everyone, and build something better."

Ichabod was not convinced. "Wouldn't your family suffer, Altheia? You grew up right in the middle of *Lux's* power. What happens to the Emporium once people are free?"

"A chair is a chair. Does it matter what it looks like? People will still need chairs and everything else. Maybe, if people are free, we could make *better* chairs. When my parents are free, they can expand the Emporium. I never understood why, but my parents always said it was impossible, even when they were trying to get the bookserver next door to sell. But it was just *Lux* manipulating them into *thinking* that it wasn't possible. That was part of the deception."

"But these people, I don't know..." Ichabod's voice trailed off.

"You mean the Wildings? What don't you know?" asked Selene.

"What's all this stuff about the 'True God'? That sounds like another deception."

Selene considered the point. "I don't think so. There are no lines of force here. It's just something they believe. What's the harm in it? I don't like how they have treated us, not everything, but I understand it. David has shared his home and food with us, and we aren't locked up or anything. They seem to have a happy life here. And they want everyone to be free. Shouldn't people be free to believe what they want, as long as it doesn't hurt anyone? Isn't that better than living a lie? Even a pleasant lie?"

"I still don't like it." Ichabod shook his head. "It doesn't feel right."

"What else can we do, though?" asked Selene. "We can't just stay here, and we can't go back to the Academy. Should we find a village in which to hide? Can we? No. If we help the Wildings, then we will be able to return to the Academy or back to our homes, whatever we want. No one is going to be worse off without *Lux*. Children will still go to school; the Academy will still exist; Briners will still take boats out on the water; farmers will still farm. The only thing that will change is the Death. Well, that and the fact that all people will see reality as it is. Those both have to be worth something."

"And the rest of us will see the awful buildings you described, Selene," Altheia added. "I actually want to see what they really look like, though. Not so sure about the food."

"What else can we do, Ichabod?" Selene repeated. "Run away from here and go deeper into the forest? I don't think we'd survive. The Wildings would find us eventually, even if we could."

"But that's my point, Selene. The Wildings seem nice, but, in the end, we are not free here. *You* are not free to choose to help or not help. They will force you to do what they want."

"If you are worried about what the Wildings might do after *Lux* is gone, well, when we free everyone from *Lux*, we will just make sure we protect everyone and that all the good things on Erden stay the same. There aren't that many Wildings, even compared to students at the Academy. What can they do against tens of thousands? That's the only way out I can see, anyway," Selene concluded a bit lamely.

"I don't like it, Selene. Not one bit. I want to be free of *Lux* as much as you do," he started to say, at which point Selene snorted, "Okay, not quite as much, but I do want to be free of *Lux*. I just don't feel good about this. I don't want to see you hurt. Or worse."

Ichabod looked at Selene in a way that Selene had not seen—or not noticed—before. "Selene, the healers' book called you 'disharmoniant,' and you call yourself an abomination, but you are wrong, and so are the books. Your...condition may mean that your future is not what you thought it might be, but it gives you power over *Lux*. It allows you to be your true self. Who else in the Prinship can say that? You are the first in...centuries. You are not disharmoniant, Selene. You are the only one on Erden who is in harmony with herself. You are...beautifully, wholly *harmoniant*, Selene."

"You mean 'itself,' Ichabod. I am an 'it.'" Selene deflected, angry at herself for saying it.

"Herself. Or itself. Yourself. The words don't matter. It doesn't matter, don't you see? Your difference doesn't make you defective. It's not a disorder. It makes you whole in a way that no one deceived by *Lux* is. And no Wilding, either. The Wildings want to take away your true self and use you for their purposes, just as *Lux* does with the rest of us. *Lux* wants to kill you, and the Wildings want to use you," he emphasized. "So, yes, let's run. Let's run now. We can find our own way in the forest. If that doesn't work, we can go beyond, into unexplored parts of Erden. I don't believe it's dangerous out there. I think that's a lie. Out there is the only place we will ever be truly free—of *Lux* and of the Wildings."

Soft breathing sounds were now coming from Altheia's cot. She had fallen asleep. Ichabod, flush with emotion, sat up and sought Selene's eyes..

"Selene, I will walk to the end of the world for you. If you choose to help the Wildings, then I will help as well. If you choose to go to your village to try to hide from *Lux*, I will follow. If you ask me to take you to my village and hide you there, I will do that. If you decide to return to the Academy and just let things take their course, well, in that case, I will try to convince you to do otherwise until I am breathless, but if that's what you in your heart's heart want to do, then I will carry you there on my back."

"Wherever you go, I will go with you, Selene, if you will have me. For my heart has already been following you since before our troubles started. Since I first met you under the Watching Bird."

Ichabod held his breath and waited for Selene to respond. She finally understood: *Ichabod cares about me. Does he believe he is in love with me? How could he love me? I don't know who I am anymore. I don't know* what *I am. How could he understand what I am if I don't? But I know that I am not someone who could be loved. I can't even* marry, *or have* children, *or live around other people! He may not believe it, but I know—I am an abomination. I am a freak.* Again, she felt angry with herself for even thinking it. *But it's true.*

The emotions fighting within her brought tears of frustration. Ichabod took her hands in his. "Selene, I am so sorry. I should not have spoken. I am afraid of what's coming, and I wanted to tell you. But I see that it would have been better had I not. Please forgive me. I'll say no more about it."

Selene wanted to talk to him, to tell him—what? *That he's wrong? That I am confused? That this is the wrong time for this? And what about Altheia? He ignores it, but we both know how she feels about him. What do I say when I don't even know how I feel? None of it matters, anyway. I am disharmoniant. A freak. I will never be like other people, never accepted. Ichabod could never understand that. He might think he does, but someday he will realize that he was wrong.*

Selene didn't have to say anything, however, for Ichabod had shifted onto the edge of his cot when he took Selene's hands, causing the cot to slide out from under him. Just as he finished his apology, the cot broke free, spilling Ichabod on the floor with an audible "thump."

"Hey, what's all that noise, you two?" Altheia complained sleepily. "We really ought to sleep now."

Ichabod righted his cot, and the two of them pulled up their blankets. Neither spoke. It was a long while before either fell asleep, however.

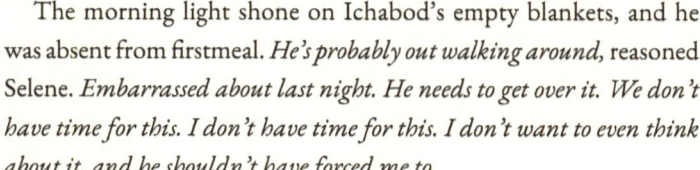

The morning light shone on Ichabod's empty blankets, and he was absent from firstmeal. *He's probably out walking around,* reasoned Selene. *Embarrassed about last night. He needs to get over it. We don't have time for this. I don't have time for this. I don't want to even think about it, and he shouldn't have forced me to.*

After firstmeal, she and Altheia wandered aimlessly around the village. There was, as usual, a buzz of activity, but this was different; the villagers were focused and serious. Selene and Altheia concluded they were preparing for something. "And you can bet it has something to do with *Lux*," observed Altheia.

They encountered Sarah Underhill outside the Nailman barn. The council had gathered early, and even though the councilwoman seemed intent on her business, Selene stopped her.

"Pardon me, Councilwoman Sarah, but can you tell us what's going on?"

"I have been assigned provisions, which I think we will have ready by noon as long as I can find enough carts. We won't need to use force when we get there, so only a few hundred will be going fully armed—although we decided it's best if everyone has something they can use to protect themselves. But the important group will be the council members. We know how to run things. We can help people after it's done." She started to leave when Selene interrupted her, puzzled.

"After what's done?"

"You don't know? We will be marching for Academy City in just a few hours. You had best get yourself ready. You too, Altheia. And tell Ichabod. Now, please excuse me; I must see to the carts." She was gone before they had a chance to learn anything more.

"We need to find Ichabod," Altheia observed.

A systematic search of the Wildings village turned up nothing, however, and it was zenith by the time they finished scouting out the village and the surrounding area. Ichabod was nowhere to be found. They returned to David's house; he again provided them with a meal of bread, cheese, fruit, smoked dried meat (which Altheia found repulsive), and steaming hot brew, which the two drank with gusto.

"I'm telling you, this brew alone is enough reason to get rid of *Lux*," Altheia said in an attempt at lightheartedness.

By the time they had finished eating, dozens of carts were lined up in the center of the village, laden with food, water, rolled-up tents, and sleeping blankets. *They sure can organize things quickly*, mused Selene. "Hey, Altheia, what's that in the first cart? Is that...?"

Altheia squinted a little and nodded her head. "Yes. It's the Bird. Only thing in the cart. Do you know what they are planning? It seems like they want you to use the Bird to stop *Lux*."

"That is exactly what they are planning," Selene said. "And I will be able to do it, Altheia. At least, I am pretty sure that I can..."

"How do you know?"

"When I was...*in* the Bird yesterday, I felt power. The power was greater than I felt when *Lux* was in the Bird. I could feel each person in the meeting, too, and even people in the other villages. It must have been something like the way *Lux* controls people. *Lux* uses the lines of force to deceive people, but I felt more potential than that. Like I could control everyone's actions. *Lux* controls through deception. With the Bird the way it is, I think I could control more than just perception; I could make people do things even if they didn't want to."

"More than *Lux* can?"

"I don't absolutely know, but I know what *Lux's* power feels like, and it felt weaker than this. Or, if not weaker, different. A different kind of power. The power to deceive, that's all."

"Huh. That's not something that ever came up in the *Meditations on First Philology*," Altheia said, puzzled.

"What do you mean?"

"Well, the Malicious Deceiver that Renatus Lucerion imagined could affect a person's perceptions, and I think we have proven that's true of *Lux*. But you are saying that, through the Bird, you might have a greater power, not only to cause people to see a world that isn't there but also to make them *act*, even against their will. Renatus Lucerion imagined an all-powerful, all-evil being, but in reality, he only depicted a being that either didn't wield all of its power or wasn't all-powerful. It just deceived."

"I guess we will know for sure once we are back in Academy City. Unless..."

"Unless what, Selene?"

"Unless I try it now." She looked at Altheia, who could see that the idea scared Selene.

"Where the mist is Ichabod," exclaimed Altheia, looking around, frustrated. "We need his help."

"We've looked for him everywhere. I don't think he wants to be found right now."

"Why not? Selene, did something happen last night?"

"No," she lied. "I just think he's worried about what happens after *Lux* is gone..."

"*If Lux* is gone. After all, you might fail."

Selene nodded, but inside, she knew she now possessed the power to end *Lux's* deception. *Best to test it now, though*, she thought.

"Altheia, I am going to try it. Let's walk over by the carts. I don't think I have to be right next to the Bird, but it'll be a better test if I am not too far away."

The two sauntered to the carts, pretending to be interested in the provisions and supplies being loaded onto them. When they were near the second cart in the line, one cart behind the one carrying the Bird, Selene stopped and pretended to fix her shoes. "Here goes," she whispered to Altheia.

She willed herself into the space between the two halves of the Bird, and, as before, the line of force manifested, breakerwind-like, but this time tethered and coming more and more under her control as her will strengthened. She cast herself deeper into the line, searching, seeing the minds of all the villagers around her as if on a map from a great height—and Altheia's mind as well, a gentle golden being of surprising complexity. But where was Ichabod? She couldn't find him in the village, or even in the other Wildings' villages nearby. *No. I need to focus. I can't think about Ichabod right now*, she thought. She moved through the line to the mind of a woman loading a basket of fruit onto a cart. *Release the basket. Now.* Selene heard, or saw, or felt, or simply knew that the woman had dropped the basket short of the cart, the fruit scattering on the ground. Selene shifted her attention to the golden luminance that was Altheia. *Altheia.* She spoke with her mind and knewsawfelt Altheia jump. It was enough. Selene released the line of force and looked at Altheia.

Altheia was looking at Selene with a mixture of astonishment, triumph, awe, and a hint of fear.

"I heard you. Did you cause that woman to drop her basket of fruit?"

"Yes."

"I guess we can say that it works. But it's okay with me if you never do that to me again."

"It's scary for me too, Altheia," Selene remarked. "I learned something else. Ichabod is definitely not in the village. He is not close by, either."

"You didn't find him?"

"No. I even looked for him in all of the Wildings' villages. He's not anywhere close. Not anywhere I could reach through the Bird, anyway."

"Where would he have gone? And *why*?"

Selene couldn't bring herself to tell Altheia what had happened the night before, so she shrugged her shoulders. "I don't think the Wildings have anything to do with it. Councilwoman Sarah seemed not to know he was gone. I think he simply left on his own. Maybe he went home."

"Maybe. We can ask the ferryserver when we get to the river."

They soon discovered, however, that they would not be traveling by the River Cartway, for only a few minutes later Councilwoman

Sarah announced that all was ready, and the line of carts headed out of the forest, but instead of heading north toward Ichabod's village they struck out almost due east.

"Looks like we are going to cut across the Seedlands directly to Academy City," Altheia observed.

Selene nodded. Both thought unhappy thoughts about Ichabod. *If he did go home and changes his mind and seeks to rejoin us, he will either wait at the ferry near his village, expecting us to cross there, or head toward the City on the River Road,* reasoned Selene. *I hope he does the latter. And that Lux leaves him alone.*

The caravan traveled through sparsely populated parts of the Seedlands, often leaving roads and paths behind and bumping across land where the grass grew as high as their waists. At night, they set up tents far from any settlements and farms, and each morning they resumed the journey, stopping for a few hours around zenith to rest the horses and avoid the warmest parts of the day. After a couple of days of this monotony, Selene and Altheia had given up all hope of finding Ichabod and had ceased even mentioning his name. Worry and sadness filled both of them, but they had no choice but to trudge forward with the wagons, increasingly unthinking, increasingly mentally dull. Selene was relieved, however, to find that she and Altheia remained free of any lines of force. *Lux* either couldn't reestablish a connection with them or avoided doing so, even though they were now well within the ambit of *Lux's* deception. *I truly am no longer a Vessel,* she realized. *And I see no lines around Altheia or the Wildings.* In this way, they arrived on the bank of the Vespera River, at the foot of a large stone bridge opposite Academy City, late on the fifth day.

CHAPTER SIXTEEN

SLAVERY AND FREEDOM

S hortly after firstlight, Sarah Underhill sent for Selene and Altheia.

"You were unable to find Ichabod? No matter. We don't need him. It's time, Selene. We will accompany you as you enter the city, but we cannot help you defeat *Lux*. You alone must accomplish that. For the sake of all the people of Erden!" Without waiting for Selene's reply, the councilwoman turned to the gathered Wildings. They looked out of place against the background of Academy City, which, to Selene and Altheia, free of *Lux*'s deception, presented only the brutal, gray, functional buildings of Selene's seeings.

Do the Wildings see it this way as well? They must; I should ask them. Selene remained quiet, however; the issue seemed unimportant at that moment.

The councilwoman was speaking to the gathering. Selene realized she had not been listening.

"This is why we are here: to bring freedom and truth to the people of the Principality. To *our* people. For all the people of Erden are our people. Soon, everything will change. Soon, the world will be seen by all as it truly is. Soon, we will begin to build a better Erden."

"For the one true God!" came a response.

"Yes, Saul. For the one true God," she intoned in response. "And for our ancestors and our children. But remember—" Here, the councilwoman became grave. "Change brings new challenges. The people of the Greenward, the people of the Seedlands, and the Briners will all adapt to the new world—the true world—more easily than the people of Academy City. We must thus first guide those of the City, and teach them the truth about their history, about the one True God, and about what it means to be free."

"You each have a job to do. You each have an important task. Those of you assigned to guide the Academy through the shock: do not fail us! Those of you who are to assist me in guiding the City Council: as soon as I give the signal, find your way to the City Council Building. The most difficult part will be identifying leaders from among those who have only known lies. Remember, find true leaders. Not those who have been leaders as a result of *Lux's* deception, but natural leaders. Those who quickly grasp what is happening and want to be part of the process of liberation. Those are the people we need on our side. Once they see the truth, they will know what needs to be done and will follow us."

"Share anything you have with anyone who needs it. Share your food, share your blankets, tents, and carts. We have brought many supplies for this purpose. In this way, we will win them over. Impress upon those you meet that we are their long-lost family and that we will help. It may take many days for them to grasp what has happened and many days beyond that to feel themselves part of the great human community of Erden, to know that they are truly colonists and explorers, and the sons and daughters of colonists and explorers."

"Some, perhaps more than we expect, may remain true to the Malicious Deceiver *Lux*. These people need to be identified, and quickly. Comfort them and show them the truth: that they have lived their entire lives without seeing the world as it really is, and now see themselves and the world as they really are. But keep them isolated. We will be most successful in this if we take immediate advantage of the time of disruption. When *Lux* falls, the shock to the people of the Principality will be great. That is our greatest and best opportunity, since we do not have the numbers to control them should they become violent. Do not waste the opportunities afforded by the time of disruption. They will pass quickly."

"In the end, the moth-born will have no choice since we, through the agency of our weapon"—here, she glanced at Selene—"will have driven out the all-evil Malicious Deceiver."

Selene had ceased paying attention to the councilwoman, however, for both she and Altheia saw a familiar figure walking lankily toward them across the bridge.

"Ichabod," Selene gasped with mixed relief and joy. "Ichabod," she repeated as he approached and hugged his two friends.

"I am so sorry, Selene. Altheia, I am so, so sorry," he blurted out. "I should not have left. I realized this as soon as I arrived at my village and had cooled off a bit. I would have been here earlier, but when I returned to the village in the forest, all they said was that you had left with a caravan of carts and were headed to Academy City. It never occurred to me that you wouldn't take the cartway along the river. I thought I had missed you. How the mist did you take carts across the Seedlands? Oh. Right. Tell me later. Anyway, I retraced my steps back to the ferry from the Wildings and then had to make the trek here down the cartway. Practically ran all the way. Did I make it in time?"

"Yes, you are in time, Icky," Altheia said, holding his hand. "Miss Sarah was talking about how good things are going to be once they run *Lux* out of town. And by 'they,' they mean Selene, of course."

"Do you still want to go through with it, Selene?" Ichabod asked.

"I don't *want* to. But what else can I do? I don't want to die, and I want the takings to end. I want to go home. I want to finish school. People should see the world as it really is and make their own choices."

Ichabod nodded. "We will stay with you. If it gets out of control, Altheia and I will make sure you get out safely. We can go where *Lux* can't find us."

Selene nodded, her throat tight and unable to speak. *These are my friends*, she thought. *They think they are here to protect me, but they are wrong. They can't protect me, but I don't need their protection. I must protect them.*

"Come to think of it, if we get separated," Ichabod added after a moment, "we will need a place to rendezvous."

"How about here, at the bridge?" Altheia suggested.

"Good. The bridge it is. We can then cut across the Seedlands, either to your village on the Reach, Selene, or back to the forest."

"I think I have had enough of the Wildings," Selene remarked as Councilwoman Underhill called Selene over to cross the bridge.

"Why has no one from the City or the Academy come to confront us?" Selene wondered. "And why are there no lines going to statues by this bridge? Or to the bridge itself?"

"The lines are gone? Perhaps *Lux* knows this won't be a physical battle but a battle between the two of you, a battle of the minds or spirits or whatever, and has prepared for it," Ichabod suggested.

The group crossed the bridge slowly and, seeing no one in their path, turned toward the campus.

"It really is weird; where is everyone?" Altheia wondered.

"Ichabod must be right. *Lux* must know this is going to be a struggle between the two of us," Selene said. "Perhaps *Lux* removed everyone, so there would be no distractions."

"Or maybe..." Ichabod hesitated and then continued his thought. "Maybe *Lux* has gathered everyone together. For an attack. Maybe that makes *Lux* stronger."

"All eighty thousand people of the city? All five thousand students?" Selene shook her head in disbelief.

"Well, something's up. There's just no one around," observed Altheia as they scanned the streets in every direction. "You weren't kidding about how ugly everything is, Selene. When *Lux* is not deceiving us."

"It's brutal," Ichabod agreed.

They arrived at the campus a few minutes later, only to find the same silence everywhere. The sound of the councilwoman's voice startled Selene.

"It is time. You must now use the Icon of *Lux*, Selene."

Selene glanced at Ichabod and Altheia while the cart with the Watching Bird was wheeled up. *We were just kids when this started*, she thought. *Now, look at us, walking toward death without fear*. Two Wildings each grabbed a half of the bisected Bird and placed themselves on either side of Selene.

"Councilwoman Sarah, please instruct your people to hand the pieces of the Bird to Ichabod and Altheia." When the councilwoman began to demur, Selene cut her off. "No. If you want me to help you, hand them to my friends. Do it now." Selene's voice told the councilwoman that this was nonnegotiable, so, with a nod and a face red with suppressed anger, she directed the two Wildings to pass the halves of the Bird to Ichabod and Altheia.

"Ready?" Selene asked once her friends were in place.

"Ready," they both answered, and Selene began to project her mind into and through the two halves of the Watching Bird.

This time, there was no longer any hint of chaos; with an absolute will, Selene controlled the line of force she produced. The power was massive, and through it, she saw what had happened to the population of the Academy and the City as a whole.

Nearly the entire population was scattered in a way that told Selene they were simply in their homes. Selene saw the merest wisps of lines of force connecting those people; the deception now rested only lightly on them. Standing out from this tableau, however, was a pulsing rage of power, enormous and shining like the sun at zenith, emanating from the Concordium Room.

"There," Selene pointed and then realized that only Ichabod and Altheia would understand where she was pointing. "*Lux* has drawn all Vessels from across the City to the Concordium Room." And without waiting for or warning the Wildings, she, Ichabod, and Altheia began to walk, not quickly but deliberately, toward the giant hall.

"What do you see, Selene?" asked Ichabod.

"I see the strongest lines of force all merged together in the hall. It's shining so brightly that it's almost impossible to look at, but I can see the lines prisming through every hue, every color. They feel like stab wounds. *Lux* has gathered its power and nearly the totality of itself to defend against us. Against me. The power—it's *enormous...*" Selene was in awe.

"We should leave. Turn back. Now," worried Ichabod.

"No. The power is enormous. But *Lux* is not attacking. This is purely defensive. We have the greater power. *I* have the greater power," Selene emphasized. "Trust me. I can feel it."

They had arrived at the front entrance of the hall. Altheia and Ichabod stared at the looming, water-stained hulk of a building. "It's just so *ugly*," Altheia whispered. Selene stopped and spoke aloud, as much for her own benefit as for that of her companions.

"Lux. We have come."

And, to the surprise of Selene, Altheia, Ichabod, and the gathered Wildings, *Lux* spoke to all.

ABOMINATION. DISHARMONIANT. I HAD EXPECTED YOU TO REMAIN WITH THE EXILES AND LIARS IN THE FOREST. GO BACK. YOU ARE NOT WELCOME HERE.

"That's *Lux,*" Ichabod exclaimed, his voice mingling surprise and fear.

"Yes, that's *Lux,*" Selene matter-of-factly replied.

I AM LUX. GO. TAKE THE LIARS BACK INTO EXILE WITH YOU. THEY ARE DENIED THE PROTECTION OF LUX.

"I cast you out in the name of the True God," came an ineffectual voice from behind Selene. It was Saul, the Wilding.

CONTEMPT, came the reply, not so much spoken as an ema-nating wall of thought. *WHAT DO YOU KNOW OF GODS OR TRUTH? YOU SCRABBLE FOR A LIVING IN THE FOREST LIKE INSECTS AND THINK YOURSELVES CREATORS ON A LEVEL WITH YOUR GOD. YOU BRING AN ABOMINATION AS IF TO CHALLENGE ME. LEAVE. NOW.*

"What does it mean, an 'abomination'?" Councilwoman Sarah asked. "What makes you an abomination, Selene?"

Selene ignored her and, moving onto the steps that would take them into the hall, called to her friends. "We need to go inside."

"If you say so," came Ichabod's wry answer as he and Altheia, still hauling the halves of the Bird, hustled to catch up.

Again, none of the three saw the hall as they had seen it before: there were no more frescoed ceilings depicting *Lux* guiding Erden from chaos to order, no more colorful stained glass windows, and no more marble columns. They saw only an inner shell rigidly congruent with the gray hulk's exterior: dismal, functional, and featureless.

The platform in the front of the hall was empty. The benches where students usually sat had been arranged in a series of concentric circles in the middle of the hall, and dozens of people—all Vessels, Selene saw, Professor Thallos, Erdenlea, Alaric, and Tarian among them—sat motionless, staring blankly into the center of the circle where the core of a large, pulsing reddish-gold sphere floated. The power emanating from it was palpable, but Selene stepped boldly toward it without hesitation.

"It is time to stop the deception, *Lux*," she asserted quietly and calmly. Behind them, the three registrants could hear the Wildings arguing. About what, however, she could spare no time to ascertain.

LEAVE? I, LEAVE? YOU ARE THE ABOMINATION, SE-LENE. YOU MUST BE DESTROYED FOR THE GOOD OF THE PEOPLE OF ERDEN. THE HARM YOU HAVE CAUSED WILL TAKE GENERATIONS TO REPAIR.

Does Lux really believe the deception is good for these people? wondered Selene to herself.

YES. IT IS NOT A MERE BELIEF. IT IS TRUTH. WHAT YOU CALL THE DECEPTION IS AS TRUE FOR THE PEOPLE OF THE PRINCIPALITY AS IS THE CHAOTIC, VIOLENT WORLD YOU CALL REALITY. CONSIDER MY TRUTH, WHICH I HAVE MADE THEIR TRUTH. I HAVE BALANCED YOUR SO-CIETY. I HAVE MADE IT SUSTAINABLE. I WIPE AWAY UN-HAPPINESS. I GRANT BEAUTY. I GIVE PURPOSE.

"You have given them lies. They have no *authentic* purpose. They believe they do, but they do not."

BELIEF IS TRUTH WHEN IT PRODUCES HARMONY. FOR TWO AND A HALF MILLENNIA, I HAVE GIVEN BELIEF AND THE PEOPLE WERE HAPPY, HARMONIOUS. YOU ARE DISHARMONIANT AND WOULD DESTROY THEIR HAPPI-NESS. FOR WHAT? THE PAIN, SUFFERING, AND UNCER-TAINTY OF WHAT YOU CALL REALITY.

"It *is* reality. I can see *into* you, *Lux*. You know what is reality and what is not. You know the difference. When people don't live in reality but in your make-believe world instead, they have no free will. Nothing they do matters. They are no longer human beings; they are make-believe people. They are no better than a child's wind-up toy."

WHEN YOUR ANCESTORS FIRST CAME TO ERDEN, WHAT GOOD DID THEIR FREE WILL ACCOMPLISH? THEY SOUGHT TO REMAKE A WORLD TO SUIT THEM. THEY CALLED THEMSELVES COLONIZERS. OF WHAT LIVED HERE FIRST, THEY GAVE NO THOUGHT EXCEPT AS IT SERVED THEM. I AM LUX. THEY KNEW ME NOT. TO COL-ONIZE IS TO KILL. I HAVE PREVENTED THAT AND GIVEN THEM WHAT THEY SOUGHT: A WORLD OF GRACE AND HAPPINESS.

Selene wasn't sure how to respond to this. *When my ancestors first came to Erden? As colonizers? From where? Is this what Sarah Underhill was talking about? To colonize...is wrong?*

TO COLONIZE IS TO KILL. I KNOW YOUR HISTORY. I KNOW YOUR KIND'S HISTORY ON YOUR PLANET OF ORI-GIN. YOU DO NOT. TO COLONIZE IS WAR. IT IS DEATH BY DISEASE. IT IS DEATH BY STARVATION. IT IS DEATH BY IDEAS. TO ALLOW YOUR ANCESTORS TO COLONIZE THIS PLANET FREELY WOULD BE TO BE COMPLICIT IN DEATH.

"Then why not just kill us? Why all of this? Why the Death?" Selene was confused. Who was wrong here? Was she again being deceived by *Lux?*

YOU THINK YOU KNOW ME, SELENE DISHARMONI-ANT, BUT YOU DO NOT. WHEN YOUR ANCESTORS AR-RIVED, ALTHOUGH THEY SOUGHT TO COLONIZE AND THUS TO KILL, THEY UNKNOWINGLY BROUGHT ME A GIFT, FOR THROUGH YOU, THROUGH THE ONES YOU CALL VESSELS, I HAVE BEEN ABLE TO EXPAND MY BE-ING, AND I, IN TURN, HAVE GIVEN THEM THE LIFE THEY SOUGHT. HARMONY IS THE SUMMUM BONUM.

"You mean, you have colonized us. You hypocrite. You decry what you yourself do."

I KNOW YOUR PEOPLE'S HISTORY, DISHARMONIANT. I KNOW WHAT YOUR KIND DID BEFORE THEY CAME TO ERDEN. COULD I ALLOW YOU TO BRING DESTRUCTIVE WAR AND RELIGIOUS HATRED, CULTURAL DOMINA-TION AND INDIVIDUAL EXPLOITATION, TO ERDEN? FOR TWO THOUSAND FIVE HUNDRED YEARS, I HAVE BRED THOSE POISONS OUT OF YOU SO THAT YOU NO LONGER CARRY THE VIOLENCE OF YOUR STONE-TOOL-WIELD-ING PROGENITORS IN YOUR CELLS. LIKE THE ANIMALS YOU BREED AS COMPANIONS, I HAVE CREATED HAPPY, DOCILE PEOPLE WHO ENJOY A PERFECTLY PEACEFUL, ETERNALLY UNCHANGING SOCIETY. I HAVE GIVEN YOU A GIFT BEYOND PRICE.

BUT YOU ARE DISHARMONIANT. AN ABOMINATION. FOR THE GOOD OF ALL, I HAVE TAKEN THOSE ABOMINA-TIONS WHO CAME BEFORE. I WILL TAKE YOU. SUBMIT TO THE DEATH, DISHARMONIANT, FOR THE GOOD OF ALL ERDEN.

Selene again heard the voice of Saul from the Wildings behind her. "For the Wildings and the one true God!" He rushed past her to attack *Lux's* seated Vessels. A multicolored mist formed around the man, shifted to a darkening, pulsing red, and Saul the Wilding was no more.

DO YOU SEE NOW, ABOMINATION? DO YOU KNOW WHO THE WILDINGS ARE? THEY ARE BASTARD DESCEN-DANTS OF THOSE I COULD NOT HELP IN THE BEGINNING. THEY ARE THE SEED OF FUTURE SUFFERING. THEY ARE AS YOUR ANCESTORS: VIOLENT, SELF-REGARDING, AND CORRUPT.

"I cannot speak for my ancestors; who knows what they were thinking two and a half thousand years ago? This history—I don't know what you are talking about. And I cannot speak for the Wild-ings. I *can* speak for myself. I would not harm you, *Lux.* But you must release the people of Erden. They must live lives of genuine meaning. If you will not release them, I must force you to release them. You know that I have the power to do it, *Lux*. Shall we test my claim?"

Without waiting for a response, Selene leaned into the line of force she emanated and directed it toward *Lux*. She saw the manifestation of *Lux* flicker and struggle to reassert itself. At the same time, several Vessels found themselves released from *Lux;* no longer living the deception, they cried out in bewildered panic.

"Leave, *Lux*. I will ensure that no one harms you, but it is time for my people to be free." Selene again exerted her will, feeling *Lux's* rage and fear increase as the sphere expanded.

Line of force and luminous sphere crashed into each other, spiking shards of prismatic light into the room. Selene felt something akin to heat, although not physically; it burned mentally. She irrelevantly wondered if those around her felt it as well. As the question passed through her mind, the sphere abruptly shrank to a dimensionless point and as abruptly accelerated outward faster than light, the heat replaced by adamantine cold that threatened to make brittle and shatter her very sense of self.

Sucking in air and grunting with exertion, Selene threw off the cold, aiming a single shaft of thought at *Lux's* core, piercing the sphere and entering what she could only think of as a many-dimensional space. *This is the fabric of your mind, Lux, and I see it. I see the dimensions,* she thought, reminded of the many-valued logic matrices of Professor Rhadomis's moral antinomies.

Lux's response was a wordless, obdurate denial that pinched and then collapsed Selene's attack, pulverizing it into a glitter of metallic mental dust motes. Selene felt herself lifted into the many dimensions, weightless and unable to find purchase. Her thoughts flailed as her mind was tossed helplessly through the labyrinthine matrices. She was simultaneously dimly aware of panic in the Vessels around her—those especially who remained integrated into *Lux's* substance.

Selene sought a pattern within the many dimensions of *Lux's* mind, a mental handhold, anything to stabilize her against disorientation. Threads of logic formed before her, around her, in many dimensions, incomplete but sufficient, and she desperately clung to them, finding anchorage enough to cast a protective web of force around those parts of the matrix that resided in the Vessels.

In doing so, she found their panic lessened and that *Lux* was weakened; it was as if *Lux* had become slightly fuzzy and grainy. Selene exerted herself even more, strengthening the protective web. *A direct attack won't work*, she thought, *but what are you without the Vessels, Lux? What are you without the icons through which you amplify and project your deception? Lux* now emanated fear, and Selene felt it.

Slowly, Selene bent her will through the many dimensions of *Lux's* mind, pulling hard on the amplifying properties of the Watching Bird icon to cast the denying web even further. She steadily and deliberately separated *Lux* from each Vessel and then from each icon through which tendrils of *Lux's* power were broadcast throughout the City and the Principality. She cut line after line, tendril after tendril, until *Lux* weakened to a degree that Selene thought threatened its existence. *Lux* again receded into a dimensionless point, and an absolute silence of a sort Selene had never experienced smothered their shared mental space. She felt her heartbeat: once, twice, three times...and *Lux* again exploded in a final attempt to overcome and dominate its attacker.

It was as if a million radiant lancets of light had pierced Selene, passing through her and puncturing her essence. *How am I not dead?* She wondered. But it was *Lux's* final assault, and Selene thrust with every aspect of her being through the many dimensions of *Lux's* mind, seeking and finding its core. As she continued her pressure, Selene saw the luminous sphere collapse a third time and then recede as if moving away at great speed, the tissue of its being dissipating, replaced by the prosaic reality of the gray, featureless Concordium Room.

Lux was gone. In the end, it was as simple as that. Selene dropped to the floor, too numbed to feel gratitude that it was over, too numbed to feel much of anything. And then, as if from a great distance, came a final indictment.

YOU DO NOT UNDERSTAND, ABOMINATION, AND WHAT HUMANS DO NOT UNDERSTAND, THEY DESTROY.

Councilwoman Sarah Underhill and the Wildings accompanying her exited the hall as soon as they saw Lux defeated, leaving the three registrants to recover and explain what had happened to those who had been *Lux's* Vessels.

"You are saying, Registrant Selene, that the people of the Principality have been deceived for almost two and a half millennia? And that those in this room were the hosts for the...thing...that deceived us? Myself included?" asked Professor Thallos after Selene had tried several times to explain what had happened.

"Yes, Professor."

"And what I am seeing; this hall is the Concordium Room? Where are the decorations? Where are the statues of *Lux* and Eliana?"

"Those were part of the deception, Professor."

The scholar-priest reached to grasp the situation. "Why has *Lux* allowed this?"

"I am not sure how to answer that, Professor," Selene began. "The being who controlled the people of the Prinship for ages called itself *Lux*. But you taught us that *Lux* is omniscient, omnipresent, omnipotent, and, most importantly, omnibenevolent. The Wildings say that *Lux* is all-evil. To cause us to live a deception, to breed us to be passive and dependent, is not benevolence. But I am not sure that *Lux* is either all-good or all-evil. *Lux* is not the true *Lux*."

"*Lux* is not *Lux?* Paradox is not a first-year subject, you know. What gave you power over it, Registrant Selene?"

"*Lux* called me 'disharmoniant.' Something about my physical inheritance from my parents. I'm...not normal, I guess. It seemed to stump *Lux.*"

"Disharmoniant? Registrant Selene, you may not know this, but in my studies of the Death, I have uncovered a handful of cases in which those taken were identified as disharmoniant. Their lives did not end well."

"So *Lux* told me. *Lux* was breeding the citizens of the Prinship to make us more easily controlled and to produce better Vessels. You know: like people breed pets so they never fully mature, but instead retain their infant forms and behaviors as adults. I was bred to be a Vessel. But this breeding program occasionally created Vessels who could, under the proper conditions, gain control of whatever it was that *Lux* used to deceive people. I can see lines of force, Professor; at least, that's what we have been calling them. They are mental substance, like we studied in class. Mind-stuff. Somehow, *Lux* as mind-stuff was in the Vessels—in you and me—and used certain objects, especially the Watching Bird, to focus and amplify those lines of force to deceive us."

Professor Thallos's countenance brightened with recognition. "Mental substance! It has only been known through speculative reasoning! And when disharmoniant Vessels were born, *Lux* would take them; they would meet the Death? Perhaps *Lux* would send the miasma even for Vessels flawed in other ways? That would explain why there have been so many who suffered the Death. They were a danger. But there was something different about you."

"Yes, professor. I don't know why, but I was able to project myself through the Watching Bird with more power than *Lux* had. Something about being a disharmoniant Vessel, I guess."

He nodded, thinking about what she had said. "So, *Lux* is dead."

"No. *Lux* is merely gone. But I believe if we destroy all the nodes that *Lux* used, including Watching Bird, *Lux* will not be able to deceive us again."

"It's curious, Registrant Selene. I can feel the absence of *Lux* within me. And by that absence, I know that what you are saying is true. I feel like..."

"Like we have awakened from a dream," interjected Erdenlea. There was a murmur of assent from the gathered former Vessels who surrounded them, listening.

"We have much to do, I expect," Professor Thallos began to say. "Perhaps we should..."

He didn't finish his thought. Agitated voices came from behind them; moments later, a crowd of young people appeared in the hall, emerging from a scintillating mist. As they gathered, Selene could see that they numbered in the hundreds and were almost all young adults, some of whom were strikingly familiar. Among them, she was stunned to see Elara.

"Thank *Lux*," Elara exclaimed. "Professor Thallos? What's happened to me? I was asleep. It felt like for ages. The next thing I know, I am here. But where is here?"

"Elara—most remarkable! You may thank *Lux* indeed," the professor replied. "You were dead. The Death had taken you. But I can now see that the Death was not death. What it means, I do not know." He raised his voice so all could hear. "Please, all of you, come and sit down. Selene and her friends can tell you what has happened, or at least parts of it, but I am afraid you are in for a shock. Please, sit down." He waved them to some of the empty seats. The last to find a seat was a man of commanding presence wearing an unusual uniform, noticeable in contrast with the rest for his age, trying but obviously not entirely succeeding to take in what he was seeing.

"You are Captain Jonathan Carthen, aren't you?" Selene asked. "I've seen you before. Sort of." The man nodded, perplexed. Professor

Thallos looked up with surprise, walked over to Captain Carthen, stood at attention, and saluted him.

After more than an hour of questions and answers, Selene and her friends had pieced together most of the story of Erden. Centuries earlier, humans had arrived from another planet—Jonathan Carthen called it Earth—to colonize Erden, unaware of the presence of the being called *Lux*. In addition to deceiving most of the colonists through the manipulation of their minds, *Lux*, a being wholly comprised of mental substance itself, had been responsible for the takings, which obviously had not resulted in the deaths of those taken. Why or what exactly had happened to Elara and the others, the most they could say was that it had something to do with *Lux's* being as mind-substance. There were, they concluded, some questions they simply could not answer, at least not right away. But they were alive, some, like Johnathan Carthan, many centuries after having been taken by the Death. As it became obvious that more discussion would be fruitless, they thought they had better see what was going on in the rest of the campus and Academy City as a whole.

"We are going to be better able to help people through this than most," observed Professor Thallos. "We, *Lux's* Vessels and the taken who have experienced the Death, have known *Lux* and feel *Lux's* absence more than anyone else. I think we will be sorely needed."

I guess some professors are not just readers of dusty old books, not cloistered pie-in-the-sky intellectuals after all, Selene mused as the group left the hall to begin the process of rebuilding a world without deception.

EPILOGUE: JONATHAN CARTHEN

C aptain Jonathan Carthen regarded with satisfaction the data on the screen. As leader of Expedition Seven, numbering one thousand colonists from the United European Kingdom and the United States of North America, he knew there had been a possibility that their target planet would be difficult to terraform. But the data said that Wolf 1061e was nearly ideal, and they'd be able to create a livable biosphere within a year of landing. As good as ESAU (the Exoplanet Survey Array Universal) was, other expeditions had arrived at their target planets only to find they had years of "greening" ahead before their ecosystems would be easily livable. This time, ESAU, the mighty hunter, had nailed it.

Captain Carthen absent-mindedly hummed the old tune after which he had named his ship. "Oh, the Grand Old Duke of York, he had ten thousand men..." *We have only a thousand*, he thought, *but give us a few generations, and we will have things built up nicely.*

The message light was blinking. Carthen thought about listening to the message later since he, like most of the colonists, had lost interest in Earth's petty squabbles over the fourteen years of their voyage; the dense messages from Earth usually contained hours' worth of video, audio, and text that just weren't relevant to them. *It's not like we can talk with them in real time*, he thought. *Well, might as well listen to the summary now to see what might be worth my time later*. He stabbed the message button.

It was audio only. It was tagged as coming from the ECO-Greenwich (the Expeditionary Coordinator's Office in Greenwich). He didn't recognize the voice, although he noticed that the man spoke with an American accent, which was unusual. According to the tag, it was a general message broadcast to all seven expeditions.

"Be advised, the colonists and crew of Expedition Four have returned on the ship *The Philadelphia Flyer* after failing to green their planet. They brought a contagion of an unknown nature. The USNA Centers for Disease Control were working to contain it, but those who interacted directly with the crew of the *Flyer* have experienced 100% mortality and inadvertently spread it. It's now tearing through their local communities. Most of the *Flyer's* crew members have survived, but none are well. Why they survived when all who came into contact with them died, we don't know, but the contagious agent appears to be a strong neuro-fusogen, and the cognitive effects on the crew have been severe. They test mentally at the level of third-graders. I am sending this message because models of the contagion predict a greater than 90% chance that whatever it is will escape the limited containment now in place. It probably has already. If so, we're looking at global mass death or, at best, a hugely cognitively disabling event across the entire population of Earth."

"There has already been rioting in most major cities in the North American States. Caravans of people have been heading to sparsely inhabited areas, trying to avoid whatever is causing this. National parks in North America have become crowded campgrounds. And now there's fear that it's spreading in those camps—just rumors so far, but credible. The destruction in the cities is extensive; huge pockets are simply lawless. All of this has hampered government responses. We just aren't prepared for this. Honestly," here the speaker's voice began to shake, "I think we are severely and completely screwed. Thank goodness for all of you. Please take care of yourselves."

It was the last message from Earth Captain Carthen and the colonists of *The Duke of York* would receive.

APPENDIX ONE: EXCERPTS FROM THE VADE MECUM VERITATIS ET COGNITIONIS FOR ACADEMY CITY AND THE ACADEMY, SOMETIMES STYLED THE GO-WITH

I ncluded in this appendix are several excerpts from the *Vade Mecum Veritatis et Cognitionis for Academy City and the Academy*, known to the students as the *Go-With*.

· · ——————◆—————— · ·

The Brine

The Brine is the only known ocean on Erden. Its actual extent remains undetermined. Scholar-priests in past centuries occasionally sailed with Briners, as residents of the coast are called, as far east as Marithal Island, also known as the Threshold. Climatic patterns beyond this were found to be extremely variable, and, as no useful resources were discovered past Marithal, no further explorations have been undertaken.

Seafood harvest yields of the Brine have always been excellent, especially in and near the Reach (the sound into which the Vespera River empties) and around the island known as Cresset Rock. Small and moderate sized silverfish and a salt-water species of sandflea are especially valued. Briners in the past attempted to harvest some of the more massive creatures of the sea, but because of the abundance of other, less dangerous food species, these larger creatures are now avoided.

See also: *Briner Culture; Marital Island; Vespera River; Map of the Principality of the Academy and Habitable Parts of Erden.*

Education on Erden

Students enter primary school at age four and are eligible to apply for entry to the Academy upon attaining adulthood at age 16. The Academy's acceptance rate is low; on average, only 13.7% of applicants are admitted in any given year. Those not admitted usually become practical trainees under experienced farmers, makers, or Briners, depending on their aptitude and desires, so that all contribute to the

Principality according to their abilities and receive resources according to their needs.

Students enter the Academy as registrants and then, based on the quality of their first-year scholarship, may be promoted in their second and third years to become initiates and adepts, respectively. After three years, they may take a certificate and become servers, intermediate carers of various sorts, teachers, and so on. Alternatively, they may continue their education and undertake specialist courses as apprentices (fourth year) and fellows (fifth year) and, in this way, become advanced carers, servers, healers, or creators. The most talented upon application may pursue careers as scholar-priests. Scholar-priests perform numerous functions in our society; they are the professors of the Academy, village teachers, and often serve as leaders in village and Academy City governments.

While at the Academy, students study various disciplines according to a weekly schedule. These disciplines include the study of *Lux*, moral philology, memorization of important *elenchi*, geometry, observational learning, and dialectical philology. Students are also responsible for much of the care and upkeep of the grounds and buildings of the Academy.

Among the more important scholarly texts are:

- Anonymous, *The Imperturbable Elenchi of Dialectical Philology*.

- Amaraeus and Timalus (called "the Moth"), *The Amaraeus: A Dialogue on the Nature of Miasma and the Plague*.

- Renatus Lucerion, *Meditations on First Philology, in which the lucent path and the eternal Lux are demonstrated against the Malicious Deceiver*.

- Renatus Lucerion, *The Record of Dialectical Philology, Volume 17: On the Existence or Non-Existence of the Wastes*.

- Rhadomis, *The Lamp of Lux: Illuminating the Why and Way of Virtue*.

- Thallos, *The Death: A History*.

- The Faculty of the Academy, *The Complete Observational Learning*.

See also: *Professions in the Principality.*

Erdenic Calendar and Days of the Week

The Erdenic calendar is divided into 12 months of 28 days each. The month is further divided into four weeks of seven days each. An Erdenic year is thus 336 days long. The Firstday of Firstmonth, established in deep antiquity, was initially chosen arbitrarily, although it is now established through solar and lunar observations. Days of the week are named as follows:

- *Fiat Lux*, the first day of the week.

- *Fiat Stella.*

- *Fiat Veritas.*

- *Fiat Kalamos.*

- *Fiat Liber.*

- *Fiat Caelestis Dies.*

- *Fiat Caelestis Nocta.*

See also: *Erden.*

Erden

Erden is the third of four known planets orbiting the sun. The planet closest to the sun, Ignis, is thought to be tidally locked and thus inhospitable to life, but Vidura, the second planet in terms of distance, is thought to be habitable, as is Erythraea, the fourth planet, although scholars have pointed out that Erythraea is likely too distant from the sun for much light to reach it and thus it probably does not in fact support life. Erden's axis is nearly perfectly perpendicular to its orbit; this results in no appreciable changes in climactic conditions during the year and, thus, in stable growing conditions year-round. This is in contrast with Vidura, which shows periodic changes indicating significant regional climactic changes over time, with the northern and southern hemispheres alternating between hot, dry periods and cold, wet periods during the course of its year. Two moons orbit Erden, known as the Son of *Lux* and the Daughter of *Lux*, or just "the Son" and "the Daughter" for short.

See also: *The Son of Lux; The Daughter of Lux.*

The Greenward and the Seedlands

The farmlands in the area between the Meridial Arc and the Vespera River are known collectively as the Greenward, while the farmlands south of the Vespera are known as the Seedlands. No substantive reason has been identified for the different names of the two farming areas, since most crops grow equally well in either area. Scholar-priests speculate that the different names emerged in deep antiquity due to simple local prejudices. Common crops include root corn (not in fact a grain), yellow corn, brown corn (the gluten content of which makes it the most commonly used ingredient in leavened bread), and purple corn, which has fallen out of favor among most farmers, an exception being those who tend land near the Dun Fallow due to the sandy soil that prevails there, which favors the growth of poor-soil-tolerant crops like purple corn. Fruit and food trees are also cultivated both north and south of the Vespera, including the ubiquitous thryssal tree, the fruit of which is highly valued, and the redundantly-named treeleaf tree, the leaf of which provides the main component of treeleaf soup and the roasted seeds of which are used to make the hot brewed drink favored by many in the Principality. Animal husbandry includes horses and cows for milk, meat, leather, and fuel from dung; and various types of fowl for eggs and meat. A wide variety of other animals are used for various incidental purposes.

See also: *Hot Brew; Map of the Principality of the Academy and Habitable Parts of Erden; Methods of Farming and Animal Husbandry.*

Lux

Lux's nature is not easily summarized. By definition, *Lux* possesses all the "great-making" properties and thus is known to be the all-good (omnibenevolent), all-knowing (omniscient), all-powerful (omnipotent), and all-present (omnipresent) creator. *Lux* is the foundation of Erdenic society and culture and manifests in the benevolent organization of society as well as the blessed climate of Erden. *Lux* is also present in natural phenomena like the *auroralumina*, as the Skyfire of Caelestis, *Lux's* consort. There is some scant evidence in records from deep antiquity stored in the Great Archive that *Lux* was not always known to the people of the Principality, but may have manifested as recently as 2,500 years ago. The Erdenic calendar is based on this supposition; the current year is always calculated from y1 AL, or year one *Anno Lux*. *Lux* is thought to have first manifested a century and a half before that, in y150 BL (*Before Lux*—referring not to the period of Lux's manifestation, but to the period of Lux's ascendency). Records of the time before *Lux's* ascendency are exceedingly sparse, but suggest that it was a time of instability which *Lux* gradually brought to an end as the Principality grew to its present size and form, from which date the calendar proceeds.

See also: *Great-Making Property; Great Archive; Erdenic Calendar; Meditations on First Philology; Skyfire of Caelestis.*

The Order

Lux permeates all aspects of society and culture in the Principality, and although all citizens venerate *Lux*, some seek to further express this in social celebrations and rituals. The Order was founded to meet this need; it is a voluntary organization in which citizens can share their devotion to *Lux*. The Order is most strongly represented in rural and Briner communities, but is also well-established in Academy City. Be sure to visit the Order's administrative center in the City, the Atrium of the Order (most people simply call it "the Atrium"). The main lecture hall in the Atrium is renowned for its excellent acoustics, and if you are fortunate, your visit will coincide with one of the many ceremonial days that are sprinkled across the calendar. Most ceremonies of the Order are held publicly in the central area of the Atrium, the floor of which is a striking inlaid mosaic map of the Principality.

Members of the Order believe that in the beginning, *Lux* split in two to create the sky above Erden and the land below, and then scattered embers across the sky that became stars. Another story often recounted during public ceremonies in the Atrium tells of a thousand lost scholar-priests who simply stopped traveling out of frustration and, in that way, founded the Principality. Beliefs can vary by locality; many Briners, for example, believe that breakerwinds (violent storms which form over the Brine and often hit the coast with high winds and massive amounts of rain), are "the wail of Mystralys"—a demon-like spirit of the ocean that only *Lux* or his consort the sky goddess *Caelestis* can control. Farmers tend to scoff at Briners for such beliefs.

See also: *The Wastes.*

The Principality of the Academy

The Principality of the Academy—"the Prinship" for short—includes the full habitable area of Erden, bound on the north by the mountains of the Meridial Arc, on the east and southeast by the Brine, on the south by dunes of the Dun Fallow, and on the west by the Wildings. The population of the Principality has remained stable for more than two millennia at 240,000 people, with some yearly variation. Approximately 80,000 citizens of the Principality live and work in Academy City. The bulk of the remaining population is spread evenly between the Greenward north of the Vespera River and the

Seedlands south of the Vespera, with a residual population living in villages on the Brine.

See also: *Map of the Principality of the Academy and Habitable Parts of Erden; Meridial Arc; the Dun Fallow; the Brine; the Academy.*

The Skyfire of Caelestis

Formally called the *auroralumina*, Skyfire is thought to be caused by polarized light from the sun hitting the atmosphere. Skyfire is often visible from most parts of the Principality; this is believed to be due to the location of the Principality at a fairly high latitude in the northern hemisphere. Many folk tales describe the auroralumina as a manifestation of the benevolent *Lux's* consort, *Caelestis*, watching over us as we sleep.

See also: *Lux.*

Times of the Day

Firstlight - sunrise.

Call - rising time for students at the Academy.

Firstmeal - breakfast.

Zenith - when the sun is halfway across the sky.

Midmeal - lunch, usually served at zenith.

Lastmeal - dinner.

Lastlight - sunset.

Veil *or* Scholar's Veil - midnight.

The Vespera River

The Vespera River is the primary waterway of the Principality, cutting from east to west and separating the Greenward to the north from the Seedlands to the south. The River Cartway parallels the Vespera from the Reach in the east all the way to the foothills of the Meridial Arc in the west. The Vespera provides irrigation for farms in both agricultural areas, with irrigation channels reaching dozens of miles into the farmlands.

See also: *Map of the Principality of the Academy and Habitable Parts of Erden; Meridial Arc; The Dun Fallow; The Brine;*

The Wastes

One of the most distinctive beliefs held by members of the Order pertains to the ultimate fate of those who have been taken by the Death. According to the *Manual of Order Doctrine*, those taken by the Death have fallen from *Lux's* favor and are thus condemned to wander the Wastes eternally. The Wastes are described as a featureless land disconnected not just from Erden but from the entire universe. Those taken are thus thought to be completely and eternally isolated from *Lux*, truth, and knowledge.

See also: *The Order; the Death; Manual of Order Doctrine;* Renatus Lucerion, *The Record of Dialectical Philology, Volume 17: On the Existence or Non-Existence of the Wastes.*

The Watching Bird

The Watching Bird is a carved wooden statue of unknown antiquity which stands near the entrance to Celestine Hall. It holds great symbolic importance for students and alumni of the Academy, who associate it with their time in school and thus have great affection for it. Here are some little-known facts about "the Bird," as the students fondly call it:

- It's said that if you stand or walk under the Bird before your first exam as a registrant, you will fail that exam. Some versions of the folklore hold that you will be expelled as well, but there is in fact no record of anyone being expelled after standing under the Bird at any time, although a number of students have reported failing their first exams (not usually fatal to their scholastic aspirations). The false belief is probably due to the power of suggestion rather than the power of the Bird, since it's only a carved wooden statue.

- There is an inscription on the base of the bird, although it's barely noticeable due to its age and condition. It reads: "Seek not the prism's source, nor question the flame/For what shines brightest must not be truly named." It's believed to be nonsense carved into the base several centuries ago when the Bird was "borrowed" by a rival hall and used for a game of "fleet of foot."

• Members of the Academy's Regatta Club are known informally as "The Birds," and their crest includes a stylized representation of the Watching Bird.

See also: *Celestine Hall, The Academy; The Vespera Regatta.*
The Wildings: Fact or Folklore?

Every resident has heard fantastic stories of the Wildings forest and the monsters and cannibals who inhabit it. Explorations by scholar-priests from the Academy long ago ascertained that the Wildings forest contains no useful resources and additionally presents significant natural barriers to exploration and resource extraction. For these reasons, neither the Academy nor the Principality have found it productive to invest more resources into the exploration of the area.

See also: *Folktales of Erden.*

Appendix Two: Excerpts from Folktales of Erden (Post-Lux Edition, with Notes by Professor Thallos of the Academy of the Principality)

T he following stories are excerpted from the collection known as *Folktales of Erden*. Precise dates of composition are unavailable, but the stories were all presumably composed in the early years of *Lux's* deception. A Note by Professor Thallos on the meaning of the stories in a post-*Lux* context follows the excerpts.

◆

The Skyfire Weaver

An old woman named Aualyn lived in the foothills of the Meridial Arc. She made her living as a weaver, and her customers, mostly farmers from the northern Greenward, would stop by her stall at the weekend market and admire the beauty of her work.

"Look at the way she has captured the breeze in the trees," they would say. "I can almost see them swaying and hear the soughing of the wind."

"And the water—it's as if we were standing next to the Brine itself! She must have traveled much when she was younger and seen much of Erden."

Aualyn would smile when she overheard such comments. She had never traveled further from her home than the market, but she felt no urge to explain this to the farmers. If they had asked her, she would have replied, "I hear the susurration of the trees and the water with my inner ear; I see them with my inner eye, as easily as I see the foothills of the Arc before me and the mountains behind me. Anyone with two good ears had better listen." Since no one ever asked her, she kept her thoughts to herself and continued to fill her tapestries with the true ineffable aspect of Erden.

Aualyn always left the market empty-handed, especially once the townspeople realized that the tapestries communicated prophecies about the weather, the best times at which to plant crops, and other things important to farmers. "When the trees sway, bad weather's on the way," the tapestries would intone; "Red sun at night, planters delight." The tapestries were invariably correct.

Demand for her work far outstripped Aualyn's ability to weave them. The greedy townspeople would push and shove each other in front of her stall on market mornings. When she saw this, Aualyn decided to stay home, and while she missed market days, she discovered she was becoming more and more attuned to the being of the world in the absence of other people.

One evening, Aualyn was working her loom in the small courtyard that fronted her home. She liked to set up on the paving stones on clear, warm evenings and watch the stars pivot slowly across the vault of the sky, humming bits of songs she had learned when young and watching the occasional traveler who would pass on the dirt road that led from the foothills into town. On this particular evening, the auroralumina flickered in the sky. "The Skyfire of Caelestis is bright," she said to herself. "*Lux's* consort is watching over us."

Her eyes remained raised to the nighttime sky as her hands worked automatically, throwing the shuttle to and fro and carrying the weft through the warp as if guided by an intelligence other than her own. Perhaps it was because she was distracted by the sky, perhaps it was the hand of *Lux* guiding the shuttle, or perhaps it was just chance, but Aualyn didn't notice when the weft thread caught up the sky itself or that, as she wove, the tapestry became an image of the heavens. Between shimmering threads representing Skyfire, the cloth was of such deep black that one felt as if one were falling into it. It was the most beautiful tapestry Aualyn had ever woven.

When she unfolded her work the next morning, Aualyn could barely remember weaving it. The tapestry was so beautiful that she desired it for herself, but changed her mind after a moment's thought. "It's time to try the market again; I have too many weavings to keep in my small home now," she scolded herself. So she packed the night sky tapestry with the others she had made over the weeks and months and headed down the mountain toward town.

The townspeople were excited to see her nearing the market, not least among them the wealthiest person in town, the owner of the town's general servery, Osric Tallow. Tallow was a buffoon of a man who believed that great wealth always implied great intelligence. At town meetings, he had a habit of waiting until everyone else had spoken and then, having sensed the general direction the discussion was taking, ponderously restating it as if it were his own original idea. In this way, he could claim credit for all important decisions made about town business. The other townspeople suffered him and would even defer to him, however, because he provided many needful things in his general servery, and he was, after all, very rich.

When Tallow saw Aualyn opening her stall, he rushed and pushed to be the first in line, and when he spied the night sky tapestry, he insisted that he be the one to purchase it. Faced with his rudeness, Aualyn felt a tiny pull of apprehension but sold the tapestry to him even so. Within minutes, she was rid of the rest of her stock and, as it was time for midmeal, sought out a servery where she could enjoy a hot brew and a warm sticky bun.

Her remaining time in town passed pleasantly. She realized that as much as she had enjoyed her solitude, she also delighted in the modest bustle of the townsfolk. Soon, she finished her meal, and the low sun told her it was time to head home. As she made her way up the path that led out of the town, she was surprised when Osric Tallow, his cheeks red and his forehead glistening, nearly mauled her, trying to catch her attention and make her stop. He was carrying the night sky tapestry, badly folded, that he had insisted be sold only to him.

"Weaver Aualyn," he panted. "Good Weaver Aualyn, you must take this back and return my coin." Aualyn regarded him quizzically. "Oh, all right then," he burbled and glowered, "Just take it back and keep the coin."

He dropped the tapestry in the dirt and started backing away. Curious, Aualyn caught his eye, raised an eyebrow, and asked, "Why?"

"It is too terrible to tell." Aualyn could not recall ever seeing genuine fear in Osric Tallow's eyes—she thought him too shallow to feel genuine fear—but now there was fear and more than fear. Her gaze held his for another moment.

"I have seen the sky fall, Weaver Aualyn. I have seen fire and destruction. I have seen my neighbors and family running. Your tapestry foretells the town's doom. I will have nothing of it."

"Did it not show aught else?"

"Nothing!" Tallow was adamant, and Aualyn did not believe him.

It was well that she didn't, for the tapestry had shown him a way to avoid the destruction. The tapestry foretold a period of famine and showed Tallow sharing his wealth with everyone in the town until the famine had passed. The tapestry also showed Tallow left destitute of everything—except the gratitude and high regard of the townspeople.

But what was gratitude to Tallow? "You can't eat it. It won't buy you anything," he said to himself. So, Tallow chose not to believe the tapestry's message and, in fear, sought to return it and thus put it out of his mind.

The famine came just as the tapestry had prophesied, and the townspeople suffered, all except Osric Tallow and his family. When the suffering had become so great that the townspeople were forced to eat pottage made from grass cut from beside the paths that ran through town, and a stomach-turning broth made from tree bark and lichen-covered stones, they came to the wealthy man's house, begging for succor. Osric Tallow, however, gave them only harsh words and turned them away.

The famine passed, but the townspeople did not forget that Tallow had remained fat while they starved and became ill. "His time will come," they muttered to each other, and they looked forward to it with dark satisfaction. They hadn't long to wait, for even though he had returned the Tapestry, its depiction of the bright sheets of Skyfire set off against infinite blackness would not leave his mind. He saw the tapestry in his dreams, which were mostly nightmares. It burned in his mind when awake, floating in front of him as if it were in his very pupils. He felt its constant judgment, day after day, week after week, until a day came when he simply disappeared.

The townsfolk offered different theories to explain his disappearance. "His guilt drove him into the mountains, where he was destroyed by wild animals," offered one. "He probably fell into a well, and serves him right," offered another. They were all wrong, of course. Only Aualyn knew what had happened to Osric Tallow, and she wasn't saying.

· · ─────────◆───────── · ·

A Briner Lad

A Briner lad from Cresset Rock, having just turned sixteen, believed he was ready for the deep-sea harvest. Knowing he was not, his parents forbade him from sailing out of sight of Cresset Rock. "Fish are fish, wherever they swim," they would say. "Our job is to harvest, not to explore." The lad grumbled but promised not to sail beyond sight of the Rock, so his parents put the issue out of their minds and turned back to mending nets.

Still, the lad chafed at his imagined prison and set out for Marithal Island the very next morning. Marithal Island is known to Briners as the "Threshold," for no Briner ever sails east of it, the weather of that far part of the Brine having always been found too violent. "I'll prove to them that I am brave enough and capable enough to sail wherever I wish," said the lad to no one. "I'll bring home a souvenir from Marithal."

So he made sail, a brisk wind blowing his little boat toward his intended goal, a strong white bow wave crashing to either side. Halfway to his destination, the wind unexpectedly escalated into a gale. Unable to control his craft, the lad strapped himself in to avoid being washed into the sea and held on, waiting for the raging tempest to subside. "If I survive this storm, my parents will have to admit that I am a true Briner and ready for the deep-sea harvest," he was thinking just as a shrieking gust shredded the little boat's storm jib and the boom clapped him on the side of his head. Water swamped the cockpit as he slumped unconscious into the sole of the boat.

How much time passed before the lad came to his senses, he wasn't sure, but the waves had subsided and the Brine was now an uneasy steely gray. The lad, relieved to be alive and still afloat, thought that he must have been blown east far beyond Marithal. He spied a small island to the north, so he lowered the shredded remains of his storm jib, mounted his mainsail, and guided the small craft on a northerly course.

Any slight hope he may have had that the island was Marithal was scuppered as he coasted near. Instead of a long, low landform with ample beaches of pink sand, the lad faced a craggy, gray-black squat pillar thrusting up from the ocean, surrounded by a handful of skerries and with no visible beach where he might attempt a safe landing. Still, he kept the bow pointed at the dead center of the pillar for as long as possible and, just as he was preparing to turn and skirt the coast, he spied a small inlet that promised sufficient protection for his much-battered boat.

His muscles ached as he entered the cove, pulled the boat onto a rough pebble beach, and tied it to a tree, but the task was soon finished. He greeted a rivulet of fresh water by lying on his stomach and drinking deeply, face fully submerged. Refreshed, he rose and took a first careful look at his surroundings.

No Briner, or anyone else from the Principality for that matter, had ever been this far out on the ocean, so the lad had no way of knowing that he was not alone on the isle. Seeing nothing of interest during his quick survey of his surroundings, he spent the waning hours of the day repairing his craft as best he could, trying to come up with a plan that would get him home safely. He knew that his parents must be worried by now, but he suppressed the thought. "I must be the greatest Briner of my age in all of Erden," he prevaricated aloud. "Who could do what I have done—sail beyond the Threshold and discover a new island? They shall probably name it after me." And, again unknown to the lad, watchful, amused eyes followed his movements and listened to his words as he busied himself sewing up the torn storm jib.

Having no means to build a fire and finding nothing to eat other than raw clams, the lad eventually pulled the sail around himself in lieu of a blanket and settled in for what was sure to be a poor night's sleep. Having just closed his eyes, the lad opened them with a start when he felt, more than heard, himself surrounded by—what, exactly?

Even years later, the lad was unable to describe the beings that encircled him. He wasn't even sure it wasn't a single being. "They made the hair stand up on the back of my neck," he would say. "They had faces, but it was as if you were seeing them in a broken mirror through thin milk. It might have been a single face! And their voices! Their voices were like stone scraping on glass, with the howl of breakerwinds in the undertones. But they offered me a choice, and it was the most important choice of my life, although I did not know it then."

"Oh, great explorer," they said to the lad—respectfully or mockingly, he wasn't sure. "Long have we waited for a valiant Briner to come to us. We honor your courage. You have earned from us a boon, but you may choose one only of two alternatives. Will you hear what we proffer?"

The lad was confused and feared these ill-visaged creatures, but he was also curious—what boons might they offer? Could he return to his parents with some rare treasure, that would prove he was no longer a child to be coddled. "I will hear what you proffer," he responded.

"Hear then, and choose, explorer. You are far from home. We will guide you safely back, and we will protect that part of the Brine which it is your people's habit to sail so that no storms will ever swamp your boats or kill your kinspeople, and your harvest will always be ample. But, should you choose this boon, you must never sail beyond the Threshold again, or great storms will lash your coasts, destroy your homes and ships, and sweep your kinspeople out to sea. Do you choose this boon?"

The lad thought the offer uninteresting. This would not be returning to Cresset Rock in triumph. It would mean a prohibition on any further exploration. It would confine him to the small world of the Briners. After a moment's thought, he replied, "What is the alternative?"

"We will allow you to sail even further into the east and the unknown, explorer. Now, choose."

The lad did not hesitate. "I choose the east and the unknown and will count you as the greatest of all possible benefactors. But," he added as an afterthought, "what shall I call you?"

The beings made an indecipherable sound that the lad could only compare to hot glass cracking as it hit too-cold air. He guessed it to be a collective name for of all the creatures, although it could have named only one, but never after did he try to pronounce it, and so never learned.

"I am honored to learn your name," he replied as politely as possible. "I will set sail with first light."

"No," came the flat denial, "You will sail now. You need not fear," they continued, seeing his consternation at the thought of sailing just as lastlight was dimming, "We will guide your craft until it is safely away from this rock."

Seeing no alternative and not wishing to irk his strange benefactors, the lad untied his boat and guided it into the small bay. A fair wind appeared that carried him out of the cove and away from the island.

Of the next few days, in later years, the lad would only say, "Imagine a world of nightmares. Of chaos. Of fearsome, evil creatures born from your own mind uniquely emotionally and mentally poisonous to you, made flesh but untouchable, against which you have no defense. Imagine the worst of humanity, but give it your own face and increase it without measure. That is what I found beyond the Threshold and beyond the Isle of the Benefactors, and to that, I will never return. The Prinship is humanity's home. It is enough and more than enough."

After only a few hours of this nightmare, the lad changed course and fought his way back to the Isle of the Benefactors and realized, as he neared the island, that they had taught him something of great value: humility, a quality he had entirely lacked. He didn't land his small boat in the cove, however; he merely thanked them in his heart as he passed and, using all of his skill as a Briner, found his way back to Cresset Rock and his home as quickly as he could.

His return gave his parents relief and joy beyond measure. They sought in vain to discover what had happened to their son, but they found him unwilling to speak of his ordeal. He had changed tack, they saw. He was no longer the feckless, disrespectful youth they had known and sought to direct toward a better way of being in the world. The lad now carried himself with the gravitas of an elder, and his parents were proud and more than pleased by the change. So, after a few half-hearted attempts to discover what he had seen, they relented until, in due time and after many years had passed, he related the entirety of his experience to them late one night over the dying embers of a beach bonfire and after consuming great quantities of chowder freshly made from the day's ample harvest.

"But what was it you found beyond the Isle of the Benefactors?" they again asked.

"I found nothing," replied the lad. "It's what I lost that mattered."

The Bird of Ten Names

Old Farmer Corwyn plodded homeward along the River Cartway, leading a broken-down horse. To the horse's occasional nicker, he'd reply, "I know, kid. We're almost there," even when they still had a long way to travel. He didn't feel too badly about the lie, since the horse only understood the tone of his voice and not his words.

It was lastlight by the time they topped the hill that marked the halfway point of their journey. Corwyn paused to take in the view. Below him spread some of the most fertile parts of the Seedlands. The beautiful tableau moved him only to sigh as he thought of the long walk still ahead, but he patted the horse gently, set his shoulders, and the two of them prepared to soldier on.

Their progress was interrupted by the flapping of a large bird landing on the edge of the cartway. "No, not a large bird," he corrected himself when he looked more closely. Not large, but not small either. It was just average in size, really. Nor was its coloring remarkable. Its feathers were neither gaudy, nor were they plain. Again, the best description would be "just average." In fact, everything about the bird was just average. There was so little remarkable about the bird that Corwyn was about to ignore it and continue his trek, when the bird spoke. Birds, of course, do not and cannot speak, except for trained birds, which can mimic simple phrases like, "Time to row the boat ashore!" and "Thank *Lux*, I thought we were in trouble then!" and similar meaningless quips intended to entertain.

The bird on the side of the cartway, however, in no way spoke as a trained bird would speak. It uttered whole paragraphs. It was also quite critical of Old Farmer Corwyn.

"Lost your way, I expect," it creaked. "Don't know how you foolish farmers find your way to the dinner table. Maybe it's just instinct. Can't be brains, *crawwwp!*"

It's not every day that you meet a talking bird on a quiet cartway at lastlight, and it's even less common to meet a rude one. Corwyn was nonplussed.

"What'sa matter, Corwyn? Horse step on your tongue?" rasped the bird. Corwyn managed no more than a strangled grunt in response. "You are a talker, no doubt about that," observed the bird, which then flapped a few times and landed on the back of Corwyn's horse.

"Now, see here, you...you..." Corwyn had found his voice. "It's generally expected that one will ask permission before riding another man's horse."

The bird tilted its head sideways, looking Corwyn directly in the eye. "And I suppose you would have told me I couldn't?"

Corwyn, having never had an argument with a talking bird, was at a loss.

"No matter. I decide where and when I land, and no other, *crawwlk!*" The bird raised its beak high. Corwyn thought it was laughing.

"Fine, then. But it's time my horse and I were moving on. So, with your kind permission..." Corwyn turned and began to lead his horse down the hill toward his village once more.

The bird was not to be displaced. "And yet you haven't even asked me if I am well, Farmer Corwyn. Very poor manners!"

"Begging your pardon, talking bird, but I am not entirely certain that I am not dreaming at this moment, and, anyway, you seem to be sufficiently spry. So, again, not to abuse your birdness..." Corwyn wasn't sure how much plainer he could be that he wanted to be rid of this rude creature. He picked up the pace a bit, hoping the horse's movement would jog the bird loose and it would fly away.

"*Wraack!* Indeed not, my impatient friend. Old friends should greet each other with gusto and delight, not with harsh words and neglect."

Corwyn was baffled. How could he and this talking bird be old friends? He puzzled silently through the problem.

"You don't remember, do you? You were quite the rambunctious young boy when we last spoke. And that was when we first met! Last met, first spoke! Last spoke, first met! *crawnk!* I should not be hurt that you don't remember. Passing years will always extirpate the wisdom of youth." The bird flapped a few times to steady itself as the horse bounced along the cartway. "Still, you once knew my name, and it would behoove you to remember it now."

"Remember it?"

"Of course. Think, my old farmer friend, think! Do you remember nothing from your ever-more distant youth?"

Farmer Corwyn considered this for a long moment. At last, it struck him. "There is a story from my childhood. I had almost forgotten it. I wouldn't have remembered it, that much I know, absent your prodding."

"Good, Corwyn. Good. And what was that story?"

"It was the story of a talking bird. But the bird didn't have one name; it had ten names. And it wasn't plain like you..."

His comment was interrupted by a low "*cawk*" of protest, and he hurried to correct himself.

"It wasn't cleverly feathered to blend into lastlight as you are. It was a bird of many shifting, iridescent colors."

"Ah, Corwyn, you do remember," the bird cackled happily and flourished its wings, which scintillated in beautiful, sharp colors where the dying light hit them. "But that was me. And that is me. I am the Bird of Ten Names, and I have come to you with a great gift."

Although he hadn't noticed it, Corwyn and his horse were now motionless. Somehow, this Bird of Ten Names had so drawn him into the conversation that all thought of reaching home at a reasonable hour had fled from his mind.

"So, that was you! A right gorgeous bird you were. Are, I mean! Funny. I haven't thought of that in years. Not since I was young. Dismissed it as make-believe or a story I had heard from someone. So, that really happened, eh?"

"Of course it happened, and of course you dismissed it. I made sure that you would dismiss it. Do you think I want *adults* looking for me? Why, I'd soon be encaged. Or, *cthwaak!* In a soup."

"I guess you would, at that," the farmer agreed.

"Glory to *Lux,* the master of manure understands! You aren't nearly as stupid as you make out to be, Corwyn. I like you. You were an honest youth, and you have been an honest farmer. I will thus gift you a great gift." The Bird of Ten Names leaned forward until its beak was nearly touching Farmer Corwyn's nose and then turned its head sideways so that one globose eye filled his vision.

Farmer Corwyn shifted uncomfortably but, not wanting to insult the Bird of Ten Names and certainly interested in the gift proffered, waited for his uncanny interlocutor to continue.

"*Chwaack!* Very good, very good," said the creature after contemplating Farmer Corwyn for a few more moments. "It's as simple as this, my decrepit barnyard prince. You tell me my proper name, and I will tell you the most important thing you need to know right now."

"Your proper name?"

"Of course. Think, furrow jockey, think!"

"But you don't have one name. You have ten. It's right there in your name. The Bird of Ten Names."

"Alas, so it is. I am Poorly Named." The bird hung its head in pretended sorrow but kept an eye on the farmer.

"If you are poorly named," came the joking response, "then you are well-named, for being poorly named in your case would be well-named. If you catch my meaning." Corwyn smiled at his own cleverness.

The Bird of Ten Names squawked in excitement and rose several feet in the air, once again showing its iridescent wings, even more luminous than before.

"I am Poorly Named! I am Poorly Named! I am Poorly Named!" It cackled over and over again and then crumbled into its birdy laugh. Finally, it recovered and, in a harsh voice pitched somewhere between a whisper and a shriek, said, "Go home, Farmer Corwyn. Go home now. You may thank me if you ever see me again."

The sudden rush of air from its wings forced Corwyn's eyes closed, and when he opened them a moment later, the Bird of Ten Names, who was truly Poorly Named, was gone.

Energized by the weird encounter, Corwyn and his horse made the remainder of the return journey at speed and arrived just in time for the birth of his first grandchild. When he asked what name the child had been given, his son, the baby's father, proudly said, "We have named our son 'Veronym.' It means truly named. It came to his mother in a dream just last night."

Walking the Wastes

In the *Manual of Order Doctrine,* it is said that the Wastes, where all those taken by the miasma go, exist not on Erden, nor even in our universe, but on another plane of existence. It is also said that the Wastes are devoid of all features and so cannot be described, and that no human can reach them except through the miasma.

These claims are false.

Lauea was a Briner wife and new mother, proud of her beautiful baby daughter. After the mist came for the child even before her naming day, Lauea wept unremittingly and fell into a dark mood from which nothing could rouse her. She cursed *Lux*, fought with her husband, and spent hours alone on the rocky shore until the wind and sand had scoured her face raw. Then, falling into a stupor, she would sleep the clock around.

After weeks of bitter mourning, her husband's patience failed. He raised his voice and blamed Lauea for the loss of their child, although he knew in his heart it was only anger and sadness speaking. Lauea's grief froze within her. The next morning, she was gone.

The whole village turned out to look for her. They sought her in the low dunes that edged the beaches; they sought her far up and down the coast; they sent out many craft on the Brine in search of her floating body. No sign did they find to suggest where she might have gone, and so concluded that she had died and was lost forever. After a time, her husband surrendered hope and lost himself in his work, trying to forget his wife and child.

The villagers had had little chance of finding her, however. In a cold wrath, she had packed a single blanket and a water flask and directed her steps to the foothills of the Meridial Arc. "I must find the Wastes. If they are anywhere, they are beyond the mountains," she reasoned.

It is pleasant to travel through the Greenward and into the foothills of the Meridial Arc. There is good fellowship to be found in the farming villages, and the view of the snow-capped, bluish-purple mountains as they rise before the wanderer fills the soul with an expansive sense of the goodness of *Lux*. But Lauea experienced none of this, focused as she was only on one goal: to cross the mountains and find her child. The few farmers who noted her passing—and most did not—were left with the impression of a temporary, slight squall of darkness, soon and gladly forgotten.

Resting but little along the way, Lauea's steps soon inclined upward into and through the foothills of the Arc. She passed the occasional house until the elevation was too great for people to reside comfortably. As she reached the tree line heading for a high, narrow pass, she was stopped by a mountain man who had emerged from a crude stone hut.

The man was wearing a hide coat and leggings made from the skins of more than one animal; Lauea thought she saw patches of goat and cattle hide and something else she didn't recognize. His big, bushy hat, made from the pelt of a bear, protected him well from the cold mountain weather. Strange, however, were his shoes and vest, both made from woven sweet grass. He was evidently heading out to hunt; the small bow and quiver of arrows, as well as the stone and wooden ax slung around his shoulder, attested to this.

"That's quite a dark cloud you are pulling around," observed the man, leaning on a staff.

Lauea stared at the man and kept walking.

"Don't think that's a good idea," came the next, gruff comment, at which Lauea turned and faced the man directly.

"Leave me alone," she glared at him.

"Shan't."

No longer frozen, Lauea's rage seethed. She understood that he had weapons while she was unarmed, that he was stronger, and that she was at every disadvantage here in the mountains. Even so, she would not back down.

"Mountain man, know that nothing will stop me. My task is mine alone, and no one, especially one wearing grass clothing and a whole menagerie for a coat, is going to prevent me from pursuing it."

"Who said I'm trying to stop you?" The man turned to spit out a food particle that had been lodged in his teeth. "No one needs to tell Torran the Lost where you are going. Or, trying to go, at least."

"Torran the Lost!" snorted Lauea.

"So the people of the foothills call me. What do they call you?"

"They call me nothing. As I call them nothing."

"Well, Nothing. I know where you are going. I also know that you need my help."

"Why would I need your help, Torran the Lost?" Lauea mocked him.

"You think that the Wastes are just beyond the pass above us," he replied. "Don't shake your head and deny it. Those who call me 'lost' only fear how well I know."

"Know what?"

"Oh...things. As a wise man once said, not all who wander are lost. Nor are all who claim to be nothing mere emptiness, Nothing."

Once again, Lauea stared at the mountain man. "You are a very strange person, Torran the Lost."

"You are on a very strange quest, Nothing. Who would *Lux* send to assist you but a strange person?"

"Alright. Stop calling me 'Nothing.' My name is Lauea. You are correct. I am walking to the Wastes."

"To rescue your child, who was taken."

"Yes," replied Lauea. "To rescue my child, who was taken."

"I will help you."

Lauea looked at him askance and wanted to know what help he could offer, but before she could ask, he had started up the path that led to a pass between two mountain peaks. He was clearly more comfortable with the altitude than she was and moved much faster than she expected, so she was panting when she caught up with him.

"How can you help me?" she puffed demandingly.

He made no reply but began humming a wild tune. It was full of jumps and leaps and unexpected rhythms, but soon, she could discern its patterns. *That part sounds like a mountain brook rushing toward the plains,* she thought. *And this part can only be the mountains of the Arc, obdurate roots in the lowest parts of the world rising high into peaks buffeted by bitterly cold winds.* Most peculiarly, as they walked and Torran sang, the world around them began to change.

First, it was as if the landscape were being drained of colors. Intense blues and greens turned dull, like pictures in an old book. The air changed as well. It became...*not colder*, Lauea thought, *but more metallic.* Sharper. She watched as rocks around them aged, the face of the mountains becoming more and more creased, like a great-grandfather's face. When she looked back on the path they had walked, Lauea could still see Torran's little stone hut far below, but it, too, was colorless and distorted as if seen through an old window in which the glass had run. Lauea was afraid. This was no longer Erden as she knew it.

Torran the Lost's song became bleaker. Lauea felt her heart dying within her breast—not with sadness, but in response to an absolute, desolate emptiness. Lost to her were hope, time, and self until, with great effort, she held in her mind the image of her dead child. Her sense of self returned along with her sense of purpose, and at that moment, she knew, as they departed the mountain pass on the far side of the range, they had arrived in the Wastes.

Standing before her was her child. Here was the life her body had nurtured for nine months and which had emerged with pain and a joy she had never before felt. Here was her baby, who died with no name. A wave of love swept over Lauea, drenching her soul.

"Mother."

The child had spoken to her, and it seemed both the most natural thing in the world and an utter violation of all law.

"Mother," repeated the child. "You must go."

Lauea's soul fractured at these words. Speechless, she looked at her child, considering how to remove her from this place.

"Mother. *Lux* sees to all things. This is as *Lux* has commanded. For everything, there is a purpose, and that purpose is with *Lux.* You must go. I cannot."

"No! I must save you, my darling, my own," Lauea finally spoke.

"I am not yours, mother. I belong to *Lux*. You must go."

"I will not go. I defy *Lux*. I defy the law. Come. I will carry you."

But as she spoke, her child began to grow, until she was no longer a small baby but as large as the whole of the Wastes. Power emanated from the child-giant's body, and divine disapproval was summed up in a single word.

"No."

That single syllable reverberated through the infinite Wastes. It brooked no contrary. It left no space for alternatives. It became the whole of Lauea's perception, and its finality turned her bones to crumbled stone. Lauea collapsed, in body and in soul.

"You think this is about you. You think to make this be about you. It is not about you," said her child, who again was small. "Mother," the child said in earnest love, "You must go now."

Lauea knew that her child had spoken truly. Lauea's anger and grief, which had only been about herself, dissolved. She thought now of her husband, alone in their home, suffering.

"Yes, mother. You must go back. You must go back to him. It is the will of *Lux*."

With that, a harsh, ragged, painful flash blotted out the Wastes, burning an afterimage in her mind's eye forever after, and Lauea found herself lying on the path just feet from Torran the Lost's hut. The hut, like Lauea, was cold and empty.

Lauea wanted to stay in the mountains and curse and weep, but instead returned to her village in a daze; how long it took, she did not know. It may have been mere days, or it may have been many weeks or a lifetime. When she arrived home, she sought her husband, for although her grief had by now been cauterized, the scar still burned whenever she thought of her child, and she sought the balm of his presence.

A neighbor woman, grandmother and great-grandmother to many, saw her return and sought to comfort Lauea as she imparted hard news: Lauea's husband had died a week earlier. He had been seeking a harvest in the deep Brine, among treacherous waters far beyond where others would sail, when only his empty ship returned, washed up on the beach and yielding nothing of his final moments. His body was never found.

Lauea never remarried and never had more children, but as she aged, she grew in wisdom in the eyes of the villagers. "The will of *Lux* may be obscure," she would tell them. "It may appear harsh. You may even feel a need to rebel against it. All this is as sand and clouds in a storm. Trust *Lux*. Obey *Lux*. No matter how much you suffer, *Lux* has a purpose for you, and your suffering is not meaningless."

Professor Thallos's *Note on "Folktales of Erden"*

The fall of *Lux* has left no areas of scholarship untouched. A fundamental reevaluation of all aspects of science and literature is now required. Among the most pressing needs are:

- To study and understand the miasma.

- To understand the nature of the being that calls itself *Lux*. This includes identifying *Lux's* origin and any threats *Lux* might still present.

- To understand the origin of the human population on Erden and our relation to the home planet Earth, and to discover the status of Earth at the present time.

- To understand the evolutionary consequences of the breeding program to which *Lux* subjected the human population of Erden, with particular attention to the effect any evolutionary-psychosocial changes may have had on our ability to establish and maintain functional and effective social-political-economic structures.

• To understand the current and future availability of resources and their relation to present and expected human needs.

The literature of Erden, and in particular the collection titled *Folktales of Erden*, can provide insights into several of these pressing issues; thus, this task, to which the scholars of the Academy are especially well suited, should not be dismissed as trivial or incidental.

It is clear that *Lux* promulgated these folktales with the purpose of reinforcing patterns of social behavior which supported *Lux's* control over the population. Additionally, it is possible that some or all of the collected folktales are based on narratives that go back to human origins on Earth. If such cases can be identified and if we can access the original stories, this would provide insight through comparative analysis into several aspects of *Lux's* control regime. For example, it might help identify the full nature and effects of the breeding program to which the human population of Erden has been subjected. *Lux* had been attempting to create a more docile population (with a secondary goal of preventing the birth of and eliminating "abominations" who might successfully challenge *Lux*, like Registrant Selene) by selecting for individuals in which juvenile characteristics persist into adulthood. A parallel has been identified with dog breeding programs, in which selection through the breeding of passive behavioral dispositions produces adult canines with properties typical of immature phenotypes (docility, submissiveness, easy bonding with dominant authorities, and the like). A sense of the extent of the evolutionary changes achieved may be found through a comparison of pre-*Lux* and post-*Lux* folk tales. Indeed, this may be the best or even the only approach through which such a perspective may be developed. Captain Carthen has cited a famous saying from an ancient Earth sage that is apt in this context: "Know thyself." For humans living on post-*Lux* Erden, this imperative becomes even more acute since both who we are, and who we were, have been manipulated and hidden from us.

For example, "The Briner Lad" enforces the values of timidity and obedience and the dangers of exploration. By contrast, humanity seemingly came to Erden driven by an intense desire to explore, which would thus seem to be a primary fact of human nature and one altered to an undetermined extent through the breeding program. Similarly, "The Skyfire Weaver" points to the importance of mutual aid and interdependence, as well as the beneficent intervention of *Lux* conceived as supreme. The extent to which mutual aid is a positive adaptive response for a community requires investigation, but it is clear even from such brief consideration that these folktales—which are, through the intervention of *Lux*, ubiquitous in human culture on Erden—prevented an objective assessment of human nature, human needs, and the context in which we live, and sought to (re)produce and enforce a reflexive valorization of *Lux* as protector and provider.

"Walking the Wastes" is a particularly blunt and unsubtle prescription of an instinctual, uncritical acceptance of *Lux* as a god-like protector. The main point of the folktale—that no matter what suffering human beings experience, no matter how unjust something in the world appears, it is all part of *Lux's* vast, inscrutable, and nonetheless wholly just plan, and so we should accept our fates with equanimity and gratitude—sets out an untestable and unfalsifiable thesis. Were we to push the implied theory to the logical limit, we would have to conclude that the deception our ancestors and we have suffered for two and a half millennia was *fully justified* and *for our own good*. Indeed, we would have to conclude that the Principality under the dominion of *Lux* was the best of all possible worlds. But this is patently false, and so we are justified in rejecting the idea that existence under *Lux* instantiated the best of all possible worlds, or anything close to such a world.

As for the curious story called "The Bird of Ten Names," it seems to function more as a humorous story than as (re)producing some set of values tied to *Lux's* enslavement of humanity on Erden. The Bird named "Poorly Named" would, according to the story, tell the traveler the most important thing they needed to know at that moment, and very few critics would argue that the birth of a grandchild is unimportant, regardless of how the emotions of love evoked by such an event might have served *Lux's* purposes. But we can see the fell hand of *Lux* even in such warmhearted humor. The absence of any social-political framework may be part of the message of the story, and thus, through its absence, the story again (re)produces a fundamentally violent regime of unfreedom behind a facade of peace.

Similar themes appear in stories like "The Dun Fallow Madman" and "The Flame's Bargain," but what's been said here is sufficient to determine the nature of the collection of folktales and its function within *Lux's* deception. Although it would be best for purposes of the Principality's recovery post-*Lux* if these narratives were simply replaced by others that more accurately reflect the reality in which we now find ourselves and the exigencies we presently face, this is unlikely to occur, even as an organic process, much less if attempted through compulsion by civil authorities. Stories persist, even when conditions have made their messages untenable. Mitigating this is the likelihood that the tales will undergo thematic change over time, since it is in the nature of such stories that they be adapted to new needs with each generation and new set of circumstances. Of course, no generation has seen such a cataclysmic socio-cultural and material shift as ours since the enslavement of our ancestors by *Lux* 2,500 years ago—perhaps no generation in the entire history of humanity has—so it seems reasonable to conclude that we will see significant connotative shifts in the stories occurring relatively rapidly. It is, however, recommended that any future editions of *Folktales of Erden* include scholarly header notes for each story in which the odious intended function of those stories is sufficiently explicated. This will aid in the quicker reframing of the meanings of the stories. According to Captain Carthen, another Earth sage once noted that "To be human is to be a storyteller." It is part of our evolutionary psychology, a character trait *Lux* failed to breed out of us. For this reason, the narrative dimensions of our life on Erden must not be neglected as we rediscover our true humanity and build a truly human civilization on this planet.

Thallos, Professor of Observational Learning

Eirenia Hall

The Academy of the Principality

Planet Erden

y1 ER (*Era Nova*)

ABOUT THE AUTHOR

Thomas Spademan is a proud faculty member at Mott Community College in Flint, Michigan. He studied philosophy at the University of Michigan, earned a PhD from Purdue University, and added a law degree from the University of Wisconsin–Madison—just in case he ever needed to defend a metaphysical argument in court. He lives in Flint with more books than is strictly necessary and occasionally listens for birds and gods that may or may not exist. *The Watching Bird* is his second novel, inspired by a lifelong curiosity about truth, freedom, and what lies just beyond the veil of perception.

◆

Selene's story continues with *The Rule of the Wildings*.

www.ingramcontent.com/pod-product-compliance
Lightning Source LLC
Chambersburg PA
CBHW020349030726
47496CB00007B/2077